STAR TREK®
K L I N G O N™
FOR THE
GALACTIC TRAVELER

STAR TREK®
KLINGON™
FOR THE
GALACTIC TRAVELER

MARC OKRAND

POCKET BOOKS
New York   London   Toronto   Sydney   Tokyo   Singapore

An *Original* Publication of POCKET BOOKS

POCKET BOOKS, a division of Simon & Schuster Inc.
1230 Avenue of the Americas, New York, NY 10020

STAR TREK is a Registered Trademark of Paramount Pictures.

This book is published by Pocket Books, a division of Simon & Schuster Inc., under exclusive license from Paramount Pictures.

ISBN: 0-671-00995-8

First Pocket Books trade paperback printing September 1997

10   9   8   7   6   5   4   3   2   1

POCKET and colophon are registered trademarks of Simon & Schuster Inc.

Text design by Stanley S. Drate/Folio Graphics Co. Inc.

Printed in the U.S.A.

SoSwI' vavwI' je quvmoHjaj paqvam

CONTENTS

INTRODUCTION

A fter years marked by increased cooperation, mutual understanding, and sharing of knowledge, a protracted period of relative amity between the Klingon Empire and the United Federation of Planets came to an abrupt end not long ago when the Empire withdrew from the peace treaty known as the Khitomer Accords over an incident regarding war with the Cardassian Union. Ironically, that same war has brought the two governments back together. Though he did so with some trepidation, Klingon Chancellor Gowron recently agreed to once again honor the accords and to engage in joint missions with the Federation. These missions have been successful, and as a result, both commerce and intellectual exchange are slowly returning to the levels that had been attained prior to the hostilities. Many feel that the time is right for travelers to once again visit various parts of the Klingon Empire.

As those who have visited the Klingon Empire in the past can attest, Klingons are an exuberant people, savoring all life has to offer. Travel to any part of the Empire offers the potential of a large number of truly invigorating experiences. On the other hand, since the Klingon inclination toward activity as opposed to passivity often is interpreted (not always incorrectly) as aggression or belligerence, one needs to be in a position to understand everything that one is likely to encounter in order to be able to participate fully in all activities as well as to avoid accidentally putting oneself in a humiliating if not life-threatening situation.

The first step toward understanding the people of another culture is learning their language. Certainly the central part of any language is its pronunciation, grammar, and vocabulary. In the case of Klingon, reference materials and courses on the language have been available for some time and, though much remains to be discovered, a traveler can, with a reasonable amount of expedience, learn the basics. Unfortunately, the basics are just that—the basics. Typically, students of the Klingon language who, after several years of study, visit the Klingon Homeworld or some other part of the Empire find that their efforts have prepared them only partially for what they actually encounter. They hear words they have not heard before and expressions that do not make any sense even though each word is familiar. They find some speakers easy to understand, but others seem to be pronouncing words most peculiarly or speaking a language that resembles Klingon only vaguely. They hear grammatical patterns their textbooks and teachers told them never occur, clear violations of the rules.

The Klingons they are meeting are not making up vocabulary, pronouncing words in a capricious fashion, or blithely ignoring the rules of grammar, however. What is going on is that most introductory courses in Klingon and most phrase books prepared for recreational travelers either fail to mention or mention only in passing the various ways the language is used within the Empire, the way it varies depending on social criteria. Of course using a language involves choosing appropriate vocabulary and following the rules of pronunciation and grammar, but the particular way language is used—the particular words chosen and the particular constructions employed—is determined partly by the meaning that the speaker wants to convey, but also partly by who the speaker is, the speaker's relationship to the addressee, the type of information being imparted, and the locale of the conversation or nature of the occasion during which it is taking place. A Klingon captain may speak one way when giving commands to his or her crew, another when speaking to a spouse or child, and another when engaged in verbal (or even physical) jousting at a bar.

In addition, introductory works on Klingon usually ignore the diversity within the Klingon Empire. This oversight is not surprising, since even the most well-informed members of the Federation often think of Klingons as a rather homogeneous group. Indeed, Jadzia Dax, science officer on space station Deep Space 9, was in a position to point out to a group of her fellow officers that "Klingons are as diverse a people as any other." She understood this because the Trill's previous host, Curzon Dax, had spent a great deal of time among, and was well admired by, the Klingons and had acquired a great deal of knowledge of their culture.

The diversity found in the Klingon Empire is to be expected because over the centuries, Klingons have conquered many worlds representing a variety of languages and cultures. Even ignoring the impact that absorbing these originally alien cultures has had, there remains variety within the Empire. There are the differences of age, of class, of region, and of participation in specialized activities. All of these differences are reflected in the way the people speak. In addition, there are occasions where strict adherence to grammatical rules and use of the most traditional vocabulary is appropriate, and other occasions where a somewhat different set of rules applies and newer words and expressions are used. There are even occasions, particularly during some rituals, requiring the use of ancient forms of the language.

Just as important as the existence of these differences is the fact that all members of Klingon society are aware of and make use of the differences. By the way a Klingon speaks, another Klingon may be able to tell what part of the Empire the speaker grew up in, whether the speaker is a member of a higher or lower class, the relative age of the speaker, and, depending on the topic of conversation, perhaps the occupation of the speaker. In the same way, a Klingon, though not predisposed to deception, may, if necessary or potentially beneficial, disguise his or her identity by imitating the speech of a member of another group.

Visitors to Klingon communities are also often ill prepared for more than superficial discussions simply because they lack the vocabulary. As in other societies, those Klingons dealing with any area of specialization, whether military skills, food preparation, or the arts, employ special words not normally used in general conversation. Furthermore, there are terms and grammatical formations used in only very special situations, and using them elsewhere is at the very least embarrassing and could be quite offensive.

Klingons take their language very seriously, and this includes not only the vocabulary and grammar but also the rules of usage. Just as a traveler who behaves in an abnormal way is an object of suspicion and probably not to be trusted, a traveler who speaks inappropriately— even if the words and grammar are, strictly speaking, correct—is sure to encounter disapproval, if not rejection or even retribution. It is against this background that this guide, *Klingon for the Galactic Traveler*, has been prepared. It is not a typical guidebook for tourists. No restaurant or hotel recommendations are made, nor is information about required travel documentation provided. Its focus is more narrow: a guide to language usage to help galactic travelers who already have at least a fair knowledge of the language get along with their Klingon hosts and get the most out of their visits. Though prepared by a staff of Federation researchers and written with a bias toward Federation Standard (that is, the language in use throughout the United Federation of Planets and, for interplanetary communication, in most parts of the Alpha and to some degree other quadrants), much of the information in this book should prove useful to travelers from other parts of the galaxy as well.

Even if one has no prior knowledge of the Klingon language, it should be possible to learn a great deal about Klingons from this book. It will be most useful, however, if the reader has familiarity with, or at least a nearby copy of, a work known as *The Klingon Dictionary*, which was prepared under the auspices of Federation Scientific Research Council a number of years ago. In particular, the spelling conventions used for Klingon words are explained there, as are descriptions of Klingon sounds. Except when needed to clarify a point, this information is not repeated here. Details of Klingon grammar, on the other hand, are explained as necessary in the discussions that follow, but comparing the descriptions here with those in the dictionary will make the specifics of the linguistic diversity more apparent. At the end of this volume, there is an addendum to the dictionary, a listing of words not known or whose accuracy was not confirmed at the time of the publication of that work.

It is understood that written explanations of spoken phenomena are inadequate for a full understanding of the topic. What is here is only a guide, a sampling, and it can in no way replace the knowledge and experience acquired by actually living among Klingons. It should be, however, an essential first step. By way of disclaimer, it should be pointed out that although every effort has been made to be accurate, the compilers of this work cannot be responsible for the behavior of Klingons who may disagree.

Once again, the Scientific Research Council has been most generous in its support of this ongoing research. Additional funding was graciously provided by the Galactic Society of Travel. A staff of Klingon consultants and Federation scholars contributed a great deal of time compiling and interpreting the data upon which the analyses in this book are based. In particular, the efforts of one Klingon contributor are to be singled out for commendation. Maltz, we are honored to still be your students. **Qapla'.**

Bruce Brimelin

THE FICTION OF KLINGON CONFORMITY

All Klingons are not alike. To an outsider, Klingon society is often regarded as rather homogeneous, as if all Klingons behave and think in the same way. In fact, although there are a good many shared basic beliefs and understandings that hold Klingon society together and define what it means to be a Klingon, there is a great deal of variation. Thus, despite the veneration shown to warriors, not everyone is a warrior. Some houses (that is, lineages) are more wealthy and powerful than others. The behavior patterns of Klingon men and women are hardly indistinguishable. Some Klingons may prefer one type of music or poetry; other Klingons, another. Older and younger Klingons find a great many areas of behavior about which they disagree.

By the same token, all Klingons do not speak alike. Some of the differences in Klingon speech are relatively trivial: rate or cadence of speech, for example, or a slight difference in the pronunciation of a specific sound. These kinds of differences, in addition to the specific audio qualities (pitch and so forth) of an individual's voice, make it possible to distinguish one speaker from another. On the other hand, some differences may be rather significant: choice of words, major differences in pronunciation, use (or avoidance) of certain grammatical constructions. Frequently, these differences mark one's place within the society. Some linguistic traits are associated with the region in which one was raised, some with age, others with levels of education or expertise in certain areas, and still others with politics.

If there are too many of these differences, intelligibility could be affected. That is, two people speaking in two extremely different ways will not be able to understand one another. This is, of course, the case when two people are speaking two different languages—with utterly different sounds, grammar, and vocabulary—each unknown to the other speaker. There are times, however, even when the same language is spoken, that some differences lead to a certain amount of intelligibility.

The current linguistic situation in the Klingon Empire is a rather complex one that can be somewhat better understood in the light of a bit of history. Klingon mythology holds that over 1,500 years ago, Kahless the Unforgettable actually created the Klingon Empire by overthrowing the tyrant Molor. Kahless gave the people laws of honor and strength and also set the tone for what was long considered, perhaps unjustly, the Klingon pattern of conquering other worlds by force and ruling them oppressively. Before Kahless united them, however, the peoples of Kronos, the Klingon Homeworld, consisted of disparate groups (despite Molor's unpopular rule over all of them), with different customs and sometimes different languages. As the Empire expanded, as other planets were—depending on one's point of view—conquered or incorporated, an even greater number of distinct cultures and languages became part of the overall mix.

Though the peoples of the Empire, except those most recently involuntarily included, have become somewhat more homogeneous as time has gone on, traces—some subtle, some obvious—of their separate histories remain. In terms of language, there are regions within the Empire where the ancestral languages are still spoken, though in a somewhat changed form. For those languages with a

A warrior who united a people: it is hoped that the clone of Kahless (Kevin Conway) will reawaken the Klingon spirit.
Robbie Robinson

great many speakers, there is regional variation; that is, people in different areas speaking the same language in somewhat different ways, following patterns dating back to the time before the unification. In short, within the Empire there are several languages, and the major languages (that is, those with the most speakers) are spoken in a number of versions or dialects.

The official language of the Klingon Empire, the language used for all official purposes, descended from that spoken by Kahless (and, for that matter, also by Molor). It is called **tlhIngan Hol**, literally "Klingon language," though this term rather effectively obscures the complexity of the situation. Before restricting this discussion to modern **tlhIngan Hol** (which is referred to as simply "Klingon" henceforth), it is important to survey, at least briefly, the role of other languages in the Empire, as well as the role of ancient forms of Klingon.

Most of the languages that are either unrelated to or distantly related to Klingon were originally spoken on planets other than Kronos and nearly all of these languages continue to live on their respective homeworlds. Few of these people are monolingual, however, since Klingon is required for commerce, interactions with the government, and so on. In some of the larger cities on Kronos, particularly the capital First City (**veng wa'DIch**), there are pockets of immigrants from these other planets who maintain their languages and customs but do so pretty much out of the hearing of the majority population. Speaking a language other than Klingon, unless everybody present understands it, is considered inappropriate because the speakers may be implying that they do not trust the nonspeakers.

Few native speakers of Klingon bother to learn these other languages (except for the names of some foods), but an occasional word or phrase does sometimes work its way into Klingon proper. For example, **qajunpaQ** ("courage, audacity") comes from *kajunpakt,* a word used in this sense but literally meaning something like "glowing lava" or "fiery lava" in a language originally spoken on Krios. In Klingon, it implies courage of a rather surprising or unexpected kind, perhaps even recklessness, as opposed to **toDuj** ("courage, bravery"), which is more neutral. Some Klingon speakers preserve the original pronunciation, though most fall into the more usual Klingon phonetic pattern. Probably very few Klingons are even vaguely aware of the original connection of *kajunpakt* with lava, glowing or otherwise. The Klingon word for lava, **vaHbo'**, has nothing to do with *kajunpakt*.

Heard far more frequently than non-Klingon languages are various archaic forms of Klingon, dating from different time periods and originating in different regions, collectively known as **no' Hol** ("ancestors' language"). The ancient forms are heard primarily, though not exclusively, in ceremonies, songs, and classical stories.

While the conventional phrases used in some rituals are uttered in modern Klingon (such as those used in the Rite of Ascension, a ceremony symbolizing a young Klingon's attainment of a certain spiritual level), those used in a great many others are in a form of **no' Hol** (such as those associated with the **bIreqtal** [*brek'tal*], the ceremony in which the killer of the leader of a Klingon house marries the widow and thereby becomes the head of the house himself). In these cases, the phrases must be studied and memorized by the participants, then repeated back accurately. Improvising or paraphrasing is entirely inappropriate. Depending on when the phrases for the ritual originated, the words and grammatical constructions may be somewhat like or very different from those of modern Klingon. If the words have survived into modern Klingon but some of the grammatical features have not, it may sound as if the celebrant is speaking improper, ungrammatical Klingon. This is not the case,

A re-creation of the historic battle between Kahless (Michael Danek) and Molor (John Kenton Shull) at a *Kot'baval* Festival.
Robbie Robinson

though the same phrase uttered away from the ritualistic context would be taken as such.

Older language forms are also often found in the lyrics of Klingon songs, particularly songs associated with rituals. Among other activities at the annual *Kot'baval* Festival, for example, the battle between Kahless and Molor is reenacted. While dueling with their *bat'leths,* the performers portraying Kahless, Molor, and other warriors sing traditional songs with words and grammatical forms that are archaic indeed, some not in everyday use for well over 1,000 years. In addition, virtually all of Klingon opera is written in **no' Hol**. In order to follow an opera even superficially, one should prepare before attending a performance by studying the story. For a deeper appreciation, however, it is essential to study also the linguistic structures used in the opera's libretto. As a result, aficionados of this musical form tend to be from the upper levels of society and rather well educated, though this is not invariably the case. Finally, there are some old but still popular songs that retain old words and old grammatical forms that are not interpretable in modern Klingon. In fact, it is not uncommon for Klingon children to think some of these songs are nonsense songs, filled with silly words, and then be surprised to find out that they are ancient hunting songs or battle songs.

Finally, Klingon myths were originally told and re-told, then later written down, in **no' Hol**. In modern times, some are read or told in the original form, though most are familiar only in their modern translations. Even in the most up-to-date versions, however, certain lines are so famous in their original form that they are seldom altered. An example of this is found in the story of Kahless and Lukara. Following the successful defense of the Great Hall at Qam-Chee, Kahless and Lukara engage in a brief conversation that marks the start of their epic romance. Students have been memorizing these lines and repeating them for so long, they have become part of the knowledge shared by all Klingons. One need only say the first line—"**mova' 'aqI' ruStaq**," a **no' Hol** way to say "today was a good day to die"—and everyone will know what is to follow. Interestingly, in the case of this particular conversation, the lines have been incorporated into a mating ritual that persists to this day, with the man and the woman taking the roles and repeating the **no' Hol** lines of Kahless and Lukara, respectively, as the prelude to a romantic encounter.

The use of older language forms is not restricted to rituals, myths, and songs. There are occasions when either as a sign of erudition or just to taunt a friend one may speak a line or two in **no' Hol**. Among some admirers of Klingon history, conversations may take place entirely in older language forms. Such conversations are usually of very brief duration, however, and restricted to a few topics for which vocabulary is known.

KLINGON DIALECTS

Even modern Klingon is characterized by variation. There is a "standard" Klingon, used in public ceremonies and official documents, taught in schools and studied by foreigners, but it changes from time to time and it is not the only way to speak. It gains its status for political, not linguistic, reasons. With a couple of exceptions, the different ways of speaking—that is, the different dialects— are not so different that speakers cannot comprehend one another. On the other hand, each has a set of peculiarities that any Klingon can easily recognize, point out, and usually mimic. For a Klingon, it is easy to tell whether someone is speaking the standard way.

Throughout Klingon history, and still today, if the leader of the Empire carries the title **ta'** ("Emperor"), the way he speaks Klingon—that is, the dialect used by his family and people from his region—is always considered the best way. The vocabulary and grammatical details typical of the leader's area become the current model for the Empire. The way other people speak, if different, is considered somehow inferior, and the more any given dialect differs from that of the Emperor, the more inferior it is considered. Not only is the way of speaking considered inferior, anyone speaking only a nonstandard dialect is considered to be inferior as well, motivating everyone to learn to speak the way the Emperor does. On the other hand, since a change in leadership tends to bring in an Emperor from a different lineage and different region, the relative status of the different varieties can easily change, with a dialect formerly associated with a certain region becoming the standard dialect spoken by all. As a result, the various dialects of Klingon have persisted, with most Klingons becoming adept at several of them. The system by which the Emperor's dialect is considered the standard dialect stayed in place even during those times when there was no official Emperor, as has been the case, until recently, for the last 300 years. Regardless of the leader's title, the leader's way of speaking is still considered the best. The term used for the standard dialect, however, harks back to the Emperors: **ta' tlhIngan Hol** (literally, "the Emperor's Klingon"), often shortened to **ta' Hol** ("Emperor's language"). It is appropriate to use these terms regardless of the official title of the leader of the Empire.

REGIONAL VARIATION

The current standard way of speaking, the **ta' Hol**, is the variety of Klingon associated with the First City on Kronos, and this is the form of the language taught to most non-Klingons, as if there were no other way to speak. This is not at all surprising, since most visitors to the Empire restrict their stay to this one city and have very little knowledge of other parts of the Empire. In the past, this was due to travel restrictions imposed by the Klingon government, though now, perhaps because residents of the First City have become accustomed to dealing with tourists and their habits, visitors simply tend to feel somewhat more comfortable there than they do elsewhere and they avoid wandering too far away.

Those unfamiliar with other parts of the Empire are likewise unfamiliar with the different dialects found in the various regions and are therefore unprepared when they hear unfamiliar speech patterns. For the most part, dialects in the various regions differ owing to specifics of pronunciation, but there are grammatical and vocabulary distinctions as well. The differences range from being rather subtle to being quite noticeable. Indeed, there are a few dialects that are so different from one another that speakers of one can barely communicate with speakers of the other. In those cases, if it were not for the fact that the Empire is a political whole, and, ever since the days of Kahless, has taken great pride in being so, the so-called dialects might be considered separate languages.

It is not possible to survey all of the regional dialects here, particularly the most divergent ones, but some of the kinds of differences that exist and that are likely to be encountered are illustrated. Before we focus on the linguistic peculiarities of some of the different areas, however, a very brief discussion of Klingon geography would seem to be in order. The Klingon Homeworld **Qo'noS**, usually rendered Kronos in Federation Standard, is a planet with basically one very large mass of land surrounded by ocean; perhaps continent is a comparable concept. Within the land mass are distinct areas, some of which are demarcated geographically (divided by a mountain range, for example), while the boundaries of others seem rather arbitrary, the result, no doubt, of ancient power struggles. A specific area whose borders are definable, by whatever means, is normally called a **Sep**, commonly translated as "region," though, since the regions were politically distinct in the past, "country" might have at one time been just as appropriate a translation. An identifiable area within a **Sep** is a **yoS** ("area, district"), and a **yoS** usually contains at least one important **veng** ("city"); though sometimes, especially in the more rugged parts of a planet, there may be only a small settlement or **vengHom** ["village"]). This terminology is also used when describing other planets within the Empire.

Regions are sometimes identified by the name of the most prominent city within the region. Thus, the region containing the First City is simply called **veng wa'DIch Sep** ("First City region") and **voSpegh Sep** ("Vospeg region," southwest of the First City—to use directional terms familiar to speakers of Federation Standard) is named after the city of Vospeg. Other regions have names that are distinct from the names of any districts or cities within them, such as the large **Sa'Qej Sep** ("Sakrej region"), several thousand kilometers east of the First City. The origins of most Klingon place names are not known, having been lost to history. Sometimes, however, the meaning of a place name is clear, such as the Sakrej region's **HuD beQ yoS** ("Flat Mountain district") and, of course, **veng wa'DIch** ("First City"). On rare occasion, a place's name can be traced to an individual or family, such as **Qotmagh Sep** ("Krotmag region"), derived from **Qotmagh**, the leader of a powerful house who, centuries ago, conquered neighboring areas, or **ruq'e'vet** ("Ruk'-evet"), a city in the **ghevchoq Sep** ("Gevchok region"), named for a warrior (whether actual or mythological is a matter of dispute) who singlehandedly defeated an invading force.

Before the time of the unification of the Empire by Kahless, the amount of interaction between inhabitants of different regions varied. When regions formed coalitions in a campaign against a common enemy, interaction was great; when they were in a period of mutual antagonism, interaction was limited. Since interaction involves people communicating with one another, this varying amount of contact is reflected in the linguistic situation. Dialects spoken in any given pair of regions have some common features (vocabulary or pronunciations, for example), developed during the periods when the people had a great deal of interaction with one another; and these same dialects have some clear differences, developed during times of discord when contact was minimal.

In addition to the regions on Kronos (and there are more than those mentioned above), of course, are the various planets that have become part of the Empire. On some, such as Morska, a dialect of Klingon has all but replaced any languages originally spoken; on others, such as Vaq'aj II, native languages survive alongside **ta' Hol**. Interestingly, the dialects of Klingon spoken on conquered planets are not as different from **ta' Hol** as are some of the dialects on Kronos itself. That is because the Klingon language came to the conquered planets relatively recently and therefore remains somewhat similar to that spoken by the conquerors, while the dialects on Kronos have been spoken for a much longer period and have had time to develop differently.

Because the dialect of the First City is the standard dialect, the **ta' Hol**, it is both customary and convenient to compare other dialects to it rather than to each other. This practice is retained in the discussions below.

Pronunciation

Residents of various regions and territories of the Klingon Empire may be identified by the way they pronounce words—that is, by their accents. Those in the Krotmag (**Qotmagh**) region, for example, have characteristic ways of pronouncing the sounds **b** and **D**, as well as the vowels. In **ta' Hol**, **b** is pronounced the same as *b* in Federation Standard *bribe*. In the Krotmag dialect of Klingon, however, **b** and **m** are pronounced identically, both of them sounding like Federation Standard *m* as in *mime*. Thus, for example, the members of the following pairs of words sound exactly alike in the Krotmag dialect; however, they sound different in Standard Klingon:

> **bup** ("quit")/**mup** ("strike")
> **boH** ("be impatient")/**moH** ("be ugly")
> **buS** ("concentrate on")/**muS** ("hate")
> **ghob** ("wage war")/**ghom** ("meet, encounter")
> **qab** ("face")/**qam** ("foot")
> **Qub** ("think")/**Qum** ("communicate")
> **teb** ("fill")/**tem** ("deny")

For the most part, this causes no problems for Krot-mag dialect speakers. There are more homonyms (words that sound alike) in their dialect than in other dialects, but, as is the case with homonyms in general, context usually serves to clarify which word is meant. Occasionally, however, two identically pronounced words can be used in such similar contexts, raising the possibilities of at least ambiguity if not catastrophic misunderstanding, that some interesting speech patterns have developed. When there are nouns that sound alike, speakers are likely to use compound nouns (that is, use two nouns where otherwise one would do). This is probably most clearly seen with the pair of words meaning "face" and "foot," both pronounced **qam** (though "face" is **qab** in Standard Klingon). Does **qamlIj vIghov** mean "I recognize your foot" or "I recognize your face"? Unless the course of the discussion clearly dictates which is meant (as it might, for example, in a conversation when buying shoes, though even here the possibility for ambiguity exists), there is no way to tell. In such a situation, "foot" would probably be rendered **'uS qam** (literally, "leg foot"); "face" would be **nach qam** (or, in the standard dialect, **nach qab**—literally, "head face"). Interestingly, though originally used only to avoid ambiguity with words containing **m** and **b**, these speech patterns have become quite common in the Krotmag region and are used even when **m** and **b** are not involved in the words at all. Thus, it would not be unusual to hear such utterances as **DeS ghop** (actually, **NeS** ghop—the meaning of **N** is explained below) meaning "arm hand" or **nach ghIch** ("head nose"), even though the single words **ghop** ("hand") and **ghIch** ("nose") need no disambiguation. Similarly, a house (lineage) is frequently called **qorDu' tuq** (actually, **qorNu' tuq**)—literally, "family house"—rather than **tuq** ("house") alone, and a sword is often termed **yan 'etlh** (or even **'etlh yan**)—literally, "sword

sword." This manner of speaking is quite characteristic of this region.

For verbs, a somewhat different tactic is employed. In **ta' Hol**, there is no problem distinguishing **bIboH** ("You are impatient") from **bImoH** ("You are ugly"). In the Krotmag region, however, both are pronounced **mImoH**. To make the speaker's intent clear, it is not uncommon to add a short sentence immediately after the potentially ambiguous one:

mImoH. yIjotchoH.
[Standard: **bIboH. yIjotchoH.**]
("You're impatient. Calm down!")

mImoH. 'oy ' mInNu'wIj.
[Standard: **bImoH. 'oy' mInDu'wIj.**]
("You're ugly. My eyes ache.")
(See below regarding Krotmag **N**.)

Krotmag dialect speakers have a distinctive pronunciation of **D** as well: it sounds like **n**, except the tip of the tongue touches a point in the middle of the roof of the mouth rather than one behind the top teeth as it does for **n**. (For the sake of clarity in this discussion, the way Krotmag dialect speakers pronounce **D** will be written **N**, to distinguish it from **n**.) The **D** sound in **ta' Hol** is also produced with the tongue pointing upward and not near the teeth (just like **N**), but otherwise the **D** sound is similar to that of Federation Standard *d* as in *did*. For speakers in the Krotmag region, the sounds **n** and **N** are distinct; the following pairs of words do not sound the same (the standard form of the second member of each pair follows in brackets):

naH ("fruit, vegetable")/**NaH** ("now") [**DaH**]
nuj ("mouth")/**Nuj** ("vessel") [**Duj**]
mIn ("eye")/**mIN** ("colony") [**mID**]
nulegh ("He/she sees us.")/**Nulegh** ("He/she sees you.") [**Dulegh**]

Though under most circumstances, speakers of the Krotmag dialect can easily distinguish between the two sounds, it is not unusual to hear a speaker add extra elements, as if to ensure clarity: **maH nulegh**—literally, "us, he/she sees us"; **SoH Nulegh**—literally, "you, he/she sees you." This does not happen anywhere nearly as frequently as it does with words with **b** or **m**, however. Speakers of other forms of Klingon, on the other hand, find the Krotmag pronunciations of **N** and **n** to be so similar as to be indistinguishable. When trying to speak in the Krotmag manner, they tend to pronounce all words with **D** as if they used **n** instead, rather than **N**, making it possible for a true Krotmag speaker to differentiate a fellow resident from an outsider, but also making communication difficult. Misunderstandings, sometimes with unfortunate consequences, are not all that uncommon.

A third characteristic of the Krotmag accent is the nasal quality of the vowels, caused by the air being expelled through the mouth and nose at the same time while speaking. This in no way impedes communication with speakers of other dialects, but it does give the dialect a distinct tone.

Although the number of speakers of the dialect of the Krotmag region is relatively small, their speech patterns are well known and easily recognized and have actually had an effect on other dialects. It is not uncommon for speakers of one dialect to imitate the speech of another, whether as a way to mock the speakers of a nonstandard dialect or as a way to learn about that dialect to be prepared for a change in leadership. A bit of dialect mixture results, with words or pronunciations of one dialect being added to another. The distinctive pronunciations of the Krotmag dialect are surely responsible for some slang and idiomatic usages in Klingon in general. For example, **chab chu'** (literally, "new pie") is another way to say "new invention" or "latest innovation." This is no doubt because the Krotmag pronunciation of **chab** ("pie") is **cham**, the same as the word for "technology." Similarly, a slang word for "sword" is **yaD** (literally, "toe"), based on the Krotmag pronunciation of **yaD** as **yaN**, which to most Klingons will sound like **yan** ("sword"). (Other examples of slang originating from Krotmag regional pronunciations are found in the chapter on Language Change and Staying Current, under "Vocabulary: Slang," pages 142–167.)

Speaking in a manner that is sort of between that of the Krotmag region and **ta' Hol** are the peoples of Tak'ev (**taq'ev**), who, though still a minority population, greatly outnumber the residents of Krotmag. These people maintain the distinction between **b** and **m** but pronounce the **b** as if it were **mb**; that is, starting off as the **m** sound but ending up at a **b**. Similarly, **D** is pronounced more like **nD** (or, more accurately, **ND**). Thus **ba'** ("sit") would be pronounced more like **mba'**; **Hub** ("defend") would sound like **Humb**; **Du'** ("farm") would be **NDu'**; **HoD** ("captain") would be **HoND**; and **Dub** ("improve") would be **NDumb**. The nasal vowel quality found in the Krotmag region is characteristic of Tak'ev speech as well.

The speech of residents of the planet Morska has some identifiable phonological characteristics also. Most striking is the absence of the sound **tlh.** Syllables ending with **tlh** in most dialects end with **ts** (pronounced the same as *ts* in Federation Standard *cats*) in the Morskan dialect; at the beginning of syllables, instead of saying **tlh,** Morskans say something that sounds very much like a combination of standard Klingon **gh** and **l**—that is, **ghl**. Compare, for example (Morskan/**ta' Hol**):

> **ghIts/ghItlh** ("write")
> **mats/matlh** ("be loyal")
> **ghlIngan/tlhIngan** ("Klingon")
> **ghlo'/tlho'** ("thank")
> **ghluts/tlhutlh** ("drink")

The Morskan dialect also pronounces **H** differently from the standard way. At the beginning of syllables, **H** sounds like Federation Standard *h* as in *hat*; at the ends of syllables, **H** is not pronounced at all:

hIv/HIv ("attack")
ba/baH ("fire [a torpedo]")
hu/HuH ("bile")

Finally, **Q** at the beginning of syllables is pronounced the same as standard Klingon **H**:

Hapla'/Qapla' ("success")
Hoy/Qoy ("hear")

Because of this pronunciation difference, sometimes speakers of the Morskan dialect and those of **ta' Hol** misunderstand one another. Words such as the following have been responsible for the loss of more than one life:

Hagh: Morskan, "make a mistake"/Standard, "laugh"
Hoj: Morskan, "make war"/Standard, "be cautious"
HoS: Morskan, "be sorry"/Standard, "be strong"

Grammar

Although the basic grammar of all dialects of Klingon is the same, there is some variation. The Morskan dialect, for example, does not put the suffix **-'e'** on the subject noun in a sentence translated with "to be" in Federation Standard (though the suffix is not missing in other contexts where it is used to focus attention on one noun rather than another within the sentence). Compare:

Morskan: **tera'ngan gha qama'.** ("The prisoner is a Terran.")
Standard: **tera'ngan ghaH qama''e'** (**tera'ngan,** "Terran"; **ghaH,** "he, she"; **qama',** "prisoner")

Morskan: **bIghha'Daq ghata qama'**. ("The
prisoner is in the prison.")
Standard: **bIghHa'Daq ghaHtaH qama"e'**.
(**bIghHa'Daq,** "in the prison"; **-taH,**
"continuous")

Sometimes the **-'e'** is heard at the end of the subject noun
in Morskan sentences of this type (**qama'** ["prisoner"] in
the examples above), leading some speakers of **ta' Hol** to
criticize speakers of the Morskan dialect for sloppiness,
claiming that sometimes the **-'e'** is heard and other times
not, with no apparent pattern. The critics are wrong: **-'e'**
added to **qama'** in the Morskan sentences would have
its usual focusing function (the sentences would mean
something like "It's the prisoner who's a Terran" and "It's
the prisoner who's in the prison," respectively), the same
as it would have in sentences of other types. This grammatical device is not available to speakers of **ta' Hol** who,
to speak grammatically, must use **-'e'** in sentences of this
type whether wishing to call extra attention to the subject
noun or not.

Another interesting grammatical difference is found
in the way prepositional concepts ("above," "below," and
so on) are expressed in the speech typical of the Sakrej
(**Sa'Qej**) region. In Klingon in general, such ideas are
conveyed by using a special set of nouns (**'em** ["area behind"], **bIng** ["area below"], and others) that follow the
nouns whose position they are indicating. Thus, "behind
the door" is **lojmIt 'em** (literally, "door area behind") and
"below the table" is **raS bIng** (literally, "table area
below"). A pronoun may be used instead of a noun: **jIH
'em** ("behind me"—literally, "I area behind"), **chaH bIng**
("below them"—literally, "they area below"). In the Sakrej region, however, possessive suffixes are used in place
of the independent pronouns: **'emwIj** ("behind me"—
literally, "my area behind"), **bIngchaj** ("below them"—
literally, "their area below"). Using the possessive suffix

construction when speaking **ta' Hol** will not lead to mis-understandings, but it will associate the speaker with the residents of Sakrej, which, depending on the political situation, may or may not be beneficial.

A third type of grammatical difference is seen in the grammar of toasting, an extremely common activity accompanying even the most casual of drinking affairs. In **ta' Hol** and most other dialects of Klingon, when a toast is made, certain grammatical rules apply that do not apply elsewhere, setting toasts off from other kinds of utterances. For example, in everyday speech, the verb suffix **-jaj** ("may") is used to express the speaker's desire or wish that something happen in the future, as in **chotwI' DaSamjaj** ("May you find the murderer"; **chotwI'** "murderer"; **DaSamjaj,** "May you locate him/her") or **jejjaj tajlIj** ("May your knife be sharp"; **jejjaj,** "May it be sharp"; **tajlIj,** "your knife"). In both cases, the normal rules of Klingon syntax are followed: the object, if mentioned, precedes the verb (as in the first sentence) and the subject, if mentioned, follows it (as in the second).

If either of these sentiments is given as a toast, however, a special rule—applicable to toasts only, and therefore better described as socially motivated than as grammatically motivated—must be followed. In a toast, the last word is always the verb (ending in **-jaj** ["may"]), even if that means the subject precedes the verb. Thus, as a toast, the first sentence, **chotwI' DaSamjaj** ("May you find the murderer") is already well formed; the last word is the verb phrase "may you find him/her." The second sentence, however, must be recast if it is to be used as a toast so that the verb comes last: **tajlIj jejjaj** ("May your knife be sharp"). If this were not a toast, this would be grammatically unacceptable. In toasts with both subject and object nouns, the order is object-subject-verb, as in the toast **wo' ghawran DevtaHjaj** ("May Gowron continue to lead the Empire"; **wo',** "empire"; **ghawran,** "Gowron"; **DevtaHjaj,** "May he continue to lead it"). If uttered as a wish, hope, or aspiration—but not as a toast—the normal word order applies: **wo' DevtaHjaj ghawran** ("May Gowron continue to lead the empire").

In a divergence from the majority of Klingon dialects, the speakers of Sakrej and No'hvadut (**noHva'Dut**) do not follow this pattern. In these dialects, there is no reforming of the sentences for toasts; the subject always follows the verb. Thus, as toasts, **jejjaj tajlIj** ("May your knife be sharp") and **wo' DevtaHjaj ghawran** ("May Gowron continue to lead the empire") are perfectly acceptable, even though the verb ending with **-jaj** is not the last thing in the sentence. Though always done in high spirits, toasting is taken very seriously. It is important, therefore, to phrase toasts correctly in order to avoid unwanted consequences, and this is done slightly differently depending upon where one is. A visitor from outside the Klingon world should be aware of the speech patterns of others present (and, to play it very safe, should avoid making toasts with overt subjects).

Vocabulary

Though most vocabulary is shared throughout the Empire, there are certain regionalisms—that is, certain words that are used fairly frequently by the speakers of some areas but only rarely, if at all, by those of others. (In the discussion that follows, all spellings are consistent with **ta' Hol**, even in exemplifying words that are from dialects with distinct pronunciation patterns.)

A good deal of variation is found among the words relating to food and food preparation. For example, in the First City and elsewhere, there is a special word, **qettlhup,** for the sauce prepared by thickening **chanDoq** ("marinade"). In some regions, the word **qettlhup** is seldom used; **chanDoq jeD** (literally, "thick marinade") is used instead. Similarly, in all regions, the word **vIy-chorgh** means "juice" or "sap"—that is, the liquid from a plant. In some regions, however, its meaning has been extended to also include any liquid that accompanies food, as if a general term for "sauce." Thus, instead of saying **ghevI'** for the sauce that normally accompanies **qagh** ("serpent worms"), the common expression is **qagh vIychorgh** (literally, "**qagh** juice" or the like). Likewise, instead of using the term **'uSu'** for the sauce traditionally offered with *gladst*, **tlhatlh vIychorgh** (literally, "*gladst* juice") is used.

Being hunters by nature and primarily carnivorous, Klingons have an extensive vocabulary for different parts of an animal, and the terminology is widespread. The word **ghab**, however, which refers to any chunk of the midsection of an animal, has slightly varying meanings depending on region. In most of the empire, including the First City, **ghab** is rather inclusive: basically, whatever was chopped off the animal as a single piece, with or without bones or internal organs. In some areas, **ghab** is never applied to a cut of meat lacking bones. Instead, the phrase **ghab tun** (perhaps translatable as "fillet," though literally, "soft **ghab**") is sometimes heard. The same concept would be expressed in most of the Empire, including by speakers of **ta' Hol**, by a longer phrase: **Hom Hutlhbogh ghab** ("**ghab** that lacks bone"). The expression **ghab tun** would probably not be used by most.

The most common utensil used in preparing Klingon food is the **'un** ("pot"), a word found with the same meaning throughout the Empire. The names for specific types of pots, however, exhibit some regional variation. For example, while a large, flat-bottomed pot is usually called a **bargh**, in some regions it is a **vutmeH 'un** ("pot for preparing [food]"), sometimes shortened to simply **vut'un**. In some regions, a **bargh** made of metal is a **mIv** (which also means "helmet," even though, historically speaking, helmets are not necessarily made of metal) or a **mIv**

The casting of Alexander's forehead displays the **Quch** of a proud house. (LeVar Burton, Marina Sirtis, Jonathan Frakes, Michael Dorn.) *Robbie Robinson*

bargh ("helmet pot"), while a ceramic **bargh** is called a **chor** (literally, "belly") or **chor bargh** ("belly pot").

A small amount of regional variation is also found among words referring to body parts, though almost always, words for the different body parts are the same in all dialects. One exception is the word for "nose," which is **ghIch** everywhere but in some regions may alternatively be called **ley'**. Another is the word for "liver," which is generally **chej** but in some regions also **mavje'**. The fact that Klingons have two livers does not seem to be relevant here, since both **chej** and, for those who use the word, **mavje'** apply to either liver.

It is a different story with the word for "forehead." The standard word for this prominent part of Klingon anatomy is **Quch**, and this word is found with this meaning throughout the Empire. In addition, however, practi-

cally every dialect has its own alternate word for
"forehead." Indeed, **Quch** is simply the word for "forehead" in the First City. Among these other forms are:
boD, **jargh**, **mIQ**, **'aQlo'**, **Huy'Dung**, **tuqvol**, **no"och**.
While the first four of these words are simply regional-
isms for "forehead," the last three can be analyzed, at
least partially. **Huy'Dung** is probably from **Huy' Dung**
("above the eyebrow[s]"). The word **tuqvol** may contain
the word **tuq** ("house [lineage]") because family resem-
blances can be seen in forehead ridges. The second element, **vol**, however, is otherwise unknown. Similarly, the
first syllable of **no"och** may derive from **no'** ("ancestors"), again suggesting something about genealogy. The
second syllable, **'och**, probably resembles **'och** ("tunnel")
only accidentally; there is no reason to think that "ancestors' tunnel" is a way to say "forehead."

For the most part, regional vocabulary is indeed restricted to a single region or set of regions. That is, a particular word is heard in, and associated with, one place
but not another. There are some words, however, that are
heard pretty much everywhere but have different meanings in different areas. As might be expected, this could
lead to confusion and misunderstanding, so it is important to use the right words in the right places. For example, the word for "stairs" or "stairway" in most of the
Empire is **letlh**. One type of **letlh** is a **choghvat**, the stairway leading to and from the doorway of a ship. In a couple of dialects in the Mekro'vak (**meqro'vaq**) region,
however, **letlh** refers only to the stairway connected to a
ship, while **ngep'oS** is any other kind of stairway but not
one used to enter or exit a ship.

Similarly, one needs to be careful in talking about
certain articles of clothing. In the First City, and in most
places in the Empire, **wep** means "jacket, coat" and **yIvbeH** means "tunic"—that is, a shirt or shirtlike garment
with or without sleeves. In the Vospeg (**voSpegh**) region,
on the other hand, **yIvbeH** refers only to a sleeveless shirt

(thus retaining much of the word's original meaning, a sleeveless protective garment worn by warriors), **wep** means a shirt with sleeves, and any jacket or coat is a **cheSvel**, a word that elsewhere refers to a specific style of coat associated with, not surprisingly, the Vospeg region.

Confusion can be caused by verbs as well as nouns. For example, while the verb **ghIH** means "be messy, sloppy" in **ta' Hol** and in most dialects, in the towns near Ruk'evet (**ruq'e'vet**), **ghIH** means "be careless." The more widespread word for "be careless" is **yepHa'**, and this word is used in addition to **ghIH** in the Ruk'evet area. To say "be messy, sloppy," the Ruk'evet inhabitants say **Soy'**, a verb meaning "be clumsy" elsewhere. The Ruk'evet word for "be clumsy" is **jat**, which is phonetically identical to the noun meaning "tongue." Even though this is probably just a coincidence, there is a slang term **jat**, used throughout the Empire but somewhat more frequently in the areas near Ruk'evet, which means "speak incoherently, mumble," a notion with negative connotations for Klingons. Enunciating Klingon clearly is always important, but one should take extra care to not accidentally say **jat** ("mumble") when intending the similar-sounding **ja'** ("say"), **jatlh** ("speak"), or **jach** ("yell").

Finally, there are some instances of a word existing in two regions with two utterly unrelated meanings, one of them quite derogatory. For example, throughout the Empire, a soup whose main component is *igvah* liver has a special name, **ghaw'**. This word is avoided in the Vospeg region, however, because there, the word **ghaw'** is a slang term meaning something like "one who is full of self-doubt or who is insecure" and is a word used only as an insult. To refer to the soup, one simply says **'IghvaH chej chatlh** (literally, *"igvah* liver soup"). In most of the Empire, to say to someone **ghaw' SoH** means only "You are *igvah* liver soup," an odd thing to say, but more incongruous than anything else. In the Vospeg region, on the other hand, to call someone a **ghaw'** is often the prelude to a fight to the death.

Though in nearly all cases using the standard **ta' Hol** will serve the visitor well, it is definitely worth putting forth whatever effort may be required to become familiar with regionalisms if one expects to travel around the Empire, especially to places distant from the First City or to regions in which there may be some dissatisfaction with the current leadership of the High Council. Not only will this make communication in these places easier, it will also facilitate building a special connection between the visitor and the Klingons with whom he or she is interacting. This is always a good idea.

Generational Variation

It should be no surprise to find that Klingon children speak differently from Klingon adults. The phenomenon is found in most societies throughout the galaxy. As children learn their language, they give distinct pronunciations to certain sounds, lack a full grasp of the grammar, and use some words in ways adults find inappropriate. Because the same patterns are followed by a great many Klingon children, however, it is possible to describe certain characteristics of children's speech.

By the time Klingon children are old enough to know many words and speak in short but well-formed sentences, most of the sounds associated with "baby talk" are gone. Nevertheless, it takes several more years for all of the sounds to disappear from their verbalizations, giving the speech of young children a distinctive sound. As a rule, before a child's First Rite of Ascension, all remaining traces of childhood speech have disappeared.

Among the most noticeable features setting children's speech apart from that of adults are the sounds of three consonants. First, the sound **j** is often pronounced

not as *j* in Federation Standard *jar*, but instead more like
the *s* in Federation Standard *pleasure* or *si* in *vision*. If
this sound is transcribed as **zh**, the verb **naj** ("dream")
would be **nazh**; **jav** ("six") sounds more like **zhav**. Second, the sound **ng**, which, for adults, is like the last sound
in Federation Standard *sing*, is pronounced as **n** at the
ends of syllables, and more like the *ni* in Federation Standard *onion* (as if *ny*) at the beginning. Thus, the children's pronunciation of **mang** ("soldier") would be **man**;
the pronunciation of **ngeD** ("be easy") would be **nyeD**.
Finally, the consonant **q**, in the speech of children,
sounds much more like Federation Standard *k* than an
adult **q** does. For example, **quS** ("chair") is more like
kuS, and **tuq** ("house [lineage]") is more like **tuk**.

Curiously, a fourth consonantal alteration, though
relatively uncommon, is the one most associated with
children's speech. A minority of children pronounce **tlh**
as **ch**, particularly at the end of syllables. For example,
qatlh ("why") is pronounced **qach**, and **botlh** ("middle") is
is **boch**. Though the resulting forms may be real, though
different, words (**qach**, for example, is "structure, building," and **boch** means "be shiny"), there is seldom any
confusion because the identically pronounced words are
used in such different contexts. If a child were to say
qach jej taj, that could mean only "Why is the knife
sharp?" (**qach**, mispronunciation of **qatlh,** "why"; **jej,**
"be sharp"; **taj,** "knife"). If **qach** were "structure," the
Klingon sentence would be as ungrammatical and non-
sensical as "The knife sharps the structure." On the other
hand, children occasionally do make unintentionally ambiguous statements. If a child who pronounces **tlh** as **ch**
were to say, for instance, **mach SuvwI'pu'**, it is not clear
whether he or she means "Warriors are loyal" (**mach**,
mispronunciation of **matlh,** "be loyal"; **SuvwI'pu'**, "warriors") or "Warriors are small" (**mach** "be small").

There are differences in the grammar children use,
too. Children employ the noun suffix **-oy** ("endearment")

with some regularity, while it is used quite infrequently in the speech of adults or even older children. It is usually used with the terms for parents and other relatives (**vavoy**, "Daddy"; **SoSoy**, "Mommy"; **vavnI'oy**, "Grandpa," etc.) but also for other people or animals for which a child feels some fondness (**targhoy**, "targy," perhaps, for a pet *targ*). Some children use it with other nouns (such as **qamoy**, perhaps "footsie," based on **qam**, "foot"), but such usage is strongly discouraged and usually falls out of a child's repertoire before too long.

Another grammatical feature of Klingon about which children frequently become confused involves nouns that are inherently plural, such as **cha** ("torpedoes") and **ngop** ("plates [for eating]"), as opposed to their singular counterparts **peng** ("torpedo") and **jengva'** ("plate"). Instead of using the special plural forms, children tend forms plurals of these words by simply adding the plural suffix **-mey** to the singular forms (**pengmey, jengva'-mey**), as would be done with most other nouns (except for those referring to body parts or to beings capable of language, for which **-Du'** and **-pu'**, respectively, would be used), such as **yuQmey** ("planets"). Adults also add **-mey** to these nouns, but they do so to indicate that the items are scattered about (**jengva'mey**, "plates scattered all over the place"). For children who say **jengva'mey**, it apparently means simply "plates"; that is, it is nothing more than the plural form of **jengva'**. Children seem to be aware of the existence of the inherently plural forms, however, for they use them as well, though usually with the suffix **-mey** superfluously appended: **chamey** ("torpedoeses"), **ngopmey** ("plateses"). Inherently plural nouns are considered singular as far as how they fit into the overall grammatical structure. Thus, the singular pronoun **'oH** ("it") is used for both **jengva'** ("plate") and **ngop** ("plates") in sentences such as **nuqDaq 'oH jengva''e'?** ("Where is the plate?") and **nuqDaq 'oH ngop'e'?** ("Where are the plates?"; **nuqDaq**, "where?"). Children, however, tend to use the plural pronoun **bIH** ("they") with **ngop** (as well as with **jengva'mey** and the redundantly suffixed **ngopmey**): **nuqDaq bIH ngop'e'?** ("Where are the plates?").

When speaking to small children, particularly babies who have not yet started speaking, Klingon adults often incorporate some or all of these aspects of children's speech—particularly the distinctive pronunciations. This form of speech is called **puq Hol** (literally, "child's language"), though a better Federation Standard translation might be "baby talk." It is entirely inappropriate for an adult or even an older child to use **puq Hol** except when speaking to a baby, though it is occasionally used when speaking to pets. Using **puq Hol** to an adult is highly insulting and degrading. Visitors from other cultures should be aware that this proscription applies to the interaction between mates or potential mates. Unlike in some other places in the galaxy, use of **puq Hol** is not a part of any Klingon courting ritual, nor is it a sign of affection between two adults.

As children grow older, their speech changes to resemble that of adults. Nevertheless, there are still some observable differences between the speech of younger and older Klingons, though mostly involving usage or vocabulary choice rather than pronunciation or grammar. One good illustration of this involves the tag question— that is, the construction in which a statement is followed by a question such as "right?" In Klingon, a tag question is formed by adding **qar'a'** (literally, "Is it accurate?"; **qar,** "be accurate"; **-'a',** the interrogative suffix) either after the verb or at the end of the sentence: **qarDaSnganpu' HIvpu' tlhInganpu' qar'a'?** or **qarDaSnganpu' HIvpu' qar'a' tlhInganpu'?** ("The Klingons have attacked the Cardassians, right?"; **qarDaSnganpu',** "Cardassians"; **HIvpu',** "have attacked"; **tlhInganpu',** "Klingons"). The tag question is found in the speech of all Klingons to one degree or another, but it is found quite a bit more frequently in the speech of younger Klingons. Indeed, some members of the older generation have accused teenage Klingons of adding **qar'a'** to the end of virtually every sentence they utter. This is an inaccurate characterization to be sure, but it does point out an awareness of the difference between the speech patterns of the older and younger generations.

The primary difference between the speech of older and younger Klingons, however, lies in the choice of vocabulary. Younger Klingons describe some of the vocabulary used by their elders as **mu'mey Doy'** ("tired words"), preferring to use what they call **mu'mey ghoQ** ("fresh words") or even **Hol ghoQ** ("fresh language"). (The word **ghoQ** ["fresh"], in its most narrow usage, applies to just-killed meat). Perhaps "slang" is a good translation of **mu'mey ghoQ**. Some older Klingons incorporate some of the **mu'mey ghoQ** into their own speech, though some claim to not understand the **mu'mey ghoQ** at all (nor are they quite sure what the term itself means).

Any visitor to a Klingon planet will undoubtedly encounter **mu'mey ghoQ** and should learn as many slang words as possible ahead of time in order to fit in easily and to avoid having to ask for explanations. New words are constantly coming into use, however, so some asking is inescapable. On the other hand, a visitor should be keenly aware that some Klingons use more slang than others, and some try to ignore the phenomenon entirely. To avert potential unpleasantness, the best tactic is to avoid using slang in conversation until someone else has first. Examples of **mu'mey ghoQ** are given in the chapter on Language Change and Staying Current, under "Vocabulary: Slang," pages 142–167.

It should be pointed out that the vocabulary associated with rituals, martial arts, literature, opera, and the like, though some of it may be genuinely archaic, is not considered **mu'mey Doy'** ("tired words"). Traditions are extremely important in Klingon culture, and the younger generation honors them fully. The term **mu'mey Doy'** is used only in reference to everyday speech.

Societal Variation

Klingon society is a stratified one. That is, there are clear distinctions between those with great wealth and influence and those with little or none. This sort of status is a matter of inheritance. Among the higher classes, one is born into an ancestral unit known as a **tuq**, normally translated "house." Some houses are particularly wealthy, controlling vast lands by means of armed forces loyal to the particular house. Other houses have far less influence and, for survival, often form alliances with the larger houses. Each house is led by the eldest male direct descendent of the previous leader (there are complex traditions dealing with what happens if there is no male heir), and the heads of the larger houses—that is, those with the greatest holdings and strongest forces—have seats on the Klingon High Council (**tlhIngan yejquv**), the body that rules the Empire. Since the number of seats on the Council is limited, many houses are not directly represented, are not as influential in Klingon society, and therefore occupy a slightly lower social position. In addition to wielding great political influence, members of the higher classes are also better educated than are others, particularly in the area of the arts.

Houses routinely contribute troops, ships, and weaponry and go into battle to help advance the Empire's objectives. On the other hand, it is not unusual for the interests of the various houses and their leaders to be at odds with one another, leading to hostilities between houses, sometimes lasting generations. Depending on a house's successes in any of these battles, its holdings—and therefore its overall influence in the society—may increase or decrease. A house's place in society may also be adversely affected by the behavior of its leadership. If the

In the mirror universe, the Regent Worf is the power behind the Emperor. *Robbie Robinson*

High Council determines an action to be dishonorable, not only may it remove the leader of a house from the Council itself, it may also seize the house's lands, forces, and other holdings.

Though members of the lower levels of society may not identify themselves as members of a house, they usually have pledged loyalty to one. Typically, members of this class work as servants or perform duties necessary for the daily functioning of the Empire's undertakings. Many serve as members of a house's military forces.

The Klingon military, of course, has a hierarchical structure of its own, with ranks and areas of authority spelled out explicitly. Various fleets and squadrons are loyal to various houses, though, as might be expected, the details of these alliances are subject to change. Within the Klingon Defense Force (**tlhIngan hubbeq**), which includes the entire Klingon military apparatus, the highest officers tend to be members of influential houses, particularly the members of the ultimate military authority, the High Command (**ra'ghomquv**). It is possible, however, for anyone to rise to higher ranks in the military and, thereby, higher levels in society in general, through particularly heroic actions in combat.

Some of this social structure influences the way Klingons speak. While social standing has no connection with pronunciation (except for the lower status associated with speakers of regional dialects differing from that of the current leadership), there are a few grammatical differences and some vocabulary differences that clearly reflect a stratified society.

The most obvious grammatical feature associated with social status is the verb suffix **-neS** (an honorific) used to express a high degree of respect or honor. For example, one might say **choQaHpu'neS**, which might be rather awkwardly translated as "You, honored one, have helped me." (Compare this to **choQaHpu'** ["You have helped me."]) Though there is no situation in which the use of **-neS** is required and its use is rather infrequent, when it is used, it is used only when addressing someone of higher rank, such as a higher officer in the military or a high political leader. It would not be used by a higher-ranking officer, for example, when speaking to a lower-ranking officer, nor would it be used when talking about a higher-ranking person. Thus, one would not describe being aided by a superior by saying **muQaHpu'neS** ("He/she, whom I honor, has helped me": **muQaHpu'**, "He/she has helped me"). Of course, one does not need the suffix **-neS** in order to speak of honor. The adverbial **batlh** ("in an honored fashion") may be used for exactly this function, as in **batlh muQaHpu'** ("He/she has helped me in an honored way" or "He/she has helped me with honor"). While it would be entirely inappropriate for a superior to say to an inferior **choQaHpu'neS** ("You, honored one, have helped me"), the superior may say **batlh cho-QaHpu'** ("You have helped me in an honored way" or "You have helped me with honor"). The relative ranking of individuals may be ascertained by noting who says **-neS** to whom.

Ironically, members of the higher social classes are more likely than their lower-class counterparts to violate the normal rule involving possessives ("my," "your," "his/her," etc.). These special constructions are formed intentionally, however, so calling them "errors" would not be accurate. As with **-neS**, this grammatical twist is not encountered very frequently, so when it is used, it carries a certain amount of force.

Normally, a possessive is formed by adding the appropriate suffix to a noun, as in **vavwI'** ("my father"), **vavlI'** ("your father"), and **vavDaj** ("his/her father") (all based on **vav**, "father"). In the case of "my" and "your," a slightly different suffix is used if the noun refers to something that is not capable of using language, typically an animal or an object, as in **tajwIj** ("my knife") and **tajlIj** ("your knife") (**taj**, "knife"). When the possessor is another noun, as opposed to a pronoun, a "noun-noun" construction is employed, the two nouns being juxtaposed in the order possessor-possessed, as in **yaS vav** ("officer's father") or **yaS taj** ("officer's knife") (**yaS**, "officer"). The grammatical diversion in which members of the higher classes occasionally indulge is to put the suffix before the noun, as if forming a noun-noun construction. Furthermore, only the suffixes not referring to beings capable of language are used. Thus, **wIj vav** would be used for "my father," though perhaps the archaic-sounding "father mine" is closer to the feel of the utterance; **lIj vav**, perhaps "father yours." Use of these otherwise bizarre constructions indicates an unusual closeness between the possessor and what is possessed, comparable to the Federation Standard practice of using a derogatory epithet to show affection (as in "John, you [epithet], it's good to see you"). Indeed, this is the best interpretation of a phrase heard among Klingons who are particularly good friends: **wIj jup** ("friend mine"). A translation such as "my very good friend" or "my dear old friend" may come closer to what is intended. It is not known with certainty why this construction is found predominantly among the higher classes, though it is probably because, among the educated elite, an intentional misuse of the language would be interpreted as a rhetorical device—even as a bit of poetry—rather than as simply careless speech. Since a visitor's place in the social scheme of things is not clear, it would be best to not use the construction at all but at the same time to refrain from expressing disapproval if someone else uses it.

Vocabulary associated with class distinctions falls into two types: words used to refer to the upper classes and words used predominantly by one class or the other. The leader of a house is afforded the title **joH**, usually translated as "Lord." This title is also used to refer to his wife, translated as "Lady." If the title is used along with the name, one puts the name first, as is the case with all titles: **Qugh joH** ("Lord Kruge"), **ghIrIlqa' joH** ("Lady Grilka"). When addressing the head of a house, a member of a lower class may use either the name plus **joH** or else **joH** plus **-wI'**, the first-person possessive suffix for beings capable of language: **joHwI'** ("my Lord, my Lady"). This title also has an alternate form, **jaw**, which is used from time to time with no known difference in meaning or connotation, though **joH** is heard far more frequently. A person of equal or close standing in the social hierarchy, perhaps the leader of another house, has two additional options: using the name alone, or using the father's name (thus Lieutenant Commander Worf may be called **mogh puqloD** ["Son of Mogh"]). If the head of a house is also a military officer, which is quite likely, it is entirely proper to use either the title **joH** or the rank itself. Both **Qugh joH** ("Lord Kruge") and **Qugh la'** ("Commander Kruge") are appropriate ways to address or refer to Kruge. Other than titles associated with military ranks, members of the lower classes are called only by their given names or by their fathers' names (**mogh puqloD** ["Son of Mogh"]; **qo'leq puqbe'** ["Daughter of Ko'lek"]).

The vocabulary used by the higher and lower classes, though for the most part the same, shows a certain amount of social variation. The lower classes are more likely to incorporate slang into their speech, though this is difficult to ascribe exclusively or even primarily to a class difference because it is true of the younger generation of upper-class Klingons as well. (For some examples of slang, see the chapter on Language Change and Staying Current, under "Vocabulary: Slang," pages 142–167.) The upper classes, for their part, incorporate a few archaic words into their speech. This is true among all age groups in the upper classes. It may be considered a sign of erudition and respect for tradition; it does not represent an aversion to change.

The archaic words tend to come up in conversations

about food. For example, the usual word for the leg of an animal, when prepared as food, is **gham** ("limb"), the same word used for the leg of the living animal. A leg served as food at a banquet in an upper-class household, however, is likely to be called a **HajDob**, an old word for "limb." In another context, such as a meal with warriors in a ship's **SopwI'pa'** ("mess hall"), only the term **gham** will be heard. Similarly, the common word for "teacup" is **Dargh HIvje'** (literally, "tea drinking vessel"). Among the upper classes, the word **tu'lum** is used with some frequency, though, strictly speaking, this archaic word used to mean only a cup made of metal.

Sometimes, a modern Klingon word is used but with an archaic meaning. Thus, the normal way to describe bland food is to call it **tlhorghHa'** ("not pungent"). In the past, the word **jot** was used in this sense, though now its meaning has changed to "be calm." An upper-class diner will, from time to time, still describe food as **jot**. Along the same lines, in an archaic form of Klingon, **ru'** meant something like "ready to collapse or die." It was used to describe weakened prey or a weakened enemy, but it was also applied to food (particularly fresh organs) meant to be eaten while still alive or just recently so, the implication being that if it were not eaten quickly, it would soon be no good. Upper-class Klingons still use the word in this latter sense, referring, for example to **qagh ru'** ("serpent worms about to die"). The modern meaning of **ru'**, derived from the earlier senses, is "be temporary." Except in upper-class settings, **qagh ru'** would be interpreted as "temporary serpent worms," which would not make much sense at all.

Among the lower classes—except for those working as servants for the higher classes—words like **HajDob** and **tu'lum** are known but seldom used, and words like **jot** and **ru'** are used only in their modern senses. Sometimes, however, a lower-class person will use an archaic word or use a word with its archaic meaning as a sign of cultivation. If, however, the words are used incorrectly, the speaker will be considered rather pretentious and regarded with contempt. It's safest to avoid such word usage.

ARGOT: SPECIALIZED VOCABULARY

The actual size of the Klingon vocabulary is unknown, even in rough numbers. Several thousand
words have been catalogued to date, most of them reasonably common, frequently heard, and used throughout
the Empire by Klingons of all social strata. A visitor
could easily get by with a knowledge of this vocabulary
alone.

Limiting oneself to everyday terminology, however,
would cut one off from an appreciation and understanding of the richness and variety of Klingon society as well
as the sophistication of Klingon art, science, and technology. Practitioners of a great many activities have developed specialized vocabulary or uses of words in order to
label the tools of their trade or to express subtle distinctions. Such specialized language is known in Klingon as
tlhach mu'mey (literally, "faction words"). A good Federation Standard equivalent would be *argot* or *jargon*. Interestingly, some fairly common words in Klingon began
as **tlhach mu'mey** and then, over time, spread to general
usage, often with altered meanings.

In some instances, the words and phrases associated
with a particular activity or group are known throughout
Klingon society. For example, knowledge of the language
of warfare is fairly widespread, as might be expected
given that the most striking characteristic of the Klingon

Empire is that it is a warrior society. Similarly, terminology associated with food is well known. On the other hand, much specialized vocabulary pertaining to other endeavors remains practically unused except by experts in the particular fields (though most well-educated Klingons probably are familiar with it).

While it is not possible to go into every aspect of the various Klingon subcultures here, some examples of the **tlhach mu'mey** associated with certain fields are presented below. Even if a visitor never engages in any of these activities directly, understanding these words is a good way to gain a more complete comprehension of Klingon culture. At the very least, these words are always useful for showing off.

WARFARE

As might be expected, the greatest degree of lexical elaboration—the most words—can be found in the area of warfare. Included here are words for weaponry, armor, martial techniques, military ranks, forms of combat, and so on. A great deal of this terminology is so widespread in society that it forms a part of any basic vocabulary and need not all be repeated here. Furthermore, much of the information about current weaponry is classified and therefore cannot be included in this guide. What remains, however, does indeed give a good indication of the importance of warfare to the Klingon way of life.

Wars, Battles, and Warriors

There are two nouns traditionally translated as "war": **veS** and **noH**. The first, **veS**, is "war" in the sense of "warfare," the concept or idea of war; **noH**, on the other hand, is used for an individual or specific war. When Azetbur, leader of the Klingon High Council at the time of the first negotiations for peace with the Federation, expressed concern that "war is obsolete," she said, **"notlh veS,"** not **"notlh noH"**; she felt the idea or nature of warfare, not a specific war, was obsolete (**notlh**). In parallel fashion, any specific "battle" is **may'**, but the concept of battle is **vIq**, often translated as "combat."

Similarly, there are several verbs for "fight," "battle," and the like. Most broadly, "do battle" or "wage war"— that is, actually engage in a conflict in which a number of combatants are involved—is **ghob**. The notion of "make war" in the general sense, referring to the *idea* of war and not a *specific* war, is **Qoj**. The verb for "fight," whether in a war or a one-on-one confrontation, is **Suv**.

In short, the nouns **veS** ("war, warfare") and **vIq** ("combat") and the verb **Qoj** ("wage war") all are used to refer to the ideas of warfare, combat, and making war, while the nouns **noH** ("war") and **may'** ("battle") and the verbs **ghob** ("make war, do battle") and **Suv** ("fight") are used when referring to specific, concrete instances of war, battle, and fighting.

Thus, it is possible to say **noH ghob** or **noH Suv**, both meaning "He/she fights a war," or **may' ghob** or **may' Suv,** meaning "He/she fights a battle," but it is not normally acceptable to say **veS ghob** ("He/she fights a warfare") or **vIq Suv** ("He/she fights a combat").

In addition to these general terms, there are a number of specific words relating to specific types of battle or engagement. First of all, there is a set of verbs that can each be translated "clash with," "encounter," "engage," and the like, but these translations do not make the differences between the words clear. They are differentiated by degree, ranging from something like "struggle in a minor skirmish" to "engage in a major melee." Arranged in ascending order of ferocity, they are: **Qor, tlhaS, vay, lul, Hargh**. If Klingons engaged in shadowboxing, **Qor** might be appropriately applied, while **Hargh** would be reserved only for situations approaching Armageddon.

Worf and Data (Brent Spiner) lead a raid against the Tilonus Institute to rescue Commander Riker. *Robbie Robinson*

Common militaristic acts also have associated terminology, both verbs (**DoHmoH,** "drive back"; **Hub,** "defend"; **yot,** "invade"; **weH,** "raid" [same as **yot**, really, but with the added connotation of surprise or speed]; **HIv,** "attack, assault"; **Sev,** "contain"; **HeD,** "retreat, withdraw") and nouns (**yot,** "invasion, raid, incursion"; **Hub,** "defense"). The noun **tuH** refers to a military maneuver of any kind. A specific plan or stratagem usually has a code name (**per yuD** [literally, "dishonest label"]) coined especially for the occasion and not necessarily used again. A **per yuD** is sometimes the name of an animal, sometimes the name of a Klingon historical figure, and it usually ends in **Qu'** ("mission, task"). Code names are the equivalent of Federation locutions such as "Operation Cougar" and are therefore often translated in that pattern: **targh Qu'** ("Operation *Targ*"), **lung Qu'** ("Operation

Dragon"; a **lung** is not really a dragon, but that is a close approximation), **'aqtu' Qu'** ("Operation Aktuh").

Since dying in battle is considered a noble aspiration, suicide missions are a part of the Klingon military repertoire, and the honorable nature of such missions accounts for their nomenclature. The honorific verb suffix **-neS**, usually used when addressing a superior, is also used when the verb refers to a suicide attack of some kind: **HIvneS**, awkwardly translated as "honor-attack," implies that suicide is part of the plan of the attack. Similarly, **HubneS** ("honor-defend") is used only when suicide is part of the defense plan. To say "attack honorably" but not refer to a suicide mission, the adverbial **batlh** is employed and the suffix **-neS** is not: **batlh HIv** ("attack honorably, attack in an honorable fashion").

Along the same lines, the verb suffix **-chu'** ("perfectly"), when used with some verbs of fighting, implies that the fight results in death. From the Klingon point of view, **Suvchu'** ("fight perfectly") is "fight to the death." A similar construction is used for dueling (**Hay'chu'**, "duel to the death"). On the other hand, **-chu'** does not add this meaning to all verbs. **HeDchu'** ("retreat perfectly") means simply that there is a full withdrawal; though death may occur as part of the retreat, it is not necessarily implied by the verb. The archaic Klingon phrase **ghIqtal** also means "to the death," though it is generally used as a sentence in its own right, a type of exclamation. For example, just before striking the first blow or firing the first shot in a battle, warriors may shout **ghIqtal!**

The participants in a war or battle are key. The quintessential Klingon person, of course, is the warrior, and there are several words for "warrior." The most commonly heard term is **SuvwI'** (literally, "one who fights" or "fighter"). This word is used in most circumstances and is never inappropriate. Indeed, it is often preferred because it states explicitly what a warrior does: fight. Other words for "warrior" are **mang** and **vaj**. The word **mang** is used when the warrior under discussion is described in terms of his membership in a fighting unit (for example, as a crew member on an attack cruiser). Perhaps for this reason it is sometimes translated "soldier." The usual plural form of **mang** is a different word altogether: **negh** ("warriors, soldiers"). The word **mangpu'** (**mang** plus the plural suffix **-pu'**) is seldom used, but it is not ungrammatical. It carries with it the notion that there are individuals (more than one **mang**) making up the group; **negh** focuses on the group as a unit. A similar word, **QaS**, normally translated "troops," is used in almost the same way as **negh**, but it excludes officers. All of the **negh** together make up something called a **mangghom**. Literally, this is "warrior group" or "soldier group," but it is usually translated as "army."

The third word for "warrior," **vaj,** refers more to the notion of warriorhood or the idea of being a warrior than it does to an individual warrior. In this way, it resembles **veS** ("warfare") and **vIq** ("combat") (see above). Thus, Captain Klaa, who took it upon himself to take revenge against the Federation's Captain James T. Kirk, remarked that he needed a real challenge to test "a warrior's mettle," or **vaj toDuj** (literally, "warrior courage"). He was not referring to his own courage or that of any specific warrior (which would have been, in all likelihood, **SuvwI' toDuj**), but rather to the kind of courage embodied in being a warrior.

Warriors are grouped according to the ships upon which they serve. A ship's full complement of personnel, crew plus officers, is called a **wey**, perhaps best translated as "company." The general word for "officer" (in addition to the specific terms for various ranks) is **yaS**. An individual crew member is a **beq**. (**QaS** ["troops"] applies to nonofficers whether or not assigned to a ship.)

There is a second term for "officer," but it is not frequently used. As is well known, it is considered the duty of officers on Klingon ships to assassinate their immediate superior if the higher-ranking officer has been judged unfit to serve, perhaps as a consequence of neglecting his or her duty, demonstrating cowardice, or behaving dishonorably. This practice extends even to the captain of the ship. As a result, there are not many officers who end their service to the Empire by simply stepping down or retiring. There are some, however, and the word **'utlh** is used to refer to an officer of this type. Perhaps "officer emeritus" is an appropriate translation.

The entirety of a government's military apparatus is its **QI'**, usually translated simply as "military." The word is rather general in that it may apply to a nongovernmental military organization as well, such as that of a group of rebels. Though many Klingons themselves are apt to describe the Federation's Starfleet as a type of **QI'**, this is not really an appropriate use of the term, since **QI'** refers to the military only, while the functions of Starfleet are scientific and diplomatic as well. This misapplication of the term may, in part, be responsible for the frequent misunderstandings between the Federation and the Empire.

The official Klingon **QI'** is the Klingon Defense Force, or **tlhIngan Hubbeq**, which is run by the Klingon High Command, or **tlhIngan ra'ghomquv**. The Defense Force is subdivided into units known as **yo'** and **nawlogh**, traditionally translated as "fleet" and "squadron," respectively, but the relationship between the two is not straightforward in terms of chain of command. While a **yo'** always consists of more than one **nawlogh**, there are a number of **nawloghmey** (the plural form of **nawlogh**) that are independent of any association with a **yo'**. Therefore, while a specific **nawlogh** may be under the command of a **yo'**, another **nawlogh** may have the same status as a **yo'** within the overall forces. Accordingly, when dealing with a troop member (**QaS**) or officer (**yaS**) of a ship, to avoid giving offense, one should either find out ahead of time how that ship fits into the hierarchical structure or else carefully avoid making references to other units as superior or inferior.

The words used as titles to denote the rank (**patlh**) within the Klingon Defense Force have caused a certain amount of confusion, largely because the system does not neatly map onto that used by Starfleet. The highest military officer, the head of the Klingon High Command, is the **la'quv**, usually translated "Supreme Commander." There are nine ranks of officers (**yaSpu'**, the plural form of **yaS** ["officer"]) serving under the **la'quv**, and below them are the troops (**QaS**), including some with titles. The officers (**yaSpu'**) are ranked as follows (from highest to lowest, each given with its usual Federation Standard translation):

'aj ("admiral")
Sa' ("general")
totlh ("commodore")
'ech ("brigadier")
HoD ("captain")
la' ("commander")
Sogh ("lieutenant")
lagh ("ensign")
ne' ("yeoman")

When used with an individual's name, a title follows the name: **tlha'a HoD** ("Captain Klaa"), **cheng Sa'** ("General Chang"), **qeng la'** ("Commander Kang"), and so on.

There is, in addition, a frequently misunderstood word, **ra'wI'**, which is correctly, though misleadingly, translated as "commander," as is **la'**. The confusion comes about because **ra'wI'** literally means "one who commands," from the verb **ra'** ("command, order") plus the suffix **-wI'** ("one who does [something]"). Thus, a **ra'wI'** is, literally, someone who gives an order. The word is generally used to refer to any officer of the rank of

Sogh or higher. It may be used as either a description (**ra'wI' ghaH qImlaq'e'** ["K'mlak is a commander"]) or a title (**qImlaq ra'wI'** ["Commander K'mlak"]), though in all cases it is understood as not reflecting the precise rank of the individual. Except for formal occasions, it is safe to use the title **ra'wI'**. In fact, if one is not sure of an officer's rank, it is probably the safest route to take.

Finally, the special title **la''a'** ("commandant") is used for officers in charge of certain specialized units within the military, such as prison camps, regardless of the officers' official ranks.

Among the troops (**QaS**), the highest-ranking are given the title **bu'**, traditionally translated as "sergeant," while the next highest have the title **Da'** ("corporal"). No specific titles are used for anyone of lower rank.

There are a number of words employed to describe the specific functions performed by officers on a ship, but none of these is used as a title. For example, the science officer is the **QeDpIn**, the communications officer is the **QumpIn**, the weapons officer is the **nuHpIn**, the engineering officer is the **jonpIn**, the tactical officer is the **ya**, and the helmsman is the **DeghwI'**. It is not correct, however, to say **qImlaq ya** ("Tactical Officer K'mlak"). On the other hand, one might say, **ya ghaH qImlaq Sogh'e'** ("Lieutenant K'mlak is the tactical officer"). Similarly, regardless of their official ranks, those closest to the captain of a ship are called **yaS wa'DIch** ("first officer") and **yaS cha'DIch** ("second officer"). Unlike the terms associated with specific duties, however, these may be used as titles as well. It is correct to say both **qImlaq yaS wa'DIch** ("First Officer K'mlak") and **yaS wa'DIch ghaH qImlaq la''e** ("Commander K'mlak is first officer"). Finally, a student may be described as a **mangHom** ("cadet"), but **mangHom** is not an official title. One should not say, for example, **qImlaq mangHom** ("Cadet K'mlak").

Weaponry: Modern

As with other technologically advanced peoples, Klingons have developed rather sophisticated weaponry. Intricate details aside, much of it is similar to the weaponry of other societies in the galaxy, notably Federation and Romulan, and therefore should be familiar to a galactic visitor.

Perhaps the most characteristic of the modern Klingon armaments—though, strictly speaking, not an armament at all—is the cloaking device (**So'wI'**). Most, if not all, Klingon ships are equipped with such a device that makes it all but impossible for them to be detected by enemies' sensors. The workings of the **So'wI'** are apparently based on the Romulan cloaking device, the Klingons having learned (some would say "stolen") the technology during their brief alliance with the Romulan Empire in the mid-twenty-third century. The **So'wI'** is not perfect, however. For one thing, ways have been developed to detect a cloaked ship, though these techniques are difficult and may not work quickly enough to allow an appropriate reaction. The device also requires so much of the ship's energy to operate that it is not possible to fire weapons while the ship is cloaked.

A cloaking device that did allow weapons to be fired while the ship was cloaked was developed by Klingon scientists and actually installed on one ship, but that ship was detected anyway and further development of the improved technology seems to have been put on hold. In this case, traditional Klingon values seem to have prevailed over potential tactical advantage. From the Klingon point of view, firing while cloaked, and therefore being unseen and unknown by the enemy, would have no honor. The **So'wI'** that must be deactivated before firing weapons remains a standard part of a ship's equipment.

The terminology associated with using a cloaking device is simply **chu'** ("activate") and **chu'Ha'** ("deacti-

General Chang (Christopher Plummer) commands the only known vessel that can fire its weapons with shields raised.
Bruce Birmelin

vate"). It is also appropriate to say **Duj So'** ("He/she cloaks the ship") or **Duj So'lu'pu'** ("The ship is cloaked"; literally, "Someone or something has cloaked the ship").

Klingon technology has produced two weapons used, as far as is known, only by the Klingons themselves. The **tuQDoq**, variously translated as "mind-sifter" or "mind-ripper," is a device that can read the contents of a subject's brain. It is considered a weapon because, at higher powers, it leaves the victim in a permanent vegetative state (though it does not seem to have this effect against those with particularly strong mental faculties, such as Vulcans). The second distinctly Klingon weapon is the **QIghpej**, a hand-held device that produces excruciating pain when pressed up against an adversary.

Scientific research has also provided the Klingons with a range of rather advanced but more familiar armaments. Among these are the disruptors or, more properly, phase disruptors, directed-energy weapons similar in function and operation to the Federation's phasers. The general term for disruptor is **nISwI'**. A disruptor pistol or hand-held disruptor (and there are several models of these) is a **nISwI' HIch**; a disruptor rifle (likewise with several models) is a **nISwI' bej**. Larger and more powerful disruptors are mounted on the ship, laid out as **nISwI' DaH** or "disruptor banks." These terms are used only for these Klingon weapons. The more general term **pu'**, "phaser," may also apply to the Klingon disruptor, but it is used just as often to refer to the Romulan disruptor, Federation phaser, and other similar devices. Since the word is short, **pu'** is heard frequently—even more frequently than **nISwI'**—especially in the throes of combat, in such formations as **pu'HIch** ("phaser pistol"), **pu'bej** ("phaser rifle"), **pu'DaH** ("phaser banks"), and even **pu'beq** ("phaser crew," the crew members responsible for the operation of the weapons). Despite the prevalence of the **pu'** words, in the strictest sense, the correct names for all of these weapons are the **nISwI'** forms.

The disruptor pistol, when not in use, may be carried in a holster, or **vaH**, worn on the side of the body and attached to the belt.

The verb used for "shoot" when referring to disruptors is **bach**. Technically speaking, one shoots the energy beam from the disruptor. The general word for any energy beam ("ray") is **tIH**, so a disruptor's beam is **nISwI' tIH**. Thus, the correct formation is **nISwI' tIH bach** ("shoot the disruptor beam"). As a practical matter, however, the **tIH** is often left out, and **nISwI' bach** is the common way to say "shoot a disruptor." Similarly, **pu' bach** is "shoot a phaser."

Ships are also equipped with an explosive weapon called a **peng**, usually translated as "torpedo," though "missile" might work just as well. The plural form of **peng** is a different word, **cha**. A **peng** is launched from a tube usually called a **DuS**, but another term, **chetvI'**, is also used, the distinction having something to do with how the projectile is actually loaded into the tube. The verb used for "launch" or "fire" a weapon of this type is **baH**, and there is even a special word, **ghuS**, meaning "prepare to launch." The warhead of the torpedo is called its **jorneb** (which seems to contain the verb **jor** ["explode"] but is otherwise not analyzable).

Weaponry: Traditional

The real distinction between Klingon weaponry and that of other societies is found among the traditional hand-held weapons used in one-on-one combat, for these best embody the true essence of the warrior. So central is the warrior to Klingon life, one might expect Klingons to actually shun high-tech weaponry, arguing that battling by means of disruptors, torpedoes, and especially cloaking devices is cowardly and contrary to the true warrior spirit. After all, touching a colored light on a control panel is hardly the same experience as staring into the face of one's enemy while lunging toward him with a drawn blade. Indeed, elements of Klingon society were highly resistant to technological innovation, but they were ultimately convinced by others of its practical advantages. Nevertheless, the traditional forms—and tools—of combat have endured, and not just as anachronistic curiosities. Along with the ancient skills and implements, of course, is the associated terminology.

A warrior's full set of armor, including weapons and clothing, is his **may'luch** (literally, "battle gear"). Traditional clothing worn in battle, known as **HIp**, the word currently used to mean "uniform," had both a protective function and a more utilitarian one, since it was from the clothing that weapons (**nuHmey**) or ammunition (**nIch**) could be hung. Klingons are not now and never have been ones to shy away from injury, considering it nothing more than a natural consequence of battle. On the other hand, lessening the severity of an injury was seen as a means to prolong a battle. Accordingly, the traditional warrior's tunic (**yIvbeH**) was made of a material (what it was is now unknown) resistant to puncture, just to add a little protection. Accompanying sleeves (**tlhaymey**), originally not parts of the tunic itself, were generally made of animal pelts (**veDDIrmey**), skin (**DIr**) with fur (**veD**) still attached. (In modern usage, the word **yIvbeH** in most places means any shirt, with or without sleeves.) A warrior's glove (**pogh**), also made of skin, had wide band around the wrist and sharp protrusions at the knuckles. If there was a special name for these protrusions, it is lost; they are now called simply **DuQwI'mey** ("spikes"). The gloves did not have fingers. They were designed to protect the palm, back of the hand, and wrist, but to not interfere with the mobility of a warrior's fingers. Modern gloves (**poghmey**) generally adhere to this design. A skin belt (**qogh**) both held pants (**yopwaH**) in place and provided a place from which to hang weapons or weapon holders. On the toe of each high boot (**DaS**), likewise made of animal hide (**DIr**), was a clawlike spike called a **pu'**. The word **pu'** now means "phaser," and the newer meaning probably developed from the older "spike" because of the lightning speed with which one delivered a blow with the sharp **pu'**. In contemporary Klingon, the spike on the toe of a boot is always called a **DaSpu'** ("boot spike"), never **pu'** alone. Finally, old armor included headgear of some kind apparently called a **mIv**, which, in modern Klingon, means "helmet." The word also survives in the word **mIv'a'** ("crown"; literally, "big helmet" or "great helmet"), a ceremonial headpiece worn by some Klingon emperors.

Perhaps the single weapon most associated with Klingons is the two-handed sword called **betleH**, or *bat'-leth* as it has come to be known in the Federation. According to Klingon tradition, the first *bat'leth* was forged

The *bat'leth* of Kahless is recovered by Kor (John Colicos) and Worf. *Robbie Robinson*

by Kahless the Unforgettable, the founder of the Klingon Empire, from a lock of his hair dipped in molten lava. Kahless created the name **betleH**, meaning "sword of honor." The word **betleH** is actually an archaic form. In contemporary Klingon, "sword of honor" would be **batlh 'etlh**, though this phrase is used almost exclusively as a translation or explanation of the older word, **betleH**.

There is an extensive vocabulary for the moves associated with *bat'leth* use. To thrust or lunge toward one's opponent, for example, is **jop**. To deflect a thrust—that is, to parry—is **way'**. To thrust either end of the *bat'leth* (as opposed to the long part of the blade) upward is **chaQ**. To change the approximate orientation of the weapon from horizontal to vertical is **ngol**; the reverse is **lev**. To slide the blade of one's *bat'leth* along the blade of the opponent's weapon is **DIj**. To twirl or rotate the *bat'-leth* is **jIrmoH** and to toss it from one hand to the other (the same word is used whether left to right or right to left) is **baQ**. When teaching someone to use the *bat'leth*, the tutor will shout out movements—for example, **yIjop! yIway'!** ("Lunge! Defend!"). Generally in such a situation, however, the tutor will use the shortened form of the language known as Clipped Klingon and skip the imperative prefix **yI-**, leaving only the bare verb: **jop! way'!** It is important to note that the tutor is giving the student direct commands ("Lunge! Defend!"), not shouting out the names of movements.

A smaller, one-handed version of the *bat'leth* is the **meqleH**, rendered in Federation Standard as *mek'leth*. For a minority of Klingons who pronounce both **b** and **m** identically, as **m**, the words **betleH** and **meqleH** sound almost the same, especially when shouted in the heat of battle. Because of the importance of the *bat'leth* in Klingon tradition, however, they have taken to calling the *bat'leth* **betleH quv** (pronounced **metleH quv**), or "honored *bat'leth*," while the *mek'leth* is **meqleH matlh**, or "loyal *mek'leth*." Although **betleH quv** might be considered a bit redundant ("honored sword of honor"), it does the job of maintaining the distinction. The longer **betleH quv** and **meqleH matlh** are sometimes heard even among Klingons who pronounce **b** and **m** distinctly, though not as frequently as the one-word forms.

The word **'etlh** is used for "sword" in general, but it really means "blade" of any kind. The **'etlh**, then, is a component of a knife and could be part of a spear as well. Another word normally translated "sword," **yan**, is more specific, referring to swords (that is, weapons with long blades) only. There is also the verb **yan,** which means "wield or manipulate (a sword)." A "swordfighter," then, would be a **yanwI'**, literally a "sword wielder"); the word for the specific type of sword may be, but need not be, included. It is thus proper to say **betleH yanwI'** (*"bat'leth* wielder") or **betleH yan** ("He/she wields a *bat'leth"*).

A **'etlh**, even if primarily a weapon, may be used in other activities as well, such as hunting and even sculpting. Indeed, to restrict the use of a **'etlh** to combat is to minimize the flexibility of its design. By the same token, a blade not designed as a weapon may be used as a weapon if need be, though to be attacked by a warrior wielding something that is normally classified as a tool is considered by some to be an insult to one's honor.

In ancient times, a warrior often wore a **Ha'quj** ("baldric"), a belt across his chest to support a sword when it was not in use. The word survives today, meaning not only "baldric" but also "sash," a common part of a warrior's uniform whether or not he carries a blade. Though originally utilitarian in nature, the **Ha'quj** has taken on symbolic functions as well, its ornamentation representing the family unit or house (**tuq**) of its wearer.

There are a good many types of Klingon knives. The general word for any knife is **taj**. The three-bladed warrior's knife (one main blade plus two smaller blades that spring out at the base of the blade) is **Daqtagh**, sometimes rendered *d'k tahg* in the Federation. In addition to the extra blades (frequently termed **tajHommey** ["little knives"]), at the end of the knife's handle (**ret'aq**) there is a spiked pommel, called simply **moQ** ("sphere"). A "spike" is a **DuQwI'** and the small spikes on the *d'k tahg* are usually called **DuQwI'Hommey** ("little spikes").

The **qutluch**, or *kut'luch* in its usual Federation Standard spelling, is a knife associated with Klingon assassins. It has a serrated blade (**Ho' 'etlh** [literally, "tooth blade"]), so it is particularly lethal. It is also used in a

Honoring his heritage, a member of the House of Mogh proudly displays its insignia. *Brian D. McLaughlin*

ritual to which it gives its name, the **qutluch tay** (*"Kut'-luch* Ceremony"), during which, as a demonstration of courage, a young Klingon preparing to be a warrior attacks someone and actually draws blood for the first time. For Klingons, bloodletting is a usual and expected part of a warrior's training regimen.

Some other knives are the wavy-bladed **QIS**, the slender-bladed **ghonDoq**, and the **tajtIq**, a knife with a particularly long blade that is used almost as if it were a sword. A knife that is relatively safe, both for user and intended victim, is the smaller **naH taj** (literally, "vegetable knife" or "fruit knife," a kind of knife used for training but also for cutting parts off of growing plants).

A knife is more than utilitarian. The knifesmith takes pride in designing a weapon that not only performs well and perfectly fits the hand of the user but that also is considered a work of art. The aesthetic value of the blade is directly related to its effectiveness, but the handle is adorned with ornamentation ranging from traditional designs to symbols that actually indicate ownership, usually by means of a family crest (**tuq Degh**).

In addition, there are also a number of knives designed not as weapons but rather as tools, used only for cutting. These are not as sharp as the weapon knives, nor as artfully decorated. While it is not uncommon to praise the workmanship or design of a warrior's knives, it is important to focus only on the weapons. To praise the tools is an insult. The general term for a knife used as a tool is the same term used for a knife as a weapon, namely **taj**. If context is unclear, this could lead to some confusion. When clarity is required, the tool knife may be called a **pe'meH taj**, a "knife for cutting."

When not in use, knives are carried in sheathes worn on the side of the body, connected to the belt. The word for this sheath is **vaH**, the same as the word for "holster" but surely representing an older meaning of the term.

The traditional Klingon arsenal also includes the ax, an implement with a heavy, flattened blade mounted crosswise at the end of a handle. The general term for ax is **'obmaQ**. Its handle is its **DeS** and its blade is its **ghIt**. These words, **DeS** and **ghIt**, when referring to humanoid anatomy, mean "arm" and "open, flat hand" (as opposed to a fist), respectively, suggesting that at one time the ax was considered an extension of the warrior himself. A double-headed ax is a **jey'naS**, while an ax with an added spike at the end is a **'alngegh**. To wield or swing an ax is **Qach**.

There exists a weapon that might be described as a cross between an ax and a *bat'leth*. The **'aqleH** has what looks like half a *bat'leth* at the end of a handle. To manipulate the **'aqleH** is **Qach**.

A general term for "spear" is **naQjej**, but, of course, there are specific types of spears. The **ghIntaq**, for example, is a battle spear, though it is also used ceremonially. The shaft of a spear is the **tIH**; the sharp tip or spearhead is the **QIn**. As might be expected, there are a great many different types of **QInmey** (the plural form of **QIn**). A plain spearhead, one that is simply a sharp point, is a **QIn pup** ("perfect spearhead"). A tip with multiple points is a **QIn vagh** ("spearhead number five"), though this is a bit odd because there may be any number of points and no other spearheads are named with numbers. A spearhead that is barbed is a **SeDveq**, a word with unknown etymological origins and otherwise unused.

Some spears are simply thrust into an oncoming enemy. Others are generally thrown. The thrower first lowers the spear to a horizontal position (the verb describing this action is **ghuS**), then hurls it with great force ("throw" or "hurl" in this manner is **chuH**). The verb **chuH**, which is more accurately translated as "spear"—that is, "hurl a spear at," can be used only if the projectile being thrown is a spear or somehow resembles a spear. The object of the verb is the intended target: **jagh chuH SuvwI'** ("The warrior spears the enemy," or "The warrior throws [a spear] at the enemy"; **jagh**, "enemy"; **SuvwI'**, "warrior"). One way to indicate that the target is actually hit is to add the suffix **-chu'** ("perfectly") to the verb: **jagh chuHchu' SuvwI'** ("The warrior spears the enemy perfectly, the warrior hits the enemy [with a thrown spear]").

There is, in addition, at least one type of spear, the **tlhevjaQ**, which employs a **chetvI'**, a stick with a hook at the end, as an aid for throwing. There is a single verb, **wob**, that is used to describe the full range of activities involved in putting the spear properly into the spear-throwing aid and using the air to hurl the spear: **tlhevjaQ wob** ("He/she puts the **tlhevjaQ** into the **chetvI'** and hurls the spear"). In speaking of this type of spear and spear-throwing technique, it is still proper to use the verb **chuH** when talking about throwing the spear at a target.

It may have been noticed that some of the terminology associated with spears is identical to that associated with modern weaponry, and certainly the vocabulary of spear-throwing was adapted for the newer technology. The meaning of **tIH**, originally "shaft" of a spear, was extended to include shaftlike energy—that is, "beam" or "ray." The verb **ghuS** means both "lower (a spear) to a horizontal position in preparation for throwing" and "prepare to launch (a torpedo)." The word **chetvI'** refers to both the tool used to help throw the **tlhevjaQ** spear and also a torpedo tube of a particular kind. Finally, though not connected to weaponry, the word **QIn** means not only "spearhead" but also "message." In this case, it is not clear which came first. Perhaps the spearhead was always thought of as the message being delivered by the spear or spear wielder.

Of similar shape to a spear, but utterly distinct, is the painstik, **'oy'naQ**, a long staff that emits a powerful (and painful) jolt of electricity (**'ul**). Though not an implement of ancient origins (its use of electricity attests to that), it is nonetheless usually used ceremonially, playing an important role in the **nentay cha'DIch**, or Second Rite of Ascension, as well as the **SonchIy**, a ceremony associated with a leader's death. Its use is not restricted to ritual, however; it is also used to help keep large animals under control. Though never part of the traditional Klingon arsenal, its potential effectiveness justifies classifying it as a weapon.

The most ancient and primitive of the Klingon weap-

Chancellor Gorkon (David Warner) carries a ceremonial staff that takes its form from the ancient **jeqqlj**. *Bruce Birmelin*

ons is the **jeqqIj**, the club or bludgeon. This weapon is made of wood, sometimes with inlaid rocks, and is heavier at one end than the other. Included in this category is the **ghanjaq**, often translated as "mace," a club with a metal head, sometimes sporting spikes (**DuQwI'mey**). As with axes, to wield or swing a club is **Qach**.

As protection against these various weapons, a warrior often carried a shield, or **yoD**, basically a large plate of metal. The verb form of "shield" is also **yoD**, and to "shield oneself" is **yoD'egh**. (Although the Federation Standard word "shields" refers to both the old hand-held protective armor and the force field protecting a vessel—the newer meaning clearly based on the older—in Klingon, there is no connection between the two. The force field on a ship is called **botjan**. To shield a ship, one must "activate the shields," or **botjan chu'**.)

A weapon that is particularly good, that is well designed and well constructed, is normally described as **vaQ**. Thus, a **taj vaQ** is a meticulously made knife and a **ghanjaq vaQ** is an especially nice mace. In speaking about a fine weapon, one could compliment it even further by adding the emphatic **-qu'** to **vaQ**. A really spectacular *bat'leth* would be a **betleH vaQqu'**. The word **vaQ** is not often used in describing the newer weapons (disruptors and the like), though such locutions are heard from time to time. The original meaning of **vaQ** has been extended to mean "effective, vigorous, aggressive" and is now heard applied not only to weapons but also to people: **SuvwI' vaQ** ("aggressive warrior").

Duels and Challenges

Dueling—that is, challenging someone to a fight, usually to the death, over a matter of honor—is a longstanding Klingon practice. The verb meaning "duel" is **Hay'**, and it may be properly used in such constructions as **Hay' chaH** ("They duel"; **chaH,** "they"), **Hay'chuq**

Insulted by Worf's "betrayal," Chancellor Gowron (Robert O'Reilly) challenges him. *Robbie Robinson*

("They duel one another"), or even **'avwI' Hay' yaS** ("The officer duels the guard"; **'avwI'**, "guard"; **yaS**, "officer"). To "duel to the death" is **Hay'chu'** (literally, "duel perfectly"), and it may be used in the same contexts: **Hay'chu' chaH** ("They duel to the death"); **Hay'chuqchu'** ("They duel one another to the death").

A duel is preceded by one party issuing a challenge to the other. This is expressed by using the phrase **qabDaj 'ang** (literally, "He/she shows his/her face," referring to the Klingon tenet that a warrior always shows his or her face in battle). To challenge someone to a duel, one will give the command **qablIj HI'ang** ("Show me your face!"), though this is often shortened to simply **HI'ang** ("Show me!"). When one does this, he or she is said to "demand" or "require" (**poQ**), a short way to say **qab legh 'e' poQ** ("He/she demands to see a face"). There is some nonlinguistic behavior that may occur along with or instead of the traditional phrases. To challenge one to a duel to the death, one hits one's adversary with the back of the hand (**chap**). If one is hitting someone for some other reason, such as simple enjoyment, one uses the fist (**ro'**).

The challenged party may agree to the duel by answering **vISo'be'** ("I don't hide it") or the lengthier **qabwIj vISo'be'** ("I don't hide my face"). This person is said to **'angchu'** ("show clearly"), the usual shorthand way of saying **qabDaj 'angchu'** ("He/she shows his/her face clearly"). One accepts a challenge (**qab 'ang** [literally, "shows face"]) in order to prove one's honor (**quv tob** [literally, "test honor conclusively"]). Though any perceived attack on one's honor may prompt one to issue a challenge, in one traditional form of duel, the goal is specifically for a man to "win the favor of a woman" (**vuv be' 'e' baj** [literally, "earn that a woman respect him"]) by competing with another man.

There are a number of weapons typically used for duels, the most common being the *bat'leth*. When the parties are ready, a third party, sort of a referee, says **moq**, the signal to begin. The verb **moq** literally means "beat" and it is a clipped form of, perhaps, **vImoq** ("I beat it") or even **vImoqpu'** ("I have beaten it"). In times past, one would hit something (such as a drum) with a stick to indicate the start of the duel; today, one simply says the word "beat."

A duel ends, normally, with death. It is often the case, however, that one of the combatants will have been outmaneuvered and will find himself in a position from which he clearly cannot recover. Should this occur, he will probably shout out **baq**, a clipped form of **yIbaq** ("Terminate it!"). It is not normal in this context for him to shout out something like **HIHoH** ("Kill me!"), even though this is what he means.

The comm system of the *Starship Defiant* rings with Klingon opera, much to the appreciation of Lieutenant Commander Worf.
Robbie Robinson

MUSIC

Although Klingon music is performed rather infrequently outside of the Empire, music plays a vital role in Klingon culture, particularly vocal music. Warriors have long celebrated great achievements and key events in song, reinforcing the importance of the accomplishments and actually reliving them while singing. Great deeds are "deeds worthy of song," as the Klingon leader

Gowron once put it, and part of the appeal of engaging in battle is the prospect that, if the battle is a really good one, it will be fought over and over again in song.

The Klingon word for music is **QoQ**. This refers to any music, vocal or instrumental or both together. A song is a **bom**, and to sing a song is likewise **bom**. The set of lyrics to a song is termed **bom mu'** (literally, "song word" or "song words"). The word for "perform music," whether instrumental or vocal and instrumental together, is **much**, which in other contexts means "present," as in "present a gift" to someone. A musician is a **muchwI'** (literally, "one who performs music"); a singer is a **bomwI'** ("one who sings").

The word used for "compose" is **qon**. This verb also means "record" and is used whether the recording is by hand (that is, written or even etched in stone), in a medium suitable for a computer, or any other form. From the Klingon point of view, a song is not the product of an individual's mind. It has somehow always existed and is waiting for someone (the songwriter or, more accurately, song recorder, **qonwI'**) to transcribe it (**qon**) and then present it (**much**) to others. There are a number of very well known songwriters, and it is quite an honor if one of them composes a song about one's exploits. Currently, perhaps the most respected **qonwI'** is Keedera.

Though one occasionally hears someone say **QoQ tIv** ("He/she enjoys [the] music") or **bom tIv** ("He/she enjoys the song"), music is not really considered something that causes pleasure. Among Klingons, pleasure is deemed quite unessential for one's well-being. More frequently, the appreciation of music is expressed in terms of something that music does to the listener rather than in terms of the listener's reaction. Thus, music is said to embolden (**jaqmoH**), excite (**SeymoH**), encourage (**tungHa'**), or to stimulate or inspire (**pIlmoH**). Another common way to say that a specific piece or performance of music has a particularly strong effect on a listener is to employ the verb **DuQ** (literally, "stab"): **muDuQ bom** ("The song stabs me," or, in a more colloquial Federation Standard form, "The song moves me"). If the music is judged positively—that is, if the listener likes it—the music is said to be **'ey**, using the word normally translated as "delicious" when talking about food. Rendering **'ey bom** as "The song is good" is acceptable, but it fails to capture the real feeling of the Klingon.

Traditional Klingon music is generally performed only by those who have had a great deal of training. The study of this type of music, whether composition or performance, is considered a discipline not unlike a martial art. There are precise forms and complex rules, and mastery of the techniques takes years of study and practice. Traditional Klingon musical forms date back to the time of Kahless, if not earlier, and have shown little variation since then.

Older Klingon music was based on a nonatonic scale—that is, one made up of nine tones. Each tone has a specific name, comparable to the "do, re, mi" system used in describing music on Earth. The nine tone names are (the first and ninth, as with Earth's "do," being the same): **yu, bIm, 'egh, loS, vagh, jav, Soch, chorgh, yu**. While the first three (and ninth) of these words apparently are used only for singing the scale, the remaining five are also numerals: **loS,** "four"; **vagh,** "five"; **jav,** "six"; **Soch,** "seven"; **chorgh,** "eight." It is possible that, at some time in the past, the numerals were "borrowed" into the lexicon of music in order to sing the scale but, for some reason, the first three (presumably **wa'**, **cha'**, **wej** ["one, two, three"]) were either changed or never used. It is far more likely, however, that the borrowing went in the other direction. As is well documented, the Klingon counting system was originally a ternary system (one based on three, with numbers higher than three formed from the words for "one," "two," and "three"). Later, owing to outside influences, it changed to a decimal system (based on ten). The independent words for the numbers three through nine were not originally a part of the Klingon counting system, but they had to come from somewhere. The musical scale is the likely source. The word for the fourth musical tone, **loS**, began to be used for the number four, and so on through the eighth tone, **chorgh**. (The origins of the words **Hut** ["nine"] and the suffix **-maH**, used in the words for "ten," "twenty," "thirty," and so on, are obscure.)

Among the traditional musical forms is what has come to be known as Klingon opera, or **ghe'naQ**. This form of music is stylistically rigorous, following specific patterns both in terms of composition and performance. There are those who vary somewhat from the tight structure, but the traditional style, sometimes called **ghe'naQ nIt** (perhaps "grand opera," though literally something like "unsullied opera") is preferred by purists.

The stories acted out in Klingon operas may be adapted from a variety of sources: legends, history (particularly military history), famous works of literature. Occasionally, an opera presents an original plot. To follow the story, one has to prepare ahead of time. First of all, the performance of Klingon opera is quite stylized—that is, unnatural. Certain actions are exaggerated, others are condensed (a certain arm movement, for example, may indicate a battle has been fought and won). Perhaps more significant, however, is that with rare exception, the libretto of a Klingon opera (**bom mu'**, the words) is in an ancient tongue heard now only in the operas and certain classic theatrical works. From time to time, a famous opera has been translated into contemporary Klingon, but this is generally considered a learning tool, hardly **ghe'naQ nIt**. True devotees will study the original libretto, often learning to sing the arias themselves.

Klingon "popular" music, for lack of a better term (there is no Klingon word referring exclusively to this type of music), is more free-form; indeed, it is character-ized by its almost rebellious nature. This is not to say that any specific song may be modified at will. Quite the contrary—the words, melody, and rhythm of any given song change very little over time. For new songs, how-ever, stylistic innovation is both acceptable and com-mendable. The words to popular songs sometimes follow the same linguistic tradition as Klingon opera and some-times are in the modern language.

There are several types of Klingon musical instru-ments. Collectively, they are known as **QoQ jan** or **QoQ janmey** (the plural suffix **-mey** is never required). **QoQ**, as noted above, means "music"; **jan** is normally trans-lated as "device" and is usually applied to some sort of sophisticated apparatus, but its use in **QoQ jan** may point to an earlier and less limited meaning, something like "implement." There are special words used to de-scribe the various techniques employed in playing spe-cific instruments, but the general term for "play a musical instrument" is **chu'**, which, when applied to technologically advanced devices, including weapons, means "activate." Indeed, out of context, **jan chu'** could mean either "activate the device" or "play the instru-ment," which may be why **QoQ jan** ("musical instru-ment") is seldom shortened to simply **jan**. When the context is clearly musical, a "player,"—that is, one who plays a musical instrument—is a **chu'wI'**, though more specific terminology may also be used, depending on the instrument being played.

There are a great many Klingon percussion instru-ments—that is, instruments that make a sound as a result of something striking something else. Klingons seem to enjoy playing the percussion instruments more than in-struments of other types. Among these are various drums and bells. The general term for a percussion instrument of any kind is **'In**. Some types of **'In** are struck with the hand, either palm (**toch**) or fist (**ro'**), depending on the particular instrument. To hit the instrument with the palm is **weq**; to strike it with the fist is **tlhaw'**. Other members of this group of instruments are hit with a stick of some kind. The stick often resembles a small hammer; when it does, it is termed **mupwI'Hom** (literally, "small striker"). A plain stick is a **naQHom** (literally, "small cane" or "small staff"). To strike the instrument with a stick is to **moq** ("beat") the instrument. The **'In** itself may be made entirely of metal (in which case it might be described as a bell, though in Klingon it is simply termed **baS 'In**, or "metal **'In**") or entirely of wood (**Sor Hap 'In,** "wood **'In**"). One kind of **Sor Hap 'In** is a tube, open on both ends, with a longitudinal slit extending not quite to either end. It is hit with a **mupwI'Hom**. Drums made of animal skin stretched over a cylinder of various materials are found but are not as common as other types of percussion instruments. Such a drum is called a **DIr 'In** (literally, "skin **'In**"). A **DIr 'In** usually has the skin stretched only over one end. A type of drum with skin stretched over both ends is called a **'o'lav**.

Wind instruments (there is no overall term for them) range from the simple flute or fife (**Dov'agh**), generally crafted from a bone, to the highly complex **meSchuS**. This is a very large instrument, not at all easily moved from place to place, which consists of a network of interlocking tubes. One tube terminates in the mouthpiece (**ngujlep**) into which the player blows (**SuS**). The instrument's pitch and timbre are modified by fingering strategically placed holes in the tubing and by moving the hands in various ways (to move the fingers in this way is to **Heng**). The sound emitted by the **meSchuS** most resembles that of large pipe organs, but that characterization is not really flattering to either instrument.

A third category of Klingon instrument is the **SuS-Deq**, the "windbag" or "bellows" type. A **SuSDeq** has a flexible bag, usually made of animal skin, which is alternately filled with and emptied of air. This air passes over

strips of various materials (**joQmey**), which vibrate as
the air goes by, producing the musical tones. For one
form of **SusDeq**, the **may'ron**, the player stretches the
bag out to fill it with air and squeezes it together to empty
it while directing the flow of air by pressing buttons
mounted on boards on either end of the bag, much like
an accordion. To finger the **may'ron**—that is, to push the
buttons—is to **Heng**, the same word applied to the
meSchuS. To alternately squeeze and stretch out the bag
part of the **may'ron** is to **rey**. Another type of **SuSDeq**,
the **DIron**, resembles and is played much like bagpipes.
The verb that means "squeeze the bag part of the **DIron**,"
usually with the elbow, is **qeb**.

Finally, a fourth type of instrument is one with
strings, a **HurDagh**. Each string is a **SIrgh**, a word also
used for any thread or filament. A **SIrgh** of the finest
quality is made from a material secreted by insects, similar to the silk produced by silkworms. To produce music,
one may either pluck (**pang**) or strum (**yach**, which also
means "stroke" or "pet") the strings. The tone produced
is varied by touching the string or strings at various
points while plucking or strumming. The verb used for
this, perhaps translatable as "to finger," is the same as
the one used for wind instruments: **Heng**. The word **Hur-
Dagh** refers to any of these stringed instruments, of
which there are several different types, the most commonly found being the relatively small **Supghew**. The
midsize **leSpal** is fairly widely used, while the large **tIng-
Dagh** is rarely heard except in conjunction with the performance of an opera.

Despite the variety and sophistication of Klingon
musical instruments, most Klingon music is vocal, with
or without instrumental accompaniment. When there is
an instrumental component, the players are said to **qat**
the song. The verb **qat** literally means "wrap, encase," the
imagery apparently being that the instrumentation adds
the final, though not absolutely necessary, touches.

Because of the feelings stirred by a **van bom**, the clerics of the monastery on Boreth created the clone of Kahless. *Robbie Robinson*

Perhaps the most important type of song is the **may' bom**, literally "battle song," which commemorates famous battles and heroic exploits. It is never inappropriate to burst into song (there is a special verb for this: **wup**) and sing a **may' bom**. At any social gathering, in addition to eating and drinking, there is no question that there will also be singing.

A **van bom**, literally "salute song" or "tribute song," is something like a hymn or anthem (indeed, "hymn" and "anthem" are common translations of **van bom**) in that it is sung at occasions where it is appropriate to express one's feelings of loyalty and dedication to someone or something. Most typically, a **van bom** praises the Klingon Empire itself, often invoking its founder, Kahless.

A song sung while going to, or returning from, a hunt is a **chon bom**, or "hunt song." Among the songs sung exclusively to or by children is the **najmoHwI'** (literally, "one that causes one to dream"), or lullaby, and the **Dap bom** (literally, "nonsense song"), which teaches and reinforces Klingon musical patterns, even though the words themselves are, for the most part, meaningless. The **bang bom**, or love song (though a more literal, and perhaps telling, translation is "beloved's song") plays an important role in Klingon courting behavior, though exactly how it fits in depends on the particular tradition being followed, and this depends, for the most part, on the region in which one or the other of the participants in the courtship ritual grew up.

Finally, despite the undisputed importance of the battle song, the most frequently heard type of song is the **HIvje' bom**, the drinking song. The word **HIvje'** really refers to a drinking glass of any kind (a goblet, tumbler, wineglass, mug), so a **HIvje' bom** is literally a "drinking glass song," perhaps so named because the glass is alternately filled and emptied (that is, the beverage is consumed) as singing continues. A **may' bom** ("battle song"), **chon bom** ("hunting song"), or just about any other kind of song may serve as a **HIvje' bom**, but there are special songs heard almost exclusively as accompaniments to drinking. The drinking songs are always sung loudly (this would probably be described by using the term **pe'vIl** ["forcefully"]), seldom with instrumental accompaniment, and they tend to be rather lengthy (**nI'**) and, from a non-Klingon perspective, repetitive.

VISUAL ARTS

Carving and, to a lesser degree, painting also play prominent roles in Klingon society. Statues are found in public spaces, weapons and uniforms are embellished with distinctive decoration, ceremonial implements feature classic patterns. A visitor to the Klingon Empire should have at least passing familiarity with the fundamentals of Klingon art.

There is no single Klingon word comparable to the general Federation Standard terms "art" and "artwork." Vocabulary associated with the Klingon arts is rather specific. The closest to a general term in this realm may be the verb **raQ**, which means "manipulate by hand, handle." It can be applied to carving, sculpting, metalworking, and the like but is really much less specific, referring to activities that involve having some control over some object. For example, in addition to saying **betleH yan** ("He/she wields a *bat'leth*"), one could say **betleH raQ** ("He/she controls a *bat'leth*"). By extension, the term **raQ** is also used when referring to controlling a space vessel "manually" (that is, when the controls are manipulated directly by a person rather than a computer): **Duj raQ** ("He/she controls the ship manually").

One of the most highly developed of the Klingon arts is sculpture. A statue of any kind, realistic or abstract, is a **Hew**. Realistic statues are found in public spaces, most notably the Hall of Heroes (**Subpu' vaS**), which features likenesses of famous Klingon warriors. Some particularly famous statues are reproduced in miniature and are found in Klingons' homes. The most frequently seen of these, commonly referred to as **ghobchuq loDnI'pu'** ("the brothers fight one another"), is a depiction of Kahless in hand-to-hand combat with his brother Morath.

Statues are carved of stone (**nagh**, "rock, stone") by various techniques. Thus, among other things, the sculptor (**Hew chenmoHwI'** [literally, "statue creator"]) may **nan** ("gouge"), **tey** ("scrape"), or **ghItlh** ("engrave"). To apply these techniques, specialized tools are employed: the **nanwI'** ("chisel"; literally, "gouger"), **teywI'** ("file"; literally, "scraper"), and **ghItlhwI'** ("stylus"). The word **ghItlhwI'** (literally, "engraver") is also used for any writing implement as well as for any person who writes. Indeed, the verb **ghItlh** is most commonly translated as "write," but it always refers to the act of writing—that is, of making marks on some surface—not to the act of composition. Its use in the contexts of both sculpting and writing suggests that writing began as carving. In addition to the specialized tools, any blade (**'etlh**), even if designed for other purposes, may be used as a sculpting tool. Kahless himself is said to have used his *bat'leth*, the original "Sword of Honor," to carve a statue for the woman he loved, presumably Lukara.

The part of a weapon with ornamentation, such as the handle (**ret'aq**) of a knife, is usually decorated by means of carving. Even modern weaponry, such as a disruptor pistol (**nISwI' HIch**) or disruptor rifle (**nISwI' bej**), is decorated. For example, typically the head of any rivet (**veragh**) used has a raised image of some kind, often that of a Klingon warrior's head. Sometimes extra ornamentation, carved of a different material, is attached. This would typically be the case with a family crest (**tuq Degh**).

Carving or incising is also done on flat surfaces, usually a stone panel or **nagh beQ** (literally, "flat rock"), a term that has been extended to mean the resulting artwork itself as well as similar pieces, including paintings. Such carvings are sometimes just ornamental, sometimes informational (if the Klingon writing system, **pIqaD**, is incorporated into the design), sometimes representational. What the Federation would classify as a painting—that is, a **nagh beQ** featuring an image not carved into it but painted onto it—is made by applying **rItlh** ("pigment, paint, dye") derived from either an animal or plant source. This may be done either by using fingers (**nItlhDu'**) or an implement called a **rItlh naQ** ("pigment stick"), a stick with flattened ends. The ends (sometimes referred to as the **nItlhpachDu'** [literally, "fingernails"]) are made in assorted sizes, making it possible to produce varied patterns. No doubt because of the phonetic similarity of the words **nItlh** ("finger") and **rItlh**

The art of embellishing metal was practiced even in Kahless's time, as evidenced by his traditional *bat'leth*. (Terry Farrell)
Robbie Robinson

("pigment"), the practice of applying pigment with fingers, and the habit of referring to the ends of pigment sticks as **nItlhpachDu'**, a pigment stick is also often called a **nItlh naQ** (literally, "finger stick"), though this term is used almost exclusively by the artisans themselves. The word **DIj** means "use a **rItlh naQ**, paint with a **rItlh naQ**." The same word is used in the context of battling with swords to refer to the sliding of one's blade along that of the opponent. The verb **ngoH**, meaning "smear" in other contexts, is used for "paint using fingers."

Compared to Federation Standard, Klingon terminology associated with colors is rather limited. First of all, there is no noun meaning "color." There is, however, a verb, **nguv**, which means something like "be dyed, stained, tinted," though it is seldom used except in the phrase **chay' nguv** ("How is [it] tinted?") or when suffixed with **-moH** ("cause") in the form **nguvmoH** ("dye, tint, stain"; that is, "cause to be dyed," etc.)—for example, **ret'aq nguvmoH** ("He/she stains the knife handle").

As for the specific colors, in addition to the verbs **qIj** ("be black") and **chIS** ("be white"), there are only two terms used: **SuD** ("be blue, green, yellow") and **Doq** ("be red, orange"). For everyday purposes, these four words suffice, since there is usually not much reason to distinguish, on the basis of hue alone, between two items that are both, say, **Doq** ("red, orange"). When it is necessary to talk about colors more precisely, as it might be for the creator of a **nagh beQ**, various devices are employed. One option is to make use of the emphatic suffix **-qu'**. The word **Doqqu'** (literally, "very **Doq**") refers to a color more red than orange. Similarly, **SuDqu'** ("very **SuD**") would probably be described as "green" in Federation Standard. Phrases containing the words **wov** ("light, bright") or **Hurgh** ("dark") further refine the description of the color. Thus, **SuD 'ej wov** means "(it) is **SuD** and light," a way to refer to a yellowish tinge; **SuD 'ach wov** ("**SuD** *but* light") is also heard. If more specificity is necessary, the item in question is generally compared to something else that typically has a particular color. For example, **Doq 'ej beqpuj rur** means "(it) is **Doq** and resembles *bekpuj*," a common mineral that is bright orange. Note that with the basic terms, the verbs, or verbs plus the emphatic **-qu'**, may be used adjectivally and modify preceding nouns: **bIQ SuD** ("blue/green/yellow water"), **HIq Doqqu'** ("red liquor"—probably blood-wine). This adjectival construction is not possible with the lengthier formations, however. To describe yellow tea (**Dargh**, "tea"), one must say **SuD Dargh 'ej wov** ("The tea is **SuD** and light") or **SuDbogh Dargh 'ej wovbogh** ("The tea that is **SuD** and light"). The fact that neither **SuD** nor **Doq** includes what is called "violet" or "purple" in Federation Standard may be related to Klingon physiology—that is, exactly how the Klingon eye processes different wavelengths of light.

FOOD

Klingons are, arguably unjustly, infamous throughout the galaxy for their cuisine. Though the gastronomically uneducated might consider Klingon food to be nothing but small animals (still alive) or chunks of barely dead animals thrown together indiscriminately with odoriferous herbs, to make Klingon food properly actually involves a great deal of study, practice, and just the right touch. There are, of course, practitioners of greater and lesser skill, but one must never be careless when preparing food. A well-fed warrior is prepared to battle any enemy and claim glory for the Empire; a warrior displeased with his meal looks to the cook for retribution.

Actually, "cook" is a convenient but misleading term. The Klingon verb **vut**, customarily rendered as "cook" in Federation Standard and used in reference to food only, might better be translated simply as "prepare, make, fix, assemble" in order to avoid association of the word with heat. This is not to say that heat never plays a role in Klingon food preparation, but rather that it is not a defining feature of the process. There are specific words for specific activities involved with food preparation, but **vut** is a general term for all of them. In fact, **vut** can also be used in reference to making a beverage, whether simply mixing ingredients together (such as putting cream in coffee) or starting from scratch (such as brewing ale). A Klingon food and/or beverage preparer is a **vutwI'** (for convenience, this will continue to be translated as "cook"). A bartender, on the other hand, is a **chom**. The term for food of any kind (including beverages) is **Soj**. An individual dish or course is called a **nay'**, and a full meal usually consists of four or five **nay'mey** ("dishes"),

though a non-Klingon might prefer to start with one or
two.

The lack of time or absence of food-preparing facili-
ties—for example, while on a lengthy hunt—is no imped-
iment to having a good meal. A larger animal may be
sliced into pieces or a section of a plant may be broken
off. This food is often described as **Soj tlhol** ("raw, unprocessed food"), as opposed to **Soj vutlu'pu'bogh**
("food that somebody has prepared"). What makes the
food **tlhol** is not that it has not been heated but rather
that no one has done anything to it; thus, "unprocessed"
might be a better translation than "raw". On the other
extreme is **Soj qub**—literally "rare food, uncommon
food" but used as the Klingon equivalent of haute cuisine, food usually served only on the most formal of occasions.

Well-prepared food is described as **'ey** ("delicious"),
the word also used to describe good music: **'ey Soj** ("The
food is delicious"); **Soj 'ey** ("delicious food"). Food also
resembles music in that if it affects one in an especially
positive way—that is, if the food particularly satisfies the
eater—one may say **DuQ Soj** ("The food stabs him/her").
All food is considered to be good in its natural state; it
takes the intervention of a "cook" to ruin it. Thus, the
word **'eyHa'**, used to describe food that is edible but is
not particularly tasty, means something like "undeli-
cious," implying that someone caused it to cease being
delicious. For food that has been prepared particularly
poorly, it is not uncommon to hear **Soj raghmoHlu'pu'**
("The food has been decayed" or "Someone has caused
the food to decay") or the more pointed **Soj Daragh-
moHpu'** ("You have caused the food to decay"), even
though the food has not literally decayed. On the other
hand, one may simply use the word **'up** ("disgusting, repugnant"): **'up Soj** ("The food is disgusting").

In terms of texture, Klingon food may be **ngal**
("chewy"), **char** ("slimy"), or **tlher** ("lumpy"), all consid-

ered positive attributes (depending, of course, on the particular dish). Other than that which is served alive, the best meat is **ghoQ** ("fresh, just killed"). A vegetable or fruit that is **baQ** ("fresh, just picked, just fallen off the plant"), on the other hand, is not as favored as one that is **DeH** ("ripe," though "overripe" might be closer to the mark) or even **QaD** ("dry, dried out").

To the Klingon palate, the best food tastes **tlhorgh** ("pungent," though some non-Klingons may prefer to translate the word as "rank" or "gamy"). The opposite of **tlhorgh** is **tlhorghHa'**, conventionally translated as "bland" but literally meaning "unpungent," the implication being that the natural punch has somehow been taken out of the food as a result of how it was prepared. The same ideas are often expressed idiomatically. When talking about the quality of a dish, one may say **jej pach** ("The claw is sharp"; that is, the food is pungent) or **jejHa' pach** ("The claw is dull"; in other words, the food is bland, where **jejHa'** ["dull"] really means something like "de-sharpened"). Klingon food also frequently tastes **wIb** ("sour, bitter") or **na'** ("salty, brackish"). The closest equivalent to "sweet" is probably **na'ran rur** ("resembles a *naran*," a fruit whose juice is sometimes added to sauces as a contrast to the other flavors.) Interestingly, many human visitors seem to really enjoy the juice of the *naran* all by itself, particularly in the morning, though Klingons find this practice most peculiar. Despite the general absence of sweet foods from their diet, Klingons tend to be quite enthusiastic about **yuch** ("chocolate"), at least in its purest forms.

The usual Federation Standard translations of the primary tastes ("pungent," "sour," "salty") are a little deceptive. From the Klingon point of view, it is not accurate to say that a particular food *is* sour; rather, it *tastes and smells* sour. That is, sourness is not an intrinsic quality of the food; it is a perception, the effect the food has upon the senses of smell and taste, the Klingon sense of smell being particularly highly developed. Translations such as "sour-inducing" (**Soj wIb,** "sour-inducing food"; **na' Soj,** "The food induces saltiness") would perhaps be closer to the feeling of the Klingon, but they are a bit clumsy.

The verb meaning "smell"—that is, "sense odors"—is **largh**. The word for "emit a smell" is **He'**. This does not necessarily imply a bad smell. Odors are not considered "good" or "bad"; they are just odors. There may be a subjective evaluation of the *source* of the odor, however. It is a compliment to suggest that someone smells like *rokeg* blood pie not because the smell itself is good, but rather because the food carries with it positive associations. On the other hand, it is most insulting to say that someone smells like rotting *forshak.*

The verb **mum** ("taste") means "sense flavors." To say **Soj vImum** ("I taste the food") is to say "I perceive a flavor or flavors," not "I try out the food to see if it is prepared properly." This latter meaning of "taste" is expressed by the verb **waH**, which can also be used more generally to mean "try out, test, use experimentally."

The Klingon diet consists primarily of animal matter. With a few notable exceptions, plants seldom form the bases of dishes in their own right, though they are used quite a bit in food preparation, particularly as seasoning. Water is consumed, but never as the beverage of choice.

It is not possible here to give detailed accounts of how to prepare specific dishes or even to list all of the ingredients. Nor is it possible to explain and compare the cuisines of different regions and planets within the Empire. For detailed information of that kind, the best source is probably **jabmeH** by J'puq (the title means *In Order to Serve*; it is a cookbook). Nevertheless, any visitor to a Klingon restaurant (or, if one is lucky, a Klingon home) should be familiar with some basics (and some basic vocabulary).

Perhaps the most representative Klingon food, certainly the one best known outside of the Empire, is *gagh* (or, in Klingon, **qagh**): serpent worms in a thick sauce (called **ghevI'**). Prior to the preparation of this dish, the worms are fed only **'Iw puj** ("diluted blood"; literally, "weak blood"), which the worms find unappetizing and therefore consume only when they are nearly starving. (The type of animal from which the blood has been taken has a great deal of influence on the eventual flavor of the **qagh**, and individual cooks, as well as individual eaters, have their own preferences.) As the final step in preparing the dish, the worms are poured into a bowl filled with the **ghevI'** (sauce), which contains, among other ingredients, pellets of an extremely flavorful herb that the hungry worms quickly ingest, even though it is toxic to them and kills them within minutes. Since **qagh** is considered best if consumed while the worms are still alive, it is important to keep the worms out of the sauce until just before the dish is served. For the same reason, it is customary to eat **qagh** as quickly as possible. If, for some reason, the **qagh** cannot be consumed before they all die, the entire mixture of **qagh** and **ghevI'** is saved and later heated up as a sort of stew (the general term for which is **tlhIq**; thus, **qagh tlhIq** may be translated as "**qagh** stew"). Although not as desirable as live **qagh**, this is a common way to serve leftovers.

Like **qagh**, other small animals are eaten whole, in great quantity (by the handful if possible), and, ideally, alive. Among these are various bugs (collectively, **ghew**). Large animals are usually chopped into pieces, sometimes with attention paid to which piece is which (thus a **tIq** ["heart"] might be served as a dish in its own right), sometimes not (the **ghab**, for example, is just a chunk of the midsection of an animal, including any organs that may have remained attached after the carving). Meat of any kind is called **Ha'DIbaH**, which is also the normal term for "animal" (and also an insult when used in reference to a person). Often the **DIr** ("skin") is still attached when **Ha'DIbaH** is served, though sometimes it is removed and prepared as a dish in its own right.

More sophisticated Klingon food preparation involves keeping anatomically identifiable parts separate. Some of the other commonly eaten parts include the **lem** ("hoof"), **namwech** ("paw"), **pach** ("claw"); **gham** ("limb"); **tagh** ("lung"), **burgh** ("stomach"), **luH** ("intestines"), **chej** ("liver"), and other internal organs not likely to be familiar to non-Klingons; **jat** ("tongue"); **mIn** ("eye"); **qogh** ("ear"—the external part, if there is one; the actual organ of hearing, the **teS**, is usually considered too small to bother with); **wuS** ("lips"), **qevpob** ("cheek, jowl"), **ghIch** ("nose"); **Hugh** ("throat"); **Somraw** ("muscle"); **QoghIj** ("brain"; another word, **yab**, also means "brain" as an organ, but in addition it means "mind, intellect" and is not used in reference to food); **to'waQ** ("ligament, tendon"); **tlhuQ** ("tail"); **Hom** ("bone"); **ghISDen** ("scales"); **veD** ("fur"); and **'aD** ("vein"). Sometimes an animal's whole head (**nach**) is served. A mixture of animal parts is **Daghtuj**, regardless of whether the parts are from the same type of animal. Curiously, eggs (**QImmey**) do not play a large role in the Klingon diet as food items in their own right, though they are mixed into many sauces, usually along with the pieces of shell (**pel'aQ**), for flavor and texture. The small eggs of the Tokvirian skink (**toqvIr lung**), however, are often eaten whole, shell and all, usually by the handful.

Let us turn, appropriately briefly, from fauna to flora. Any part of any plant that is eaten may be termed **naH**, usually translated "fruit" or "vegetable." Any nut (a fruit with a hard shell) is called a **naHlet** (literally, "hard fruit"), a thistle (a flower with dangerously sharp leaves) is a **naHjej** (literally, "sharp fruit"), a bean (which, in this case, may mean the pod or the seed or seeds in it or both) is a **qurgh**, and a root or tuber is a **'oQqar**. Otherwise there are no known generic names for different types of

naH (though there are terms for specific plants and parts of a plant). A plant's sap or juice is called **vIychorgh.**

The outer covering of a fruit or vegetable (**yub,** "husk, rind, peel") is always consumed, except in the case of the **naHlet yub** ("nut shell"). Klingons typically gnaw (**choptaH**—literally, "continue biting") on the nut until it cracks open, and then they spit out (**tlhIS**) the pieces of shell (occasionally at a nearby diner, as a gesture of sociability) before chewing and swallowing the rest. Similarly, they will usually gnaw on the hard pit of some fruits (**naHnagh**—literally, "fruit stone") until it can be chewed and swallowed, but it is not considered out of place to treat the pit as a shell and spit out the pieces.

Agriculture (**Satlh**) is practiced to a certain extent, though it is common to gather uncultivated plants as well. Fruit or vegetables that come from a farm (**Du'**) are called either **naH** alone or **Du' naH** ("farm fruit or vegetable," or "produce"); the wild variety is termed **naH tlhab** (literally, "free fruit or vegetable"). The verb **yob** ("harvest") is used to refer to gathering up plants or plant parts, whether from a field (**yotlh**) that has been sown or out in the wild. The verb meaning "farm" is **wIj**; that meaning "plant" (referring to vegetation of any kind) is **poch**. One may say **Sor poch** ("He/she plants a tree"), **lav poch** ("He/she plants a shrub"), and even **naH poch** ("He/she plants fruit or vegetables"), referring to the ultimate use of the plant as a food source. Animals to be eaten are generally acquired by means of a hunt (**chon**; the verb "hunt" is **wam**). On the other hand, Klingons generally **Sep** ("breed") small animals such as **gharghmey** ("worms").

There is actually quite a large repertoire of food preparation techniques, only a few of which are noted here. Let us focus only on nonliving animal matter: if it is fresh, the "cook" may **pID** it, which involves coating it with herbed granulated cartilage (not necessarily from the same animal) mixed with some kind of **tIr** ("grain")

As he describes the thrill of his first hunt, Toq (Sterling Macer) reminds his elders of what it is to be Klingon. *Robbie Robinson*

and doing very little else. The name of the granulated cartilage is **ngat**, which has also come to mean "gunpowder." Meat prepared in this way is sometimes described as **wamwI' Ha'DIbaH** ("hunter's meat"), but the specific animal name is usually used instead of the word **Ha'DIbaH** ("meat"); for example, **wamwI' mIl'oD** ("hunter's sabre bear"). If the meat is somewhat older, a common preparation technique is to **HaH** ("marinate") it in any of a wide variety of concoctions containing **'Iw** ("blood") and/or **vIychorgh** ("sap") as a base, along with assorted animal parts. Meat prepared in this style is also called **voDleH Ha'DIbaH** ("emperor's meat"), again with the specific animal used instead of **Ha'DIbaH**; for example, **voDleH lIngta'** ("emperor's *lingta*"). (Presumably there was an emperor at one time who liked his meat prepared in this fashion.) All but the least experienced cooks have **chanDoq** ("marinade") prepared well in advance of a meal, keeping a large container of the brew around at all times and constantly adding new ingredients to it as they become available. A special sauce (**qettlhup**) that accompanies many dishes is often a thickened version of **chanDoq**.

The verb **HaH**, though once restricted to this form of food preparation, is now often used in the more general sense of "soak, drench." It is frequently heard in the reflexive form (**HaH'egh**, "soak oneself") in reference to such activities as drinking a great deal, which has positive connotations, and bathing, an occasional undertaking with negative connotations.

Almost as common as food that has been soaked in a marinade is food that has been set aside to **rogh** ("ferment"). It is important to distinguish **rogh** from **ragh** ("decay"). Food that has decayed (**raghpu'bogh Soj**, or, more succinctly, **Soj non**—"rotten food") is food that has become inedible and must be thrown away, though it is sometimes given to animals. (Note that **Soj woD** ["He/she throws the food away"], which refers to a regrettable activity, is very different from **Soj jaD** ["He/she throws or hurls the food in the manner of a projectile"], which, under certain circumstances, is considered a reasonable pastime.) To ferment food is to **roghmoH** (literally, "cause to ferment"). Fermented meat is also known as **qeyvaq Ha'DIbaH** ("Kayvak's food"), named, for now forgotten reasons, after a famous ancient warrior. As with hunter's and emperor's food, the specific meat is used rather than the word **Ha'DIbaH** ("meat"), as in **qey-**

vaq lIngta' ("Kayvak's *lingta*"). The Kayvak naming style does not apply to fermented plants; its use is restricted to meat.

One way to bring fermentation about is to mix the food with a fungus (known as **'atlhqam**) usually scraped off the bottom of certain animals' feet, though it also grows on trees. The fermentation process is monitored so that the food is served at just the right time, even though the process is actually still going on (the verb meaning "serve fermented food at its peak" is **wech**). The shell of an animal (**nagh DIr**—literally, "rock skin"—not to be confused with **yub** ["husk, rind, peel"], the word applied to the shell of a nut, or **pel'aQ** ["eggshell"]) is commonly separated from the animal meat, fermented, and served at another time. Finally, the way to prepare a common dish called **qompogh** is to mash (**tap**) a mixture of various types of **naH** ("fruit, vegetable"), with or without some animal matter, into a rather lumpy paste and then to let it **rogh** ("ferment").

A distinctive Klingon culinary technique similar to fermentation involves using a living animal as a food processor. Once again, timing is critical. A number of different kinds of foods are mixed together, along with various flavorful herbs, and the concoction (called **Su'lop**) is fed to an animal. After just the right amount of time (a good cook knows from experience when this is), the animal is killed and its parts are used for various dishes, as would be expected. The stomach, however, still contains the now partially digested **Su'lop**, which is removed, used as a sauce (called **quD**), and served with great flourish. To prepare a sauce in this manner is described as **Su'lop Suqqa'** (literally, "reacquire **Su'lop**," often shortened to just **Suqqa'**. There is an alternate way of preparing **quD** that involves using chemicals to do the job of the animal's stomach enzymes. Klingon gourmets distinguish between the two by referring to **quD** made in the natural way as **burgh quD** ("stomach **quD**"), as opposed to the artificially produced **'un quD** ("pot **quD**"). Though nutritionally identical, **burgh quD**, when available, is always preferable to **'un quD**.

If heat is used as part of food preparation, the cook is most likely to **mIQ** ("deep-fry") the food. This involves first acquiring **tlhagh** ("animal fat") from any available source and then heating it up so that it boils (the general word for "boil" is **pub**, but the verb used specifically to refer to the boiling of fat is **'Im** ["render"]). After it has been boiling for a while, the food to be fried is tossed in (sometimes having been coated in some kind of paste), and it stays there until it has soaked up as much of the **tlhagh** ("fat") as possible. A particularly popular dish, **tlhombuS**, requires that the cook coat a block of **tlhagh** with a mixture of **ngat** ("herbed granulated cartilage") and **tIr** ("grain") and then briefly immerse the block into the already boiling fat, just until the coating hardens.

Some dishes are prepared by heating meat in a liquid consisting of the animal's blood along with some choice condiments. To prepare food in this way is to **Qev** it. Livers of *bokrat*s are typically prepared in this manner. Though the dish is heated, in order to properly make **boqrat chej Qevlu'pu'bogh** ("stewed *bokrat* liver"; literally, "*bokrat* liver that has been stewed"), the livers should be from an animal that was killed only minutes before. The difference in flavor between fresh and nearly stale livers is most noticeable.

Another popular dish, **qul DIr** ("fire skin"), is made by soaking cut up pieces of animal skin, from whatever animal is available, in a strong liquor, then removing them from the solution and setting them afire just before serving. The dish is eaten quickly, while the pieces are still burning.

It is also not unusual to **HaH** ("marinate") or **roghmoH** ("ferment") various sorts of **naH** ("fruit, vegetable"). One common dish is a torpedo-shaped fruit called **peb'ot,** which is soaked in a **chanDoq** ("marinade"). The fully marinated **peb'ot** is called a **Hurgh**. Experienced cooks will **mIQ** ("fry") the **DIghna' por** (*"digna* leaf"), though this is risky, since if the leaf is heated for too long, it will wilt.

Certain dishes are typically prepared in certain ways, so it is not necessary to describe the preparation technique when naming it; the name of the plant, animal, or animal part is enough. Thus, **pIpyuS pach** (*"pipius* claw") is always prepared the same way; it would be peculiar to hear **pIpyuS pach HaHlu'pu'bogh** (*"pipius* claw that has been marinated; marinated *pipius* claw"), since such phrasing would be redundant. By contrast, the claw of the *ka'raj* is prepared in a variety of ways, so saying that dinner will consist of **qa'raj pach** (*"ka'raj* claw") is not giving enough information. If a dish with a standard preparation technique (a **nay' motlh**, "usual dish") is being offered, asking how it is to be prepared is a demonstration of cultural ignorance. Thus, in addition to *pipius* claw, questions about **bIreQtagh** (*"bregit* lung"), **targh tIq** ("heart of *targ"*), **raHta'** (*"racht"*), **tlhImqaH** (*"zilm'kach"*), and **Qaj tlhuQ** (*"kradge* tail") should be avoided. On the other hand, asking whether the **quD** is naturally produced (**burgh quD**) or the artificially produced type (**'un quD**) or specifying whether one prefers **tlhatlh** (*"gladst"*) with or without sauce shows both knowledge of and interest in Klingon cuisine.

Klingon drinks may be divided into two types: those with and those without an intoxicating effect—basically, those with and those without alcohol. There is no known noun referring to drinks in general (though, as noted above, beverages are considered a type of **Soj** ["food"]). Any alcoholic beverage is called **HIq**. Federation Standard makes a distinction between the various forms of liquor; Klingon does not. Thus, the word **HIq** is translated in various ways in names of different drinks, particularly, though not exclusively, those of non-Klingon origin: **romuluS HIq** ("Romulan ale") **'Iw HIq** ("bloodwine"), **Sorya' HIq** ("Saurian brandy"). On the other hand, many native Klingon alcoholic drinks have names that do not contain the word **HIq**. Among these are **wornagh** (*"warnog"*), a kind of ale; **baqghol** (*"bahgol"*), consumed heated and out of rather small glasses; and the very strong **chechtlhutlh** (*"chech'tluth"*). (The fact that **chechtlhutlh** seems to be made up of two verbs related to drinking—**chech** ["be drunk"] and **tlhutlh** ["drink"]—is no doubt coincidental.) Imported alcoholic beverages are made of various ingredients, some of them not available in the Klingon Empire. Domestic **HIq** is distilled from a number of different kinds of grain (**tIr**), with some additional constituents (of both plant and animal origin, including **'Iw**, "blood") adding flavor and strength. **'Iw HIq** ("bloodwine") is served warm to hot (best is **porgh Hat**—"body temperature," though it is not clear whose body) and should be very dark red in color. Drinking **HIq** is usually accompanied by toasting.

There are a number of common nonalcoholic drinks (though no single word refers to the entire collection of them). As already pointed out, any drink made of the liquid that circulates through any part of a plant is **vIychorgh** ("juice"). Animal blood (**'Iw**) is found primarily in alcoholic beverages, but the milk (**nIm**) of some creatures (such as the **targh** [*"targ"*]) is combined with other ingredients to form drinks of rather complex flavor, though it is seldom consumed by itself. A popular effervescent drink, black in color, is called **'awje'**. This is frequently, though not accurately, translated as "root beer," probably because of its superficial resemblance to the Federation soft drink, but it is made from, among other things, the marrow (**melchoQ**) taken from the bones of a **teghbat** (*"teg'bat"*). It is considered relatively mild, even for a Klingon nonalcoholic drink.

Though not native to the Empire, Klingons have developed a way to make coffee (**qa'vIn**) particularly strong, both in flavor and in its effect as a stimulant, and it is a very popular beverage. As a rule, coffee is consumed plain—that is, black—but some Klingons prefer to mix other ingredients in with the coffee. If some kind of **HIq** ("liquor") is added to the coffee, the drink is called **ra'taj**. It is said that the drink was originally nicknamed **ra'wI' taj** ("commander's knife," suggestive of its potency), and that the name was shortened over time. This often repeated story cannot be confirmed. In any event, **ra'taj** became one of the few Klingon foods to become popular outside of the Empire, though in an altered form. Instead of containing liquor, as does the genuine Klingon **ra'taj**, the "export" version (which came to be pronounced *raktaj* in Federation Standard) consists of strong Klingon coffee plus a nutlike flavoring. Eventually, a new fashion developed—adding cream to the *raktaj*—and with this innovation came yet another name, *raktajino*, modeled after the name of another popular coffee drink, cappuccino. *Raktajino* is now served hot or iced, with or without extra cream, and with or without the rind of some fruit to add even more flavor. Though it is sometimes called "Klingon coffee," it is quite different from both plain **qa'vIn** and the alcoholic **ra'taj**.

Tea (**Dargh**) is another common Klingon beverage. There are many types of tea, some based on vegetable matter, some on animal. The word **Dargh** refers to the beverage only. If plants or animal parts are dried and, if necessary, chopped up before being steeped in boiling water to produce **Dargh**, this preparation is called **Qenvob**. Often, however, there is no **Qenvob**; the tea is made by simply picking thorns, leaves, petals, or seeds off of a plant and immediately immersing them in the water. Usually brackish water (**bIQ na'**) is best. Tea may be made either in a teapot (**runpI'**) or directly in the teacup (**Dargh HIvje'**, or, if not a cup specifically designed for drinking tea, just **HIvje'**).

Though one may drink tea at any time, Klingons observe a very solemn Tea Ceremony in which a tea that is somewhat toxic (for a Klingon—but quite deadly for humans) is both prepared and consumed according to certain ritualistic procedures. During the Tea Ceremony, two friends drink the tea partly as a test of bravery and partly as a reminder of the Klingon maxim that "death is an experience best shared."

The equipment needed for the preparation of Klingon food is rather minimal, consisting pretty much of pots or vats plus cutting and stirring implements of various sorts. The general term for a pot is **'un**. Pots that may be put on top of a fire in order to heat their contents are made of metal (**baS**); others may be made of either metal or ceramic material (**nagh** [literally, "stone"]). A **bargh** is probably the most frequently used pot. It is rather large and has a flattened bottom. The smaller **nevDagh** is characterized by its V-shaped handles, termed **DeSqIvDu'** ("elbows"; note that **-Du'**, the plural suffix for body parts, is used here even though the handles are not literally body parts). A square or rectangular tub used to hold food while it is fermenting is called a **'Ib**, and a cook's ever-present supply of **chanDoq** ("marinade") is kept in a large **bal** ("jug, jar, bottle").

If the food must be cut up before cooking or eating, a knife (**taj**) is used, though, as noted earlier, the knives used for this purpose are different from those used as weapons. Food-preparation knives, of which there are many types, come in different sizes and shapes for different cutting tasks. For example, a **warjun** is a large, extremely sharp, square-bladed chopping implement (but for its short handle, it would probably be considered a kind of **'obmaQ** ["ax"]). For finer work (such as making the slits in limbs needed to extract veins), a small **SIjwI'** (literally, "slitter") is commonly employed. A general, all-purpose knife that seems to be able to cut through practically anything is a **'aqnaw**.

The stick used for stirring in a **'un** ("pot") is usually called a **DuDwI'** ("mixer"), though sometimes the term

Surrounded by what he believes are loyal warriors, Chancellor Gowron lifts his **HIvje'**. *Brian D. McLaughlin*

'un naQ ("pot cane") is heard. If the end of the **DuDwI'** is flattened out, paddlelike, the device may also be called a **ngawDeq**. A scooping implement, much like a garden trowel, used to remove food from a pot, is a **bo'Dagh**.

A container from which drinks are consumed is a **HIvje'**. This word is used for any sort of drinking vessel: glass, cup, mug, stein, goblet, tumbler, and so on. If necessary, **HIvje'** can also be used to refer to drinking vessels normally not associated with Klingon culture—for example, crystal stemware. Since certain drinks are typically associated with certain containers, saying the type of drink plus **HIvje'** indicates the type of cup or glass as well: **'Iw HIq HIvje'** ("bloodwine glass"), **qa'vIn HIvje'** ("coffee mug"), **baqghol HIvje'** (*"bahgol* cup"). Unless specified further, **HIq HIvje'** ("liquor glass") usually means a tankard or stein for beer or ale. A **bal** is any bottle or jug used to store liquid. Usually one will pour (**qang**) the drink directly from the **bal** into the **HIvje'**, but it is not considered uncivil to drink directly from the **bal**. Ale is often stored in a large vat (**qegh**) rather than in a **bal**. Some drinks are served in special containers, such as the **runpI'** ("teapot") used in the making of **Dargh** ("tea"), and are then poured into the appropriate **HIvje'**.

Each dish is brought to the table (**raS**) on a platter ('**elpI'**), usually made of metal. The food is arranged not haphazardly but in a way that helps the food look appealing. For example, in some dishes, pieces are placed with the veins clearly visible so that the blood still inside them can be seen. A diner transfers a portion to his or her plate (**jengva'**, though the plural form is **ngop** ["plates"]), if one is available, by simply grabbing the desired quantity of food with a hand. If the '**elpI'** ("serving platter") is not close by, it is quite acceptable to just reach across the table or to walk around the table to a more convenient position. If necessary, two hands may be used to break off (**wItlh**) a slab of the desired fare. If **ngop** ("plates") are provided, they will probably be in a pile somewhere on the table. It is acceptable to reach over and grab one; it is not acceptable to ask someone else to grab a plate and pass it down. If there is no pile of plates, none will be furnished, and it is quite improper to ask for one.

Eating is done with hands only. There is no Klingon fork or spoon. If the cook has prepared the food properly, there should be no need to use a knife either, though, from time to time, one is quite useful. If the particular dish is somewhat soupy (a dish of this kind is termed a **chatlh**, roughly translated as "soup," though the amount of liquid is far less than what the Federation Standard term "soup" would suggest), it will arrive at the table in a large bowl (**maHpIn**) and a diner will pour its contents into a smaller bowl (**Duq**), from which he or she will consume it. Since this sort of dish is still primarily solid food as opposed to liquid, using the verb **tlhutlh** ("drink") to describe ingesting it is not quite right. There is another verb, **'ep**, which refers to eating food of this kind.

When the food arrives, it should be eaten as is; nothing equivalent to a saltshaker will be found on a Klingon dining table. On the other hand, if a dish comes with a sauce, it is appropriate to use as much or as little sauce as one desires.

Klingons tend to eat quickly, taking rather large amounts of food into their mouths and swallowing in big gulps. This is true of food eaten at any of the four daily meals (**nIQ** ["breakfast"], **megh** ["lunch"], **'uQ** ["dinner"], and **ghem** [usually translated as "midnight snack," but really a late-night meal of some substance]), as well as food eaten at any other time. Unless one is dining alone, a meal is typically quite noisy, with a great deal of talking (and often singing) accompanying the clattering of plates and bowls. This is particularly true of a **'uQ'a'** ("banquet, feast"; literally, "great dinner" or "big dinner," but used regardless of the time of day of the banquet). By the end of the meal, there should be a good amount of food scattered all about, mostly as a result of food spilling or dropping as it makes its way from various plates and platters to mouths. Indeed, if one eats too neatly or if one does not eat with gusto, it will probably be assumed that one is not enjoying the food. (The verb **noS** ["eat in small mouthfuls, nibble"], unless applied to small animals or very young children, is always used derogatorily.) Also, at the end of a meal, one should avoid picking bits of food out of one's teeth. To do so is to insult the cook by implying that the food was not well prepared and that the eater wants to get the flavors out of his mouth.

Any visitor to a Klingon city, or even outpost, will undoubtedly want to spend some time sampling Klingon food in a restaurant (**Qe'**). Reservations are not accepted, and the means of payment is arranged upon being shown a table. Tipping is unknown. In some restaurants, the menu (**HIDjolev**) is posted (seldom are individual copies

The atmosphere of a Federation reception is deadly dull compared to dining in a **Qe'**. *Robbie Robinson*

available), but in most, the patrons know the regular fare and ask about specials, including the **DaHjaj gheD** (literally, "today's prey"), a dish whose components depend on what animals the restaurant's hunters were able to bring in. The person who takes the order and brings the food is the **jabwI'** ("server") and the chef is the **vutwI'** ("cook"; in a large restaurant, the head chef is referred to as the **vutwI' quv,** the "honored cook"). In small establishments, the **jabwI'** and **vutwI'** are likely to be the same individual. If there is a separate bar (**tach**), the bartender (**chom**) will mix drinks; otherwise, these chores fall to the **vutwI'**.

When taking a table's order, the **jabwI'** neither writes anything down nor enters data into a computer. It is considered the duty of the **jabwI'** to remember (**qaw**) the choices and to bring the correct food, and servers tend to be quite skilled at this. On the rare occasion when the

jabwI' has remembered incorrectly (**qawHa'**), the patron may reject (**lajQo'**) the dish. If the patron rejects a
dish that the server believes has been properly remembered, however, the misunderstanding could develop
into minor combat. For most of the other diners in the
restaurant, this is regarded as an exhilarating diversion.

The actual eating of a meal at a restaurant is done in
accordance with the same rules of etiquette as any other
meal, as described earlier. If anything additional is desired during the meal—more food or drink, for example—the server is called over by shouting **jabwI'!**
("Server!") If a refill of the drink order is all that is
needed, some time can be saved by adding **wI'oj** ("We're
thirsty") to the shout. By the end of the meal, all of the
ordered food should be gone (except, for, of course,
whatever may have been spilled, dropped, or thrown).
Soj chuv ("leftover food") is rare unless all members of a
dining party were called away midmeal.

If the restaurant is large enough to have a separate bar
(**tach**), the dining party, upon completion of the meal, is
likely to move to the bar and continue drinking and, probably, toasting and singing. In a smaller establishment, diners tend to remain at the table for quite a while.

Some restaurants post a sign reading **moD Soj** (literally, "the food hurries"). This means that the restaurant,
sometimes called a **Do Qe'** (literally, "velocity restaurant"), caters to those who have a limited amount of time
to eat before returning to their various duties. In such
an establishment, the menu is limited and changes quite
infrequently. Orders are given and taken quickly, and lin-
gering is uncommon. Each dish is prepared and served
in one way and one way only, so it is inappropriate, for
example, to say whether sauce is desired. The person taking the order is, in this case, called not a **jabwI'** ("server")
but, instead, a **tebwI'** (literally, "filler"), presumably because he or she fills a platter (**'elpI'**) with the requested
food. Customers, even those who have never been in the

During a *Kot'baval* Festival, Alexander (Brian Bonsall) and his father enjoy **leng Soj**. *Robbie Robinson*

establishment before, are assumed to be familiar with all details of the fare and procedures. It is not uncommon for a **tebwI'** to become a bit testy (a subtle change in temperament, to be sure) if a customer hesitates or asks questions while giving an order. Other customers will probably show their annoyance as well. A regular patron of a **Do Qe'** tends to order the same dishes on each visit.

At many restaurants, it is possible to order food packaged in boxes to be eaten elsewhere. This sort of food is called **leng Soj** ("voyage food"). The term **leng** ("voyage") may be applied to any specific meal—for example, **leng megh** ("voyage lunch"). It is unwise to order a dish that should be eaten live as **leng Soj**.

John Shannon

IDIOMS

Klingon culture is known as a rather straightforward one in which people speak in a forthright manner, saying exactly what they mean and never using an indirect expression when a blunt one will do. When a Federation citizen on Earth says "It's rather chilly in this room," he or she may really mean "I am uncomfortably cold and want somebody to close the window." The Klingon sentence **pa'vamDaq jIbIr** means "I am cold in this room" (**pa'vamDaq,** "in this room"; **jIbIr,** "I am cold")—nothing more, nothing less. If it is desirable to close the window, the Klingon will simply say, **Qorwagh yISoQmoH** ("Close the window!"; **Qorwagh,** "window"; **yISoQmoH,** "Close it!"). Similarly, if a Klingon wants to know something, he or she may simply demand that the information be given. For example, a common way to say "Which weapon do you want?" is not as a question at all but instead as a command: **nuH DaneHbogh yIngu'!** (literally, "Identify the weapon that you want!"; **nuH,** "weapon"; **DaneHbogh,** "that you want"; **yIngu',** "Identify it!").

On the other hand, there are a great many Klingon expressions that, interpreted literally, are likely to make little or no sense to a non-Klingon visitor. For example, the Klingon phrase **wa' DoS wIqIp** ("We hit one target") or the shorter **DoS wIqIp** ("We hit a target"; **wa',** "one"; **DoS,** "target"; **wIqIp,** "We hit it") is frequently heard in conversations that have nothing to do with shooting, targets, or even weaponry. It is a way of saying "We agree." By the same token, **cha' DoSmey DIqIp** ("We hit two targets") or the shorter **DoSmey DIqIp** ("We hit targets"; **cha'**, "two"; **DoSmey**, "targets"; **DIqIp**, "We hit them") normally means "We disagree."

These expressions that cannot be interpreted properly from the individual meanings of their components are *idioms*, and they are used just frequently enough in everyday Klingon that a visitor needs to be aware of at least some of them. To understand an idiom, one must learn the phrase as a whole. In using an idiom, one must repeat it exactly; paraphrases will be interpreted literally, not in the idiomatic sense. Thus, in the last example above, the word for "targets" must be **DoSmey** (**DoS**, "target," plus **-mey**, "plural"), never **ray'**, an inherently plural noun meaning "targets." The phrase **ray' wIqIp** means only "We hit targets"; it would never be interpreted as having anything to do with agreeing or not agreeing. (Inherently plural nouns like **ray'** are grammatically singular, so the verb form is **wIqIp**—literally, "we hit it"—rather than **DIqIp**, "We hit them".) Incidentally, the word **DoSmey** brings with it connotations of "scattered all about," so **DoSmey DIqIp** really means something like "We hit scattered targets," an image that fits the idiomatic meaning of "We disagree" quite well.

It is important to note that an idiom usually cannot be translated from one language into another and carry with it the same meaning. Thus, to a speaker of Federation Standard, "We hit a target" conveys information only about hitting a target and has nothing to do with agreeing. By the same token, literally translating a sentence such as "The restaurant changed hands" into Klingon, presumably as **ghopDu' choHpu' Qe'** ("The restaurant has altered hands") or perhaps **ghopDu' tampu' Qe'** ("The restaurant has exchanged hands"; **ghopDu'**, "hands"; **choHpu'**, "has altered, has changed";

Qe', "restaurant"; **tampu',** "has exchanged"), does not tell the Klingon that the restaurant is now under new ownership, which is what the Federation Standard phrase really means. Assuming that a restaurant can do anything at all (which it probably cannot—only a being of some sort can do something), the only meaning a Klingon would glean from these sentences is that the restaurant acquired hands (meaning only body parts) that it previously did not have. Even given Klingon cuisine, this would be highly unusual. Idioms are very much language (and culture) specific.

Among the common Klingon idioms are some phrases taken from mythology and literature. For example, the expression **Hoch jaghpu'Daj HoHpu'** ("He/she has killed all his/her enemies"; **Hoch,** "all"; **jaghpu-'Daj,** "his/her enemies"; **HoHpu',** "He/she has killed them") is used to describe a person who is leading a meaningless, empty life, one lacking any challenge. It is derived from a line in the poem "**lu qeng**" ("The Fall of Kang"; literally, "Kang falls") by G'trok: **Hoch jaghpu'Daj HoHbogh SuvwI' yIvup**, the classic Federation Standard translation of which is "Pity the warrior who slays all his foes."

Normally, an idiom follows the rules of Klingon grammar (for example, the verb takes the prefix appropriate to the meaning intended), but occasionally, one will be grammatically aberrant. Thus, the phrase **mIv je DaS** (literally, "helmet and boot") is used to mean fully dressed, as for a ceremonial affair (as in **mIv je DaS tuQ ra'wI'** ("The commander wears helmet and boot"—that is, "The commander is in full dress uniform"). Normally, the conjunction **je** ("and") would be expected to follow the second noun (here, **DaS** ["boot"]), but in this phrase, it does not. The grammatically correct **mIv DaS je** also means "helmet and boot," but it would not be used in the sense of full dress. The sentence **mIv DaS je tuQ ra'wI'** would mean simply "The commander is wearing a helmet and a boot" (or, since the plural need never be overtly indicated, perhaps this would mean "The commander is wearing a helmet and boots"). How the odd grammatical construction came to be is not known with certainty, but it probably is based on an older form of the language. The fact that the expression for "full dress" includes the word **mIv** "helmet" also suggests that the phrase has been in use for a long time, since helmets are no longer commonly part of Klingon attire. Finally, it is important to note that the idiomatic expression is always **mIv je DaS** ("helmet and boot"), never **DaS je mIv** ("boot and helmet"). As is frequently the case in idioms, the order of elements cannot be changed.

Klingons are sometimes aware of the source of an expression, as is the case with the line from G'trok just noted, but more often the origin of the phrase is known only to scholars or is lost altogether. In the list that follows, the sources or probable sources of the idioms are given when possible. There are a great many idioms other than the ones in this list (some are cited elsewhere in this book), but the collection here should give the visitor a good start on speaking the language in a way that sounds natural.

COMMON IDIOMS

ngaQ lojmIt. ("The door is locked.")

This phrase has two meanings: (1) "The situation has an unavoidable outcome"; (2) "The plan or commitment is firm and cannot be changed." A door (**lojmIt**, though this word may also be translated as "gate") is a symbol of escape, so a door that is locked (**ngaQ**) means there is no escape or no way out.

Hoch nuH qel ("consider every weapon")

This is an idiom cloaked in the terminology of the military that has a wider application. It is used to mean

Despite his commander's assurances to the contrary, Worf considers the possibility of ambush by a surprise party.
Robbie Robinson

"Consider every possibility" or "Consider every option," with the word **nuH** ("weapon") standing metaphorically for "possibility." (**Hoch** means "all, every" and **qel** is "consider, take into account.") It is not a set phrase, so it is heard in various forms, such as a command (**Hoch nuH yIqel!**—literally, "Consider every weapon!" but meaning "Consider every possibility!"), question (**Hoch nuH Daqelّaؘّ?** ["Did you consider every weapon?"]), or statement (**Hoch nuH wIqelpu'** ["We've considered every weapon"]), and it can be negated (**Hoch nuH qelbe'** ["He/she does not consider every weapon"]). The regular word for "possibility" is **DuH**, and, grammatically, there is no reason it could not occur instead of **nuH** in these sentences (**Hoch DuH yIqel** ["Consider every possibility!"] is a perfectly well formed sentence), but this is simply not the normal way to express the advice. The use of **nuH** ("weapon") for **DuH** ("possibility") may have been influenced by the Krotmag dialect pronunciation of **DuH** as something very close to **nuH** (see The Fiction of Klingon Conformity, under "Pronunciation," pages 18–23).

> **qul DIr yISop!** ("Eat the fire skin!")

This phrase means "Hurry up! Move quickly!" It comes from the necessity of eating **qul DIr** ("fire skin"), a dish consisting of flaming pieces of cut-up animal skin, quickly, before the fire goes out.

> **naH jajmey** ("vegetable days")

The phrase "vegetable days" (or "fruit days," since **naH** means both "vegetable" and "fruit") refers to one's youth, a time before reaching an age considered appropriate for marriage. The imagery is of a plant, rooted but growing, just as a Klingon youth still needs grounding (the home) for nourishment (teaching) in order to grow spiritually. The phrase is used in sentences such as **naH jajmeywIj betleH vIyanbe'** ("In my vegetable days, I did not wield a *bat'leth*"; **naH jajmeywIj,** "my vegetable days"; **betleH,** "*bat'leth*"; **vIyanbe',** "I do not wield it"). This expression was actually first heard in a speech in the original Klingon version of Shakespeare's "**'antonI' tlhI'yopatra' je**" in which the heroine refers to her own youth in this way. In the popular Federation Standard version of this play, **naH** is translated as "salad."

> **qutluch patlh** ("*kut'luch* rank")

This phrase means "hierarchical structure." The *kut'-luch* is a knife associated with Klingon assassins, so the imagery is one of a list, presumably in a specific order, of intended victims of the *kut'luch*. To determine one's place in Klingon society or to understand who has authority over whom, one must be aware of the **qutluch patlh** of the military, the government, the house with which one is associated, and so on.

ngem Sarghmey tlha' ("chase forest *sarks*")

A Klingon *sark* (**Sargh**) is an animal somewhat resembling a Terran horse, both in appearance and in that Klingons (generally individually) often ride on the animal's back. A "forest *sark*" (**ngem Sargh**) is a *sark* found in the forest (**ngem**)—that is, in the wild, usually one that has never carried a Klingon around. A Klingon game played on *sark*back involves one rider and *sark* executing a particular maneuver, and then the other players copying this maneuver. The idea is to make the movement somewhat erratic—in the manner of a wild, not a domesticated animal—so that it is difficult to duplicate. In other words, the players all follow or chase (**tlha'**) the lead rider on his or her wild *sark*. The phrase (often in the form **ngem Sarghmey tlha'laH** ["be able to chase forest *sarks*"]) is now used to indicate that one is capable of following anyone or anything—that is, that one is capable of understanding even the most complex of discussions or of solving the most intricate of problems.

vIHtaH gho. ("The hoop is moving.")

This expression means that an activity of finite (though perhaps indeterminate) length has started. It is used to encourage somebody to make a decision or to perform a process more quickly. The implication is that the activity will soon end, so that one should be sure to do whatever is required before it is too late, before the opportunity passes. The phrase might be used, for example, after a ship has been attacked. The captain might say, **vIHtaH gho** ("The hoop is moving"), meaning the battle has begun and it is time for each warrior to play his part. On the other hand, it may be used to ask a friend to join one for a dinner that has already started: **bISop DaneH'a'? vIHtaH gho** ("Do you want to eat? The hoop is moving"). In other words, "If you want to eat, say so now before the food is gone." The expression comes from a maneuver used for hunting practice known as the **qa'vaQ** in which a hoop (**gho**) is rolled and one tries to throw a stick through it while it is moving. The verb **vIH** ("move, be in motion") can be applied to any sort of motion. In this case, it refers to the motion associated with the hoop in this exercise, namely rolling. In the idiom, the verb occurs with the suffix **-taH** ("continuous"), implying that the hoop continues to roll for a period of time (though it will not do so forever).

pe'vIl bI'chu' ("forcefully sweep away")

The verb **bI'** ("sweep") refers to the action of pushing something out of the way by using an implement or the forearm as if it were a broom. If whatever is pushed is cleared away completely, one is said to **bI'chu'** ("sweep [something] away"; literally, "sweep perfectly"). In the Mekro'vak region, for example, a common courtship ritual requires the male to use the leg of a *lingta* to forcefully (**pe'vIl**) sweep away (**bI'chu'**) whatever is on the dinner table before declaring his feelings to the female. In addition to its literal interpretation, the phrase has come to mean "do something all at once, as a single event." It is used in such constructions as **romuluSnganpu' Dujmey DIQaw'pu'; pe'vIl DIbI'chu'pu'** ("We destroyed the Romulans' ships all at once"; **romuluSgnanpu'**, "Romulans"; **Dujmey**, "ships"; **DIQaw'pu'**, "We have destroyed them"; **pe'vIl**, "forcefully"; **DIbI'chu'pu'**, "We have swept them away"; thus, literally, "We've destroyed the Romulans' ships; we've forcefully swept them away").

mevyap! ("Stop, [it is] enough!")

This expression, usually considered a single word, is used as a command meaning "Stop! Cease!" It comes from two Klingon verbs, **mev** ("stop, cease") and **yap** ("be enough, be sufficient"). No doubt in the past, the locution was longer, perhaps **yImev, yap!** ("Stop! It is enough!") Actually, **yImev!** ("Stop!") is the imperative form if the command is given to an individual; to tell a group to stop, one would say **pemev!** The dropping of the imperative prefix (**yI-** or **pe-**) is what would be expected in Clipped Klingon, the abbreviated form of the language frequently used in giving military orders or when under duress; **yap** ("be enough") is used as if an exclamation or a single-word sentence meaning "It is enough." The two words have been used in juxtaposition (**mev, yap**) for so long, they have come to be accepted as a single, though grammatically peculiar, word. If the order of the components were reversed (**yapmev**), the utterance would be meaningless.

vaj Duj chIj ("navigate a warrior ship")

This is a way to say "have strength of character." This sense clearly came about because of the existence in Klingon of two words pronounced **Duj**, one meaning "ship, vessel," the other meaning "instincts." If **Duj** is taken in its "ship" sense, then **vaj Duj** means "warrior ship," something that is certainly appropriate to navigate (**chIj**). On the other hand, if **Duj** is taken to mean "instincts," then **vaj Duj** means "warrior instincts" and the phrase **vaj Duj chIj** ("navigate warrior instincts") makes no sense unless interpreted idiomatically. To a Klingon, this would be to set and direct the course or use of these instincts—that is, to be in control of them. The phrase **vaj Duj** ("warrior vessel" or "warrior instincts"), even without the verb **chIj** ("navigate"), is taken to mean "strength of character," though it can also be used liter-

Unbowed by the battering of the Borg, Lieutenant Commander Worf takes his old station on the *Starship Enterprise*. *Elliott Marks*

ally. It is noteworthy that in this idiom the word for "warrior" is not the frequently heard **SuvwI'**, which would denote an individual warrior, but rather is **vaj**, which refers to the whole idea of being a warrior. Thus, when **Duj** is taken to mean "instincts," **vaj Duj** refers to the instincts associated with being a warrior or the instincts needed for combat; **SuvwI' Duj** would mean the instincts of a specific warrior. If **Duj** is taken to mean "ship," **vaj Duj** ("warrior ship") would suggest that the ship itself has the characteristics of a warrior, a perfectly reasonable notion. To express that a ship is that of a specific warrior, the word **SuvwI'** is appropriate: **SuvwI' Duj** ("warrior's ship"). The idiom, referring to strength of character, may be used in sentences such as **vaj Duj DachIj** ("You navigate a warrior ship"—that is, "You have strength of character") or **vaj Duj chIjbe'** ("He/she does not navigate a warrior ship"—that is, "He/she lacks strength of character").

Dujmey law' chIjpu' ("has navigated many ships")

This expression means "be experienced." It is similar to the previous one in that it is phrased in terms of the navigation of ships. This time, **Duj** (here in its plural form **Dujmey**) means only "ship," not "instincts," and the focus is on the fact that someone has navigated (**chIjpu'**) many (**law'**) of them, presumably successfully. To have navigated many ships is to have gained a great deal of experience. When used, the subject of the sentence is the person who is being characterized as experienced: **Dujmey law' DachIjpu'** ("You have navigated many ships"— that is, "You are experienced").

jop 'ej way' ("lunge and deflect")

This idiom, which means "have an argument," is based on movements associated with the *bat'leth*. During the course of a bout, both parties, among other things, alternately lunge (**jop**), that is, push the *bat'leth* toward the opponent, and deflect (**way'**), or use the *bat'leth* to push the oncoming one away. Each side, then, engages in both offensive and defensive movements, and this alternation of roles is likened to a verbal duel. In using the expression, the appropriate verbal affixes are attached; for example, **wIjoppu' 'ej wIway'pu'** ("We have lunged and we have deflected"—that is, "We have had an argument"). If the two verbs are reversed (**way' 'ej jop** ["deflect and lunge"]), the idea of "have an argument" is not present, though the phrase is perfectly well formed if referring to a *bat'leth* bout.

In a re-creation of the historic battle, the actor playing Molor (John Kenton Shull) temporarily triumphs. *Robbie Robinson*

pollaH pagh polHa'laH ("can either keep it or discard it")

This is a way to say "The matter is unimportant" or "It does not make any difference." The phrase is usually used in response to someone who expresses a concern about something, and the "it" in the translation refers to the matter under discussion. It is sometimes phrased in terms of the speaker, as in **vIpollaH pagh vIpolHa'laH** ("I can either keep it or I can discard it"; **vIpollaH,** "I can keep it"; **pagh,** "or"; **vIpolHa'laH,** "I can discard it"), or the listener, as in **DapollaH pagh DapolHa'laH** ("You can either keep it or you can discard it").

ghe'torvo' narghDI' qa'pu' ("when spirits escape from Gre'thor")

According to mythology, when a dishonored Klingon dies, his or her spirit goes to a place called Gre'thor, there to remain. To speak of spirits escaping from Gre'thor is to speak of an impossibility. The phrase usually follows the statement of what it is that supposedly cannot happen: **jIjegh ghe'torvo' narghDI' qa'pu'** ("I will surrender when spirits escape from Gre'thor"; **jIjegh,** "I surrender"; **ghe'torvo',** "from Gre'thor"; **narghDI',** "when they escape"; **qa'pu',** "spirits"). Note that the word for "spirit," **qa',** takes the plural suffix **-pu',** which is used for beings capable of using language. Spirits do speak.

yItaD! or petaD! ("Be frozen!")

These are idiomatic ways to give the command "Don't move!" The word **yItaD** is used when speaking to an individual; **petaD** is used when giving the command to a group. The verb **taD** means "be frozen," and it is used here in a peculiar, though not really ungrammatical, way. Generally, when a verb describing a state of being (for example, **tuj** ["be hot"]) is used in the imperative form, the suffixes **-'egh** (reflexive suffix) and **-moH** ("cause") are used as well: **yItuj'eghmoH** ("Heat yourself!"—that is, "Cause yourself to be hot!"), **yItaD'eghmoH!** ("Freeze yourself!"—that is, "Cause yourself to be frozen!"). When **taD** is used in the idiomatic sense of "not move," however, it is treated as if a verb describing an activity, such as **yIt** ("walk"): **yIyIt!** ("Walk!").

qagh HoH ("kill *gagh*")

Gagh, the Klingon delicacy consisting of serpent worms in a sauce, is ideally eaten while the worms are still alive. To kill *gagh* (**qagh HoH**), therefore, is counterproductive, to say the least, and that is the notion this idiom conveys. The phrase is applied to a person and means that he or she is doing something counterproductive: **SuyDuj DaQaw'chugh qagh DaHoH** ("If you destroy the merchant ship, you kill *gagh*"; **SuyDuj**, "merchant ship"; **DaQaw'chugh**, "if you destroy it")—that is, destroying the merchant ship is contrary to the best interests of the current mission.

latlh HIvje'Daq 'Iw HIq bIr yIqang! ("Pour the cold bloodwine into another glass!")

This means something along the lines of "I don't believe you; maybe someone else will" or "That is irrelevant to me; maybe someone else will care." The circumstances that prompted the first usage of this saying are unknown, but the imagery is pretty straightforward, especially with the understanding that bloodwine should never be served cold. The expression is always used in this imperative form (**latlh,** "other one"; **HIvje'Daq,** "into a drinking vessel"; **'Iw HIq,** "bloodwine"; **bIr,** "be cold"; **yIqang,** "Pour it!"). A sentence such as **latlh HIvje'Daq 'Iw HIq bIr vIqang** ("I pour the cold bloodwine into another glass") would be interpreted only literally, though perhaps also as a statement about the poor quality of the beverage.

may' bom pIm bom ("sing a different battle song")

This expression means "speak of another matter entirely." It is used when someone changes the topic or offers clarification on an existing one or when some new information comes to light. When uttered, it is frequently preceded by **DaH** ("now") or **toH** ("Aha!"). For example, if a Klingon warrior who has chosen to ignore a messenger bearing what he thinks will be an irrelevant communiqué finds out that the message is from the leader of the High Council himself, the warrior may say **DaH may' bom pIm Dabom** ("Now you sing a different battle song"; **may' bom,** "battle song"; **pIm,** "be different"; **Dabom,** "You sing it")—that is, "Well, that's another matter altogether." The idiomatic meaning comes across regardless of who is said to be "singing" (**may' bom pIm wIbom,** "We sing a different battle song"; **may' bom pIm lubom,** "They sing a different battle song," etc.).

to'waQ yIv ("chew ligament")

This is an idiomatic way of saying "take some time to consider a matter." The origins of the phrase are unknown, but the imagery makes sense, since even with Klingon teeth, to chew (**yIv**) gummy ligament or tendon (**to'waQ**) takes longer than to chew most other types of food. The expression may be used as a command, as in **to'waQ yIyIv!** ("Chew ligament!"—that is, "Take your time thinking about it!") or as a statement, often with the verb suffix **-taH** ("continuous"), implying an ongoing activity, as in **to'waQ vIyIvtaH** ("I'm chewing ligament"—that is, "I'm in the process of taking my time considering the matter"). Though not necessarily derogatory, it is frequently used with negative connotations: **to'waQ yIyIvQo'; DaH yIwuq!** ("Don't chew ligament; decide now!"; **yIyIvQo',** "Don't chew!"; **DaH,** "now"; **yIwuq,** "Decide!") or **HoD QaQbe' ghaH; reH to'waQ yIv** ("He/she is not a good captain; he/she always chews ligament"; **HoD,** "captain"; **QaQbe'** "not be good"; **ghaH,** "he, she"; **reH,** "always").

maj ram ("good, [it is] night")

When going to sleep, Klingons generally have nothing in particular to express to one another. There are a few set phrases, however, that parents frequently say to their children, and the same expressions are commonly used by good friends, particularly on a night before a battle. One of these phrases is **yInajchu'** ("dream well"; literally, a command: "Dream perfectly!"). The other, **maj ram**, is an idiomatic expression usually rendered in Federation Standard as "good night," though this translation obscures the real meaning of the sentiment. The Klingon word **maj** is an exclamation expressing satisfaction, generally translated as simply "good," and functioning as a sentence in its own right. The second word, **ram**, is a noun meaning "night," and it is all that remains of two formerly used longer expressions, **ngaj ram** ("The night is short"; **ngaj,** "be short in duration") and **nI' ram** "The night is long"; **nI',** "be long in duration"). The original full expressions, then, were **maj, ngaj ram** ("Good, the night is short"), suggesting that it would not be long before the next day's activities could begin, or **maj, nI' ram** ("Good, the night is long"), suggesting that there was ample opportunity for rejuvenation and meaningful dreaming. Over time, as result of frequent repetition of the phrases, the original intent of both versions was lost. People said them but did not give much thought to what they meant. They came to be used interchangeably, as if they meant the same thing, namely "Good, it is night." Later, the expressions were shortened by dropping the superfluous (and, by then, meaningless) **ngaj** and **nI',** leaving the contemporary **maj ram.** As a practical matter, Klingons still do not think about what **maj ram** means; they just say it, if they say anything at all, upon retiring.

bIQ ngaS HIvje'. ("The cup contains water.")

This idiomatic expression means "be quite mistaken, be totally wrong." It has its origins in the disdain Klingons generally have for water as a beverage. For a Klingon, drinking anything is better than drinking water.

Thus, it is always undesirable for one's glass or cup (**HIvje'**) to contain (**ngaS**) water (**bIQ**), and, by extension, it is inappropriate as well. When the phrase is used, the person who is being characterized as mistaken is the one whose cup it is: **bIQ ngaS HIvje'lIj** ("Your cup contains water"—that is, "You're all wrong.") This is a reasonably strong expression, and it would not be unexpected for a rather substantial fight to break out shortly after the phrase is uttered.

wa'maH cha' pemmey wa'maH cha' rammey je ("twelve days and twelve nights")

This is a rather long-winded way to say "a long time" (which would be **poH nI'** in nonidiomatic speech). It implies a bit more than that, however, for it is used to mean not only that the length of an event is long but also that the event is an important one, worthy of taking up so much time. The expression comes from the well-known story of Kahless the Unforgettable, the founder of the Klingon Empire, and his brother, Morath, who fought for the fabled "twelve days and twelve nights" because Morath had broken his word and brought shame to the family. The word used for "days," **pemmey**, is the plural form of **pem** ("day, daytime"), a word referring to the part of the day when it is light out (as opposed to **ram** ["night"]). Another word, **jaj** ("day") refers to the full period from dawn to dawn.

bIQ'a'Daq 'oHtaH 'etlh'e'. ("The sword is in the ocean.")

This is another expression based on a story about Kahless. After Kahless's brother, Morath, killed their father, Morath threw their father's sword into the ocean, saying that if he could not have the sword, no one could. After that, the brothers never spoke again. The idiom **bIQ'a'Daq 'oHtaH 'etlh'e'** ("The sword is in the ocean"; **bIQ'a'**, "ocean"; **'etlh,** "sword") is used to mean that something has ended, that it is impossible to return to a prior condition, just as Kahless and Morath never spoke to each other again. The expression might be used, for example, in reference to a treaty that was just signed, suggesting that a former state of antagonism has ended forever. Of course, simply saying that something will last forever does not make it so. If an alliance ends, the phrase is equally apt: the era of peace has ended, and the sword is in the ocean—there is no going back.

ghaH vuv SuS neH ("want the wind to respect [someone]")

A well-known Klingon myth tells of a man in the ancient city of Quin'lat who dies because, during a storm, he remained outside the walls of the city in order to show that he was not afraid of the storm and to make the storm respect him. Kahless, who was in the city at the time, remarked **qoH vuvbe' SuS** ("The wind does not respect a fool"), which has become a frequently repeated proverb. The idiomatic expression **ghaH vuv SuS neH** ("he/she wants the wind to respect him/her"; **ghaH,** "him/her"; **vuv,** "respect"; **SuS,** "wind"; **neH,** "he/she wants") comes from the same story; it is used to mean "He/she is foolish" or "He/she is a fool." For example, one might answer the question **qatlh betleHDaj tlhapbe'?** ("Why doesn't he take his *bat'leth?*"; **qatlh,** "why?"; **betleHDaj,** "his/her *bat'leth*"; **tlhapbe',** "He/she does not bring it") by saying **ghaH vuv SuS neH** ("He wants the wind to respect him"—that is, "He's a fool." The expression can be modified to apply to different persons or situations: **muvuvpu' SuS vIneH** ("I wanted the wind to respect me"—in other words, "I acted like a fool"); **bImaw''a'? Duvuv SuS DaneH'a'?** ("Are you crazy? Do you want the wind to respect you?"—that is, "What's with you? Are you an idiot?").

Ha'quj nge' ("take away a sash")

This is the Klingon equivalent of "wound one's pride." The sash represents a Klingon's heritage. If the sash is removed, so is the Klingon's ancestral identity, and, along with it, his or her dignity and self-esteem. It is generally used with a possessive pronominal suffix attached to **Ha'quj** ("sash"): **Ha'qujwIj** ("my sash"), **Ha'-qujlIj** ("your sash"), and so forth. Thus, the phrase **Ha'-qujlIj nge'** (literally, "take away your sash") means "wound your pride."

Doq bIQtIq bIQ. ("The river water is red.")
Doq bIQtIq. ("The river is red.")

This expression, heard in both variants, means that something momentous has happened, perhaps a major victory. One might say **romuluS yo' wIjeyta'** ("We've defeated the Romulan fleet"; **yo'**, "fleet"; **wIjeyta',** "We have succeeded in defeating it") and then add, to point out the significance of the occasion, **Doq bIQtIq bIQ** ("The river water is red"; **Doq,** "be red"; **bIQtIq,** "river"; **bIQ,** "water"). The phrase can be traced back to an old drinking song that commemorates the slaying of the tyrant Molor by Kahless. On that day, according to the song, the River Skral ran red; that is, it was filled with the blood of Molor. As noted earlier (see the chapter on Argot: Specialized Vocabulary, under "Visual Arts," pages 78–83), the Klingon word **Doq** ("be red"), which occurs in the song as well as in the idiom, really means much more than "red." It refers to a rather wide spectrum of colors ranging from deep red to bright orange and includes pink. Nearly all Klingon bodily fluids, including blood, can be described as **Doq**.

cha' qabDu' ("two faces")
qabDu' law' ("many faces")

The first of these similar phrases means that two individuals are involved in some activity and no one else is. Common Federation Standard equivalents are "face-to-face" (which is based on the same imagery) and "one-on-one." Grammatically, it usually functions as the subject of a sentence, such as **Suv cha' qabDu'** ("Two faces fight"—that is, "They are fighting one-on-one"; **Suv,** "fight"; **cha',** "two"; **qabDu',** "faces"). The similar idiom **qabDu' law'** ("many faces"; **law',** "be many") may be used to refer to a group participating in a single activity. Thus, a brawl may be described by saying **Suv qabDu' law'** ("Many faces fight").

quSDaq ba' ("sit in a chair")

Probably influenced by the homophony of verb suffix **-ba'** ("obviously") and the verb **ba'** ("sit"), this expression has come to mean "that's obvious." It is used only in a condescending manner as a response to something that the hearer deems so self-evident that it need not have been stated in the first place. For example, upon hearing an obvious remark, one might say, **quSDaq bIba'** ("You sit in a chair"—that is, "What you said is quite obvious") or **quSDaq ba'** ("He/she sits in a chair"—that is, "What he/she said is quite obvious"; **quSDaq,** "in a chair").

pel'aQDaj ghorpa' ("before it breaks its shell")

This idiom means something like "before it's too late" or "while there's still time." The literal meaning of the phrase evokes the image of an egg with a baby animal inside who will, at some point, break (**ghor**) the shell (**pel'aQ**), get out, and presumably pose some kind of threat, or at least inconvenience. One might use the expression in a sentence such as **pel'aQDaj ghorpa' qama' yIHoH** ("Before it breaks its shell, kill the prisoner"—that is, "Kill the prisoner now, while you've got a chance"; **qama',** "prisoner"; **yIHoH,** "Kill him/her!").

bo'Dagh'a' lo' ("use a big scoop")
bo'DaghHom lo' ("use a little scoop")

The phrase **bo'Dagh'a' lo'** is another way to say "exaggerate," though it has negative connotations of exaggerating when it is inappropriate to do so. If a warrior, for example, boasts about his recent exploits in a way other warriors find unbelievable, someone might say **bo'-Dagh'a' lo'** ("He's using a big scoop"—that is, "He's exaggerating"). It is not uncommon to confront someone by making use of this phrase (for example, **qaHarbe'; bo'-Dagh'a' Dalo'** ["I don't believe you; you're using a big scoop"—that is, "You're exaggerating"]) or to use it to assert one's veracity, as in **bo'Dagh'a' vIlo'be'** ("I am not using a big scoop"—in other words, "I am not exaggerating"). The "scoop" (**bo'Dagh**) in the phrase is the implement used to remove food from the pot in which it was prepared and place it on a serving platter. This is hardly a delicate operation, so scooping with a **bo'Dagh** entails transferring as much food as possible on each trip from pot to platter. Using a "big scoop" (**bo'Dagh'a'**) would imply transferring even greater quantities of food, perhaps more than the serving plate can handle. An altered form of this expression substitutes **bo'DaghHom** ("little scoop") for **bo'Dagh'a'** ("big scoop"). The phrase **bo'-DaghHom lo'** ("use a little scoop") means "make less of something than it really is" or "minimize the importance of something," again with the connotation that this is inappropriate.

mIvDaq pogh cha' ("display a glove on [one's] helmet")

This idiom is used to convey the idea that a matter has been postponed or rescheduled. It has nothing whatsoever to do with a helmet (**mIv**) or a glove (**pogh**), but it came about because of an incident in literature that did deal with these articles of clothing. In Shakespeare's original Klingon version of **HenrI' vagh**, known in Federation Standard as *Henry V*, HenrI', the Supreme Commander, gets into an argument with one of his troops the night before a great battle. Knowing that they are needed for combat the next day, and not wishing to jeopardize what they both know will be a most glorious battle, they agree to put off their fight until a better time. Each gives the other a glove as a reminder, and they put the gloves in their helmets. Thus, a glove on one's helmet has come to stand for an acknowledgment that a matter is pending, but that there is a more important matter that must be attended to first. It is a statement about both honoring one's obligations and setting priorities, both Klingon virtues. The phrase can be heard in a number of forms, depending on the parties to the commitment. For example, **mIvwIjDaq poghlIj vIcha'** ("I display your glove on my helmet"; **mIvwIjDaq,** "on my helmet," **poghlIj,** "your glove," **vIcha',** "I display it") implies that the postponed matter is between the speaker and the addressee.

> **jej pach.** ("The claw is sharp.")
> **jejHa' pach.** ("The claw is dull.")

As discussed earlier (see the chapter on Argot: Specialized Vocabulary, under "Food," page 85), these two idioms refer to the taste of food. To say **jej pach** ("The claw is sharp") is to say that the food is pungent—that is, good. If the food is bland, one may say **jejHa' pach** ("The claw is dull").

> **cha'maH cha' joQDu'** ("twenty-two ribs")

Klingons have 23 ribs (**joQDu'**). The idiom **cha'maH cha' joQDu'** ("twenty-two ribs"; **cha'maH cha',** "twenty-two"), leaving one rib out, is used to indicate that something is missing or not quite right, especially when it is difficult or impossible to explain the problem. It can be used in varied circumstances. For example, referring to a situation, one might say **naDev cha'maH cha' joQDu'**

tu'lu' ("There are twenty-two ribs here"; **naDev,** "here"; **tu'lu',** "there is/are")—that is, there is something out of the ordinary going on, even if no one can say exactly what. Referring to a person, one could say **cha'maH cha' joQDu' ghaj qama'** ("The prisoner has twenty-two ribs"; **ghaj,** "have"; **qama',** "prisoner"), suggesting that the prisoner is somehow a bit strange. If any other number is used, such as **cha'maH wa' joQDu'** ("twenty-one ribs"), the phrase is always interpreted literally—that is, as a statement about anatomy. If, by chance, a Klingon really does have only 22 ribs, owing to a prior injury, for example, reference to this fact is usually phrased in a way to avoid saying **cha'maH cha' joQDu'** ("twenty-two ribs") and having to deal with the snickers. A common alternative is **wa' joQ Hutlh ghaH** ("He/she lacks one rib").

SIMILES

There are a number of common Klingon expressions similar to such Federation Standard phrases as "stubborn as a mule" or "busy as a bee." In Klingon, however, such similes, as such rhetorical devices are known, are constructed as if two sentences. The first attributes a quality to someone or something; the second makes use of the verb **rur** ("resemble") to link the quality to something that presumably epitomizes the quality. For example, "trivial as a glob fly" would be **ram; ghIlab ghew rur** ("He/she/it is trivial; he/she/it resembles a glob fly"; **ram,** "be trivial, insignificant"; **ghIlab ghew,** "glob fly").

Some Klingons are rather creative in their use of this construction, making up a new simile on the spot for a given occasion, sometimes coming up with rather poetic images, such as **let mInDu'Daj; Separmey rur** ("Her eyes are hard; they resemble *separ* [a type of gemstone]"; **let,** "be hard"; **mInDu'Daj,** "his/her eyes"; **Separmey,**

Valkris (Cathie Shirriff)—her heart was as hard as her eyes.
John Shannon

"separs"). This facility is an admirable one, demonstrating the speaker's wit and mastery of the language. Indeed, several drinking games are built around devising ever more inventive phrases with **rur**. There are, in addition, a number of set phrases that are used repeatedly and are known by everyone. Most of these have been heard so often that they have become overused—that is, they are clichés. Employing a smattering of clichés in one's speech is both natural and acceptable, but using too many makes one's speech less effective and is not at all desirable. To be on the safe side, a visitor should be familiar with the clichés in order to understand what is being said, but at the same time he or she should remember to actually use them only once in a while.

Some of these comparisons can be understood only if one if familiar with various aspects of Klingon culture, such as mythology, history, proverbs, cuisine, weaponry, and so on. For example, for a Klingon, a hammer is a symbol of power. The phrase **HoSghaj; mupwI' rur** ("powerful as a hammer") is based on this notion. (Here, and in the discussion that follows, translations of the similes with **rur** are given in the familiar Federation Standard form, as in "powerful as a hammer," though a literal translation would be more like "He/she/it is powerful; he/she/it resembles a hammer.") The following similes also find their origins in Klingon culture:

bIr; bortaS rur ("cold as revenge")
puj; bIQ rur ("weak as water")
HoS; 'Iw rur ("strong as blood")
'oj; bomwI' rur ("thirsty as a singer")

The likening of "cold" to "revenge" comes from the old Klingon proverb "Revenge is a dish which is best served cold." Water, to Klingons, has long been a symbol of weakness or lack of control, especially when it is contrasted with blood, a symbol of strength. The association of thirst with singing is probably due to the custom of accompanying drinking with singing and the usual practice of continuing both of these activities for a great length of time.

ghung; qagh rur ("hungry as *gagh*")
jeD; ghevI' rur ("thick as *gagh* sauce")

The serpent worms known as *gagh* are considered to epitomize hunger because, in preparing them to be eaten, they are virtually starved so that, at the last minute, they will ravenously eat the delicious but toxic (to them) sauce into which they are placed. This sauce (**ghevI'**), in turn, symbolizes thickness, although, in truth, there are sauces that are thicker.

mIgh; molor rur ("evil as Molor")
ngo'; QI'tu' rur ("old as Qui'Tu")
qej; veqlargh rur ("mean as Fek'lhr")
quvHa'; ghe'tor ngan rur ("dishonored as an inhabitant of Gre'thor")
wov; ghI'boj Sech rur ("bright as the Torch of G'boj")

These expressions are based on Klingon history and mythology. Molor was the tyrannical and hated ruler of the Homeworld until he was killed by Kahless, who in turn established the Klingon Empire. **QI'tu'**, sometimes translated "Paradise," is the mythological source of all creation, hence its association with antiquity. The word **ngo'** in the phrase above means "old" as opposed to "new." Thus, it would be applied to objects or ideas, but not to animals or people. To say that a person is extremely old, the phrase would be **qan; QI'tu'** ("He/she is as old as *Qui'Tu*"). Fek'lhr is a somewhat ferocious mythological beast that guards the entrance to Gre'thor, the place where the spirits of the dishonored go. Finally, the Torch of G'boj is one of the most revered historical objects in the Empire, though exactly why is seldom revealed to outsiders.

jej; Daqtagh rur ("sharp as a *d'k tahg*")
lo'laHbe'; chetvI' chIm rur ("worthless as an
    empty torpedo tube")
yuD; jey'naS rur ("dishonest as a double-headed
    ax")

These similes make reference to Klingon weapons.
The **Daqtagh** (*d'k tagh*) is the quintessential warrior's
knife. It would approach irreverence to think of one in
any condition other than sharp and ready for combat.
Significantly, the usual phrase used to describe the opposite condition—that is, "dull, blunt"—makes reference
not to a weapon but to a tool: **jejHa'; naH taj rur** ("dull
as vegetable knife"). A **naH taj** ("vegetable knife" or "fruit
knife") is hardly a dull instrument, but it does not come
close to the sharpness of a *d'k tagh*. The word **chetvI'**
("torpedo tube") in the second expression is also the
name of a hooked stick used in throwing certain type of
spear, the **tlhevjaQ**. In the set phrase, however, it refers
only to a torpedo tube, not the stick, which suggests that
the phrase came into use only after the introduction of
torpedoes. While the **chetvI'** stick is certainly most useful when used to hurl a spear, it cannot be said that it is
worthless otherwise. For example, if necessary, it can
serve as a weapon in its own right, as if a long cudgel. An
empty torpedo tube, on the other hand, is a most ineffec-
tive weapon. The connection of dishonesty to the **jey'naS**
ax is symbolic rather than literal: the two heads of the ax,
facing in different directions, represent duplicity. Because the double-headed ax is connected with dishonesty, the opposite quality—that is, honesty—is commonly
associated with a single-headed ax: **yuDHa'; ghIt rur**
("honest as an ax head"). The word **ghIt** ("ax head, ax
blade") also means "open, flat hand," and this fits into the
imagery as well. An honest person will have his or her
hands open, with nothing to hide. Thus, "honest as an
open hand" is an equally good rendition.

In a second type of simile, the quality is associated with animals that stereotypically behave in a manner consistent with or otherwise exhibiting a particular quality. For example:

Dogh; tIghla' rur ("foolish as a *t'gla*")
tlhIb; toppa' rur ("incompetent as a *topah*")
tIb; tI'qa' vIghro' rur ("nervous as a *tika* cat")
tun; reghuluS 'Iwghargh rur ("soft as a Regulan bloodworm")
naS; norgh rur ("vicious as a *norg*")

Perhaps this list should also contain **tlhab; ngem Ha'DIbaH** "free [or independent] as a forest animal"), though this refers to how or where any animal lives rather than to a specific animal. There is one more exceedingly common expression that falls into this animal category, not so much because of the inherent characteristics of the creature, but rather because of Klingons' normal reaction to it: **'up; yIH rur** ("disgusting as a tribble").

Another set of similes link humanoid species of various kinds to certain qualities:

matlhHa'; romuluSngan rur ("disloyal as a Romulan")
qur; verengan rur ("greedy as a Ferengi")
wIH; Hur'Iqngan rur ("ruthless as a Hur'q")
Hoj; tera'ngan rur ("cautious as a Terran")
Hem; tlhIngan rur ("proud as a Klingon")

One simile of this type associates a people with a quality opposite from one they actually typify: **nong; vulqangan rur** ("passionate as a Vulcan.") This would be used to describe somebody who was not passionate. As far as can be determined, this is the only use of irony in expressions of this type, and what led to this unique occurrence is not known.

Finally, there are some common similes whose

meanings are obvious, such as **tam; Hew rur** ("quiet as a statue"), while still others suggest no explanation whatsoever:

> **val; Huy' rur** ("clever as an eyebrow")
> **lugh; Sor rur** ("correct as a tree")
> **'IQ; rav rur** ("sad as a floor")
> **Sagh; Ho"oy'** ("serious as a toothache")
> **boch; ghIch rur** ("shiny as a nose")

Robbie Robinson

LANGUAGE CHANGE AND STAYING CURRENT

K lingon society is one in which tradition plays a highly significant role. Ancient customs, rituals, and beliefs are painstakingly, conscientiously, and successfully passed on from one generation to the next. Klingons revere their ancestors, respect their elders, and have unparalleled veneration for heritage. Nevertheless, over time, change does occur in all aspects of Klingon life, and there are observable differences—some subtle, some rather obvious—between the older and younger generations. The more established members of Klingon society (generally speaking, older Klingons) tend to see change as indicating the gradual downfall of the society, the loss of values and traditions. "The warrior ethic is deteriorating" is a common lament. Younger Klingons, while accepting their heritage and observing the ancient rites, see some aspects of their elders' behavior and beliefs as, if not obsolete, then just old-fashioned. This state of affairs was not brought on by recent technological innovation such as galactic travel; it has been this way for centuries.

The differences between younger and older Klingons are mirrored in the way members of the different generations speak. While everyone does speak the same language (and this discussion is restricted to **ta' Hol**, the standard dialect), there are still certain speech patterns clearly associated with younger speakers, and other patterns with older. Paralleling the differing attitudes about other aspects of society, the Klingon spoken by older members of society is considered by some to be "proper and eloquent" and by others to be "stilted and confining"; the Klingon spoken by the younger generation is either "sloppy and ungrammatical" or "innovative and expressive." Though it is safe to say that much of this innovation is heard among younger speakers, there is no clear line of demarkation separating the generations, no age at which one crosses over from "younger" to "older." Attitude and stake in the status quo play greater roles than does chronological age. Indeed, there is a great deal of disagreement as to which newer features of the language (generally, those associated with younger Klingons) are acceptable innovations and which are simply errors. It is therefore probably best for the visitor to avoid taking a stand on what is "correct" Klingon and, when asked to settle a dispute, to defer to the wisdom of the native speakers, all of whom enjoy a good fight anyway.

Depending upon one's age (or, more importantly, upon the age group with which one most identifies), one may or may not want to adopt the pronunciation patterns or grammatical peculiarities associated with the younger generation. It is worthwhile for a visitor to be familiar with these patterns, however, if for no other reason than to be able to understand what a younger Klingon is saying.

When it comes to vocabulary, on the other hand, knowledge of prevailing terminology is essential if one is to understand and participate in everyday conversation. There are words and expressions, usually dubbed *slang*, that are infrequently used in scholarly or scientific writing or in formal presentations, such as judicial proceedings or governmental ceremonies, but they are quite common otherwise, both in conversation and in popular writing, such as romance novels. Such words are often not included in textbooks or in classroom

Although training to attain the mettle of a warrior, Alexander still maintains his own identity. *Robbie Robinson*

instruction because they are not considered "proper."
Proper or not, to communicate successfully with Klingons and to be comfortably accepted into their company, one must be aware of, understand, and use at
least some slang. To speak in a manner totally deficient
in the more colloquial forms of Klingon speech is to
betray one's status as an outsider.

GENERATIONAL DIFFERENCES: PRONUNCIATION AND GRAMMAR

The differences in pronunciation between younger
and older Klingons are rather subtle. As a result, the
characteristic patterns of younger people's speech, if noticed and commented upon, are more likely to be judged
"sloppy" or "careless" rather than "wrong." First of all,
some younger speakers tend to pronounce doubled consonants as if they were single, while older speakers pretty
much maintain the distinction between single and doubled consonants. For example, in the word **qettaH** ("He/
she keeps on running"; **qet,** "run, jog," plus **-taH,** "continuous"), an older Klingon would either pronounce each **t**
distinctly, releasing the first one with a puff of air before
articulating the second, or else he or she would hold the
t just a bit before releasing it, so that the time taken up
would be about the same as if each **t** were articulated
separately. A younger speaker, on the other hand, may
pronounce the word as if it were **qetaH,** though with the
stress remaining on the first syllable as it is in **qettaH.**
Similarly, an older speaker would probably maintain the
mm in **bommey** ("songs"; **bom,** "song," plus **-mey,** plural
indicator) by either pronouncing each **m** distinctly or,
more likely in this case, prolonging the **m**; some younger
speakers (though a smaller number than in the case of
tt) might say **bomey,** again with stress remaining on the
first syllable. Only in the case of " (as in **pa"a'** ["big
room"]: **pa',** "room," plus **-'a',** an augmentative) is there

a tendency in both groups to reduce the " to a single ', though " (a somewhat prolonged gap between the preceding and following **a**) is hardly unknown or archaic-sounding. The reduction of doubled consonants to single follows a clear pattern. Those most likely to be reduced are **pp**, **tt**, , and, as noted above, "; least likely to be reduced are **ll**, **mm**, **nn**, **ngng**, **vv**, **ww**, and **yy**.

Younger speakers also have a slight tendency to change the pronunciation of the vowel **a** in nonstressed syllables to something that sounds a bit like the *u* in Federation Standard *but*. If this sound is transcribed with the symbol **U**, a word like **qaleghpu'** ("I have seen you") might sound more like **qUleghpu'**. This particular phonological inclination seems particularly bothersome to older Klingons and is generally considered an error worthy of correction. Students who speak this way are customarily reprimanded.

When it comes to grammar, the younger generation is innovative as well. One of the more noteworthy characteristics of their speech is the placement of conjunctions joining nouns (**je,** "and"; **joq,** "and/or"; **ghap,** "either/or"). In standard Klingon grammar, the conjunction follows the last noun of the conjoined set; for example, **naQjej 'etlh taj je** ("spear, sword, and knife"; literally, "spear, sword, knife and") or **tlhInganpu' romuluSnganpu' ghap** ("either Klingons or Romulans"; that is, "Klingons Romulans or"). Instead of putting the conjunction after the last noun of the phrase, younger Klingons are often heard putting it before the final noun: **naQjej 'etlh je taj**, **tlhInganpu' ghap romuluSnganpu'**. This is a common young person's error, and teachers seem to be constantly correcting it, with reasonable success. It is interesting to note that in earlier stages of the language (and the form of language still used in many rituals and in some forms of writing), at least under certain circumstances, the conjunction did indeed precede the final noun, meaning it was not always a mistake to use that phrasing.

Younger Klingons also tend to use the imperative prefix **yI-** in circumstances judged inappropriate by older Klingons. In standard Klingon, the prefix **yI-** is attached to a verb to form a command given to one person if there is either no object or a singular object, as in, for example, **yIjatlh!** ("Speak!") or **jagh yIHIv!** "Attack the enemy!"; **jagh,** "enemy". Also, it is used to form a command given to more than one person if the object is singular: **jagh yIHIv** ("[all of you] attack the enemy!") When the object is plural, however, the prefix **tI-** is used instead, whether the command is given to one or more than one: **jaghpu' tIHIv!** ("Attack the enemies!") Some younger Klingons are apt to use **yI-** rather than **tI-** when the object is plural, saying, for example, **jaghpu' yIHIv!** for "Attack the enemies!" This construction is heard with increasing regularity, though hardly a majority of the time. It leads to no misunderstanding as long as the object noun (**jaghpu'** ["enemies"] in the examples above) is marked for plural—that is, as long as it has a plural suffix (here, **-pu'**) or is a word that is inherently plural (such as **cha** ["torpedoes"]). Since marking the plural is never required, however, **jagh** could mean "enemy" or "enemies." While in standard Klingon there is no ambiguity in these kinds of commands—**jagh tIHIv!** must mean "Attack the enemies!" because **tI-** is used specifically for plural objects—in the younger generation's way of speaking, **jagh yIHIv!** could be either "Attack the enemy!" or "Attack the enemies!", since **yI-** is used with both singular and plural objects and **jagh** could be either. On the other hand, this ambiguous use of **yI-** makes it possible to be vague on purpose. That is, in Klingon (and in Federation Standard also, for that matter), there is no easy way to say "Attack the enemy or enemies, however many there may be." The younger Klingons' **jagh yIHIv**, however, means exactly that. Despite this debatable advantage, and despite the slow but ongoing spread of the practice among younger speakers, most Klingons still consider the ambiguous use of **yI-** an error.

One habit of younger speakers that seems to be taking hold among speakers in general involves planet names. Though no official treaty or agreement exists, Klingons generally follow a naming scheme used throughout the galaxy whereby a planet's name is really the name of its sun (or one of them) followed by a number referring to its orbit. Within a solar system, the planet orbiting closest to the sun is numbered "one," the next is "two," and so on. Thus **lIghon wa'** ("Ligon I") is the planet orbiting closest to the Ligon sun; **lIghon cha'** ("Ligon II") is the second closest. There are a couple of other ways planet names are derived. Sometimes the Klingon name is simply a rendition of the name used by the inhabitants of the planet, such as **tera'** ("Earth, Terra"). On other occasions, a name is a Klingon version of the name used not by the natives of a planet but by another alien culture. Thus, **romuluS** ("Romulus") is based on the Federation name of the planet; the actual Romulan name is something quite distinct.

A name for the inhabitant of a planet (and, therefore, the name of a race of beings) is formed by adding **ngan** ("inhabitant") to the planet name (excluding the number, if any): **lIghonngan** ("Ligonian"), **tera'ngan** ("Earther, Terran"), **romuluSngan** ("Romulan"). (Actually, there is some phonetic variation here. "Ligonian" is often pronounced **lIghongan**, dropping the final **n** of **lIghon** before the initial **ng** of **ngan**. This is not considered an error, only an alternate pronunciation.)

Occasionally, and no doubt owing to influence from Federation Standard, from which names, as noted, are often taken, an extra syllable, **-ya'-**, comes between the planet name and **ngan**. Thus, "Denebian"—that is, an inhabitant of one of the Deneb planets—is both **DenIb-ngan** and **DenIbya'ngan**. The planet name itself is also heard in two forms: **DenIb** (formed from the name

Deneb) and **DenIbya'** (formed by dropping the **ngan** from **DenIbya'ngan**). The syllable **ya'** seems to be used as if it were a suffix meaning "place name." Thus, Ligon has sometimes been called **lIghonya'** in addition to **lIghon**, Organia is both **'orghenya'** and **'orghen**, and Cardassia is both **qarDaS** and **qarDaSya'**. The **-ya'** cannot be added to all planet names, however. No one ever says **romuluSya'** ("Romulus") or **tera'ya'** ("Earth") and certainly not **Qo'noSya'** ("Kronos"), the Klingon Homeworld itself.

For a long time, the two forms of planet names were used with roughly equal frequency, with the **-ya'** variants having just a slight edge in formal and scholarly contexts, and one might have considered **-ya'** to be simply a place-name suffix. More recently, however, younger speakers have been favoring the shorter forms (that is, those lacking **-ya'**), and this habit seems to be slowly spreading to older speakers as well. Though the longer names are certainly still heard and are unobjectionable, **-ya'** may, over time, fall out of usage altogether.

Which, if any, of the other speech patterns currently associated primarily with younger speakers will become acceptable among Klingons at large as time goes on cannot be predicted with certainty. Some will probably wind up as simply fads of the current era; others will be used with increasing frequency and ultimately replace current standards. For a visitor to a Klingon settlement, of course, the fate of any given trait is only of academic interest. What is important is to be aware of the differences so that communication is not impeded.

VOCABULARY: SLANG

Except in formal situations, the speech of younger Klingons is apt to contain a fair amount of slang, or **mu'mey ghoQ** (literally, "fresh words"). Though the term *slang* can be defined in a number of ways, here it is used to refer to words used in colloquial speech in the place of or in addition to standard words. Choosing to express a concept by means of slang rather than a standard word or phrase is a way to show social identity. That is, using a common set of special terms marks the users as members of the same subgroup within the society. Such a subgroup could be occupational (such as artists or warriors) or geographic, but in the case of Klingon **mu'mey ghoQ**, the innovative vocabulary is used primarily, though hardly exclusively, by the younger generation. As with other aspects of the speech of the younger Klingons, many older Klingons, particularly those most resistant to any change in Klingon society, avoid using slang and deride its use. There are some older Klingons, on the other hand, who use slang quite comfortably, especially when communicating with younger Klingons. The disagreement about the status of slang is reflected in the terms used for "standard" or "proper" Klingon words. As noted earlier, those who tend to favor the use of slang often call standard words **mu'mey Doy'** ("tired words"). Those who dislike the use of slang, on the other hand, refer to standard words as **mu'mey qar** ("accurate words").

Anyone who participates in the Klingon-speaking community is aware of slang, whether or not he or she uses or understands specific words. A speaker's choice of words associates him or her with a specific group. For example, a younger Klingon who wants to appear more grown-up may use relatively little slang, or a commanding officer may use quite a bit to show that he fits in with his younger troops.

An important characteristic of slang is that for the most part, the nonstandard terms do not come about because a word or phrase is missing from the standard vocabulary. Though slang expressions are often vivid or imaginative alternatives to standard vocabulary, there are almost always standard ways to express the same thing, though sometimes in phrases rather than individual words.

Slang also tends to be transient. That is, a particular expression may be in common use for a while—sometimes for only a year or so—and then fall out of fashion, to be replaced by a newer term or a return to the standard expression. Using an antiquated term marks the speaker as being out of step with Klingon society, a cause for rejection by some other Klingons. Not all slang expressions have short lives, however. Some remain in use for years, some become outmoded only to be in fashion again some time later, and some, after a while, actually become accepted as "proper." Sometimes, a slang expression shifts from one group within the society to another. A word once used primarily by, say, members of the military may be adopted by the younger generation in general. What may be passé in military circles may be au courant among kids.

In order to fit into Klingon society as much as possible, a visitor should be comfortable with a good deal of slang, but because of its ever-changing nature, staying current is a difficult task. Any available list of slang expressions will lack the newest terms and will also probably contain several expressions that have become old hat or associated with different groups. The best course of action is probably to study and become familiar with the expressions before traveling to a Klingon planet, but then to avoid using any expressions that Klingons themselves do not use. Using only standard Klingon will not brand a speaker as old-fashioned or out of touch, only as somewhat more formal and traditional.

The following is a listing of some of the current slang expressions used pretty much throughout the Klingon Empire; others have been noted in previous sections. It must be remembered, however, that between the time this list was compiled and the time it is being read, new expressions have no doubt come into common use and some of the expressions on the list may have become obsolete. The origins of the expressions are indicated when known.

bachHa' ("err, make a mistake")

This word literally means something like "misshoot"—that is, "shoot wrongly." It is used in such constructions as **jIbachHa'pu'** ("I have made a mistake"; literally, "I have mis-shot"; **jI-,** "I"; **-pu',** perfective). The standard word meaning "err, make a mistake" is **Qagh**, as in **jIQaghpu'** ("I have make a mistake").

bej ("be sure, definite, positive, certain")

The verb **bej** literally means "watch," though its slang usage is probably influenced by the verb suffix **-bej** ("certainly, undoubtedly"; compare **voq,** "trust," and **voqbej,** "certainly trust"). It is used in such forms as **jIbej** ("I am positive [about something I just said]"—literally, "I watch" [**jI-,** "I"]) or **bIbej'a'?** ("Are you sure?"—literally, "Do you watch?" [**bI-,** "you"; **-'a',** interrogative). Unlike the verb **na'** ("be salty"), which has an identical slang meaning (see below), the verb **bej** may be used when there is an object: **HIvrup 'e' vIbej** ("I am positive they're ready to attack"; literally, "I watch that they're ready to attack"; **HIv,** "[they] attack"; **-rup,** "ready"; **'e',** "that"; **vI-,** "I [do something to] it"). The notions expressed by **bej** can be conveyed without slang with a word such as **Honbe'** ("not doubt") or by making use of the verb suffix **-bej,** as in **HIvrupbej** ("They're certainly ready to attack").

bochmoHwI' ("sycophant, flatterer, one who
    tries to curry favor by flattering a superior")

Literally "shiner, one who shines (something)," this word is all that remains of an earlier expression, **'etlh bochmoHwI'** ("blade shiner"). It was originally used to refer to someone who shined somebody else's blade, as

Garak (Andrew Robinson), a Cardassian operative in the mirror universe who is a **bochmoHwl'**. *Robbie Robinson*

opposed to one's own, suggesting the idea of flattering a superior rather than simply doing one's own work. A nonslang equivalent might be **naDwI'** ("one who praises"), though this lacks the overtones of "self-serving."

bolwI' ("traitor")

This word actually means "drooler"—that is, "one who drools" (**bol,** "drool"; **-wI',** "one who [does something]"). The nonslang word meaning "traitor" is **maghwI'** (literally, "one who betrays" [**magh,** "betray"]). Probably because of the parallel formation of **bolwI'** and **maghwI'** (that is, verb plus **-wI'**), the verb **bol** ("drool") is sometimes used to mean "betray," as if it were equivalent to **magh.** In this usage, **bol,** like **magh,** may take an object; that is, the sentence may indicate who is betrayed: **mumaghpu'** ("He/she has betrayed me"); **mu-,** "He/she [does something to] me"; **maghpu',** "has betrayed") or **mubolpu'** ("He/she has betrayed me"; literally, "He/she has drooled me"; **bolpu',** "has drooled"). In its nonslang sense, **bol** does not take an object: **bolpu'** ("He/she has drooled").

buy' ngop. ("It is good to hear that.")

This expression is often uttered when one has just been given good news, such as a report of victory in a battle. Literally, the phrase means "The plates are full" (**buy',** "be full, filled up"; **ngop,** "plates"), suggesting an abundance of food. If the information is particularly good, one may add the emphatic suffix **-qu'** to the verb: **buy'qu' ngop** ("That's *really* good news"; literally, "The plates are very full"). Similarly, if the information is considered only partially good, or only the forerunner of good news to come, one might use the suffix **-law'** ("apparently"): **buy'law' ngop** ("That seems to be good news"; literally, "The plates are apparently full"). In standard Klingon, one might say **De'vetlh vIQoy, vaj jIQuch**

("I am happy to hear that information"; **De'vetlh,** "that information"; **vIQoy,** "I hear it"; **vaj,** "so, therefore"; **jIQuch,** "I am happy").

chatlh "nonsense, balderdash"

This word literally means "soup." It is not known why **chatlh** took on this slang meaning. The standard word for "nonsense" is **Dap**.

chelwI' ("someone who deals in finances, accounting, etc.")

Mildly derogatory in its slang usage, this word literally means "adder, one who adds." There is no known nonslang counterpart, though **HuchQeD** (literally, "money science") is often used for "economics."

chong ("be profound, thorough, careful"; also "good, excellent")

Literally "be vertical," this word is used to refer to one's intellect, as in **chong tlhIngan SuvwI'** ("The Klingon warrior is profound"—literally, "The Klingon warrior is vertical"; **tlhIngan,** "Klingon"; **SuvwI',** "warrior"). In its literal sense, this word is the opposite of **SaS** ("be horizontal"), and as a slang term, it is an opposite as well, as **SaS** is used to mean "be shallow, superficial." It is most likely that **chong** took on its slang meaning because of the prior existence of **SaS,** which has been used as slang for a much longer time. An equivalent meaning may be expressed without slang by using a word such as **Qubchu'** ("think perfectly, think clearly"; **Qub,** "think"; **-chu',** "perfectly, clearly"), as in **Qubchu' tlhIngan SuvwI'** ("The Klingon warrior thinks clearly"). The word **chong** may also be used as an exclamation expressing approval or satisfaction, somewhat like standard **maj** ("good"). Thus, one may describe one's feelings about a skillfully made knife or about an upcoming social event by saying simply **chong** (literally, "vertical" but meaning "good, excellent, admirable"). See also **qu'** (literally, "be fierce"), another slang term used to express approval.

chuH ("explain clearly to, clarify for, specify for, spell out for")

The literal meaning of **chuH** is "throw a spear at, hurl a spear at." The object of **chuH** is usually the intended target, the person or thing at which the spear is thrown. In the slang sense, the object of the verb is the person who wants clarification, as in **HIchuH!** ("Clarify for me!" "Spell it out for me!"; literally, "Throw [a spear] at me!") or **yaS chuH** ("He/she clarifies [it] for the officer"; literally, "He/she throws [a spear] at the officer"). The verb **QIj** ("explain") is a standard term somewhat close to this in meaning, though the object of **QIj** is that which is explained, while the person to whom the explanation is given is the indirect object: **yaSvaD nab QIj** ("He/she explains the plan to the officer"; **yaSvaD,** "for the officer"; **nab,** "plan").

Dach ("not pay attention, be distracted, lack focus")

The verb **Dach** literally means "be absent," but when applied to a person who is obviously present or otherwise accounted for, it is usually interpreted to mean that the person's mind has wandered. It does not mean "absent-minded," which involves forgetfulness. Rather, it means that the person is, for whatever reason, not focusing on the task at hand. Nonslang equivalents are **qImHa'** ("not pay attention") and **buSHa',** ("not focus [on], ignore.")

Degh ("take action without a plan, improvise")

This expression may be based on **DeghwI'** ("helmsman"). There is no known verb **Degh**, but if there were such a word, presumably it would mean "steer," and **DeghwI'**, then, would be literally "one who steers," formed from **Degh** plus the suffix **-wI'** ("one who does [something]"). There is a related noun **Degh** ("helm"), but since **-wI'** follows only verbs, there must have been a verb **Degh** at one time that has fallen out of use, at least in the sense of "steer." It is the absence of a verb **Degh** from the standard vocabulary that makes this term slang and that also allows it to have a specialized meaning: not "steer" in the usual sense of guiding a vessel along a set course or defined path but rather in the sense of maneuvering without a plan, without a set course or path. In the standard vocabulary, there is no single word equivalent meaning "improvise" or the like, but the idea can be expressed in a phrase such as **nab Hutlh 'ach vang** ("He/she lacks a plan, but he/she takes action"; **nab,** "plan"; **Hutlh,** "He/she lacks it"; **'ach,** "but"; **vang,** "He/she takes action").

> **Duj ngaDHa'** ("person who is wildly
>   irresponsible, out of control, undisciplined")

This expression means literally "unstable vessel, unbalanced vessel." **Duj** is "vessel"; the verb **ngaD** ("be stable, balanced," here followed by the negative suffix **-Ha'**) normally applies to a ship or a physical object, not to a situation or a person. It would be inappropriate to refer to a person as **ngaD** or **ngaDHa'** in a phrase such as **tera'ngan ngaDHa'** ("unstable Terran"). A standard verb that is close in meaning is **ngIj** ("rowdy, unruly"), as in **tera'ngan ngIj** ("rowdy Terran").

> **ghIgh** ("assignment, task, duty")

As this word literally means "necklace," perhaps the slang usage is based on the old practice of identifying one's position within a military unit—for example, one's assignment on a ship—by means of a symbol hung on a chain worn around the neck. On the other hand, it may be based on the idea that assignment to a specific task holds one in that position as if by means of a line around the neck. The usual nonslang word for "assignment, mission" is **Qu'**.

Haq ("intervene in [a situation]")

The word **Haq** actually means "perform surgery on (someone)." Even though Klingon doctors generally have thriving practices and a doctor is always part of a ship's crew, not only is being under a doctor's care considered a sign of weakness, but it is also regarded as a relinquishing of self-control. Klingons tend to avoid visiting doctors except under the most serious of circumstances and, as a result, doctors spend a great deal of their time tending to critically wounded patients and relatively little time performing routine examinations or practicing preventive medicine. The general term for "doctor" or "physician" is **Qel**, but a "surgeon," a doctor who actually manipulates the internal organs or bones of the patient and thereby is the most invasive, is a **HaqwI'**, "one who performs surgery." The slang term **Haq** developed from the association of surgery with invasion of the person, hence "intervene." Just as **Haq** in the nonslang sense of "perform surgery" has negative connotation, the slang term **Haq** ("intervene") is likewise disparaging, implying that the intervention was unnecessary and/or that the party doing the intervening somehow handled the situation badly. Thus, if one were to say **jagh HIvrup SuvwI' Haqpa' DIvI' qeSwI'** ("The warrior was prepared to attack the enemy until the Federation advisor intervened"—literally, "The warrior was prepared to attack the enemy before the Federation advisor performed surgery"; **jagh,** "enemy"; **HIvrup,** "be prepared to attack"; **SuvwI',** "warrior"; **Haqpa',** "before he/she performed surgery"; **DIvI',** "Federation"; **qeSwI',** "advisor"), the implication is that the advice was unnecessary, counterproductive, or both. The common nonslang term for "intervene" is **mun**.

Ha'DIbaH ("dog, cur, inferior person")

Ha'DIbaH means "animal" in general (also "meat" of any kind), but when applied to a person, it is an insult. It is most frequently used epithetically—that is, in name calling—as in **romuluS Ha'DIbaH!** ("Romulan dog!"; literally, "Romulan animal!").

Hom ("weakling, runt, scrawny one, skinny one")

This word literally means "bone," but its slang usage is no doubt influenced by the noun suffix **-Hom,** a diminutive that adds a meaning of smallness or lack of importance (compare **taj** ["knife"] and **tajHom** ["little knife," the extra small blade in the handle of a *d'k tahg* knife]). There are a number of standard counterparts to **Hom**, such as **pujwI'** ("weakling"), **langwI'** ("one who is thin"), and **runwI'** ("one who is short").

Ho' ("idol, someone worthy of emulation,
       something deserving of respect")

This is actually the word for "tooth," but it is applied to someone who is admired or revered. It might be used in a phrase such as **Ho' SoH** ("You are an idol" or "You are someone worthy of emulation"; literally, "You are a tooth" [**SoH,** "you"]) or **Ho' ghaH HoD'e'** ("The captain is an idol"; literally, "The captain is a tooth"; **ghaH,** "he/she"; **HoD,** "captain"; **-'e',** "topic"). Grammatically, even as slang, **Ho'** follows the rules appropriate to its literal meaning. Thus, even though it may refer to a person, its plural is **Ho'Du'** ("teeth"), making use of the plural suffix for body parts (**-Du'**), not **Ho'pu'**, with **-pu'**, the plural suffix for beings capable of using language. Similarly, it never takes the possessive suffixes associated with beings capable of using language. That is, "my idol" (literally, "my tooth") is **Ho'wIj** (with **-wIj**, the general suffix for "my"), not **Ho'wI'** (with **-wI'**, the suffix for "my" used with beings capable of using language). The slang meaning of **Ho'** is no doubt influenced by the identically sounding verb **Ho'** ("admire"), and, indeed, the closest nonslang counterpart is probably a phrase with this verb: **HoD Ho'lu'** ("The captain is admired"; **Ho'lu'**, "someone admires").

Hur'Iq ("outsider, foreigner")

This word originally referred only to the people known as the Hur'q, a race of humanoids from the Gamma Quadrant who developed a reputation as ruthless invaders who would attack other societies primarily for the purpose of robbery, stealing whatever they could and destroying the rest. The Hur'q invaded the Klingon homeworld some 1,000 years ago, and the loss to the Klingons was so disastrous, not to mention humiliating, that Klingon society became increasingly intolerant of other races. In time, the Hur'q came to symbolize any non-Klingon. Actually, in Klingon, a Hur'q person would be **Hur'Iqngan**, while **Hur'Iq** refers to Hur'q society or their homeland. This shorter word took on the slang meaning of "outsider, foreigner." The standard term for "foreigner, alien" is **nov**.

jav ("prisoner")

The origin of this slang usage of **jav** (literally, "six") is unknown. The usual word for "prisoner" is **qama'**.

luH "cause [someone] to confess, cause
     [someone] to reveal a secret")

This verb literally means "yank" and is used in such sentences as **jav luHpu' 'avwI'** ("The guard has caused a prisoner to confess"—literally, "The guard has yanked a six"; **jav**, "prisoner" [slang, see above]; **luHpu'**, "has yanked'; **'avwI'**, "guard"). Standard words expressing the same notions are **DISmoH** ("cause to confess") and **peghHa'moH** ("cause to not keep a secret").

moH ("exert undue influence on [somebody,
     something]")

The verb **moH** (literally, "be ugly") normally does not take an object. In its slang meaning, however, it is used only if there is an object, as if it were "(somebody) uglies (somebody)." For example, it is found in such expressions as **DamoH** ("You exert undue influence on him/her"; literally, "You ugly him/her"; **Da-,** "You [do something to] him/her"). The word **bImoH**, with the prefix **bI-** ("you [no object]"), can mean only "You are ugly." The slang usage of **moH** is probably influenced by the verb suffix **-moH** ("cause"), as in **mevmoH** ("cause [someone] to stop"—(compare **mev,** "[someone] stops"). In standard Klingon, the verb meaning "influence" is **SIgh**.

mo' ("motive, motivation, grounds, reason, rationale")

This word literally means "cage," suggesting that one's reasons for accomplishing a particular act are somehow restrictive or confining, as if preventing "escape" into other forms of behavior. The slang meaning is no doubt also influenced by the noun suffix **-mo'** ("due to," as in **HeSmo'**, "due to the crime") and verb suffix **-mo'** ("because," as in **HIvmo'** ["because he/she attacks"]). The slang term **mo'** is used in sentences such as **jaghpu' mo' wIyajnIS** ("We must understand the enemies' motive"; literally, "We must understand the enemies' cage"; **jaghpu',** "enemies"; **wIyajnIS,** "We must understand it"). A close standard equivalent is **meq** ("reason")—that is, "logical thinking."

naQ ("ponytail")

The usual word for the popular hairstyle called a "ponytail" in Federation Standard is **DaQ**, but the word **naQ** (literally, "cane, staff") is frequently heard instead. This may have originated with the Krotmag dialect's pronunciation of **DaQ**, which sounds like **naQ** to most Klingons (see the chapter on The Fiction of Klingon Conformity, under "Pronunciation," pages 18–23). Incidentally, a slang expression for "ponytail holder," usually **choljaH**, is **Qeb**, the regular word for "ring" (for the finger).

natlh ("be reprehensible, disgusting, contemptible, shameful, objectionable")

The slang term **natlh** is a frequently heard expression of disapproval or disgust, the speaker's comment on an event, another person, or a situation. Though by no means a curse and having no overtones of vulgarity, it is nonetheless a rather forceful term, used to express a strong emotion. Literally meaning "consume, use up, expend," **natlh** is normally applied to energy, fuel, supplies, and the like and is used in phrases such as **nIn Hoch natlhlu'pu'** ("All the fuel has been consumed"), with **nIn Hoch** ("all the fuel"; **nIn,** "fuel"; **Hoch,** "all") functioning as the object of the verb **natlhlu'pu'** ("someone/something has consumed it"). In its slang usage, however, the verb never has an object and the subject is what is being disparaged: **natlh 'Iw HIq** ("The bloodwine is disgusting"; literally, "the bloodwine consumes"); **natlh romuluSnganpu'** ("Romulans are objectionable"; literally "Romulans consume"); **bInatlh** ("You are contemptible"; literally, "You consume"). Often, the word is used with no overt subject, as if an exclamation: **natlh** ("It is objectionable," or "That is shameful"; literally, "It consumes"). Nonslang counterparts, none of which carries the impact of **natlh**, might be **quv Hutlh** ("lack honor"), **qab** ("be bad"), or **Do'Ha'** ("be unfortunate"). The word **'up** ("disgusting, repugnant") may also be used, most commonly in reference to food or drink. See also **SaS** (literally, "be horizontal"), another slang term used to voice disapproval. Slang terms expressing the opposite of **natlh**—that is, approval—are **chong** (literally, "be vertical") and **qu'** (literally, "be fierce").

na' ("be sure, definite, positive, certain")

The word **na'** literally means "be salty," but its slang usage is probably influenced by the noun suffix **-na'**

Worf assures Duras and his associates that they will not have the *bat'leth* of Kahless. *Robbie Robinson*

("definite"), which is used when the speaker wants to indicate that he or she is absolutely sure about what is being said (compare **maghwI**, "traitor," and **maghwI'na'** "definite traitor, without a doubt a traitor"). The slang word, a verb, is used in such constructions as **jIna'** ("I am positive [about something I just said]"; literally, "I am salty"; **jI-**, "I"] and **bIna''a'** ("Are you sure?"; literally, "Are you salty?" [**bI-**, "you,"; **-'a'**, interrogative]). These kinds of meanings may be expressed without using slang by employing such verbs as **Honbe'** ("not doubt") or **Sovbej** ("know for certain"). See also **bej**, a slang term with similar meaning, page 145.

> **ngIb** ("ankle" [derogatory term])
> See **yeb** ("wrist"); page 166.

> **ngup** ("authority, power, one in authority, one in power, one in charge")

Literally meaning "cape," this slang term is an example of metonymy, whereby one word (or phrase) stands for another with which it is associated. In this case, the leader of the Klingon High Council typically wears a ceremonial cape. The slang sense of **ngup** does not refer only to this position on the High Council, however, but to anyone in power or even to "the power structure." Someone unsatisfied with the status quo, a rebel, might be said to want to **ngup qaD** ("challenge those in charge"; literally, "challenge the cape"). Nonslang equivalents of **ngup** are **woQ** ("authority, political power") and **qum** ("government").

> **paw'** ("butt heads")

This verb describes a very common habit among Klingon warriors, particularly at festive occasions. Two Klingons stand close together, facing each other, and, with great joviality, slam their foreheads together. The word literally means "collide" and is usually (though hardly exclusively) heard when referring to vehicles. In both its literal and slang usages, **paw'** takes a plural subject: **paw' tlhIngan SuvwI'pu'** ("The Klingon warriors butt heads"; literally, "The Klingon warriors collide"; **tlhIngan,** "Klingon"; **SuvwI',** "warrior"; **-pu',** plural suffix); **paw' lupDujHommey** ("The shuttlecraft collide"; **lupDujHom,** "shuttlecraft"; **-mey,** plural suffix). To refer to a something in motion colliding with something stationary, a different verb, **ngeQ** ("bump into, collide with") is used, as in **raS ngeQ tera'ngan** ("The Terran bumps into the table"; **raS,** "table"; **tera'ngan,** "Terran"). When the subject of **paw'** is persons, the most common interpretation of the verb is the slang one—that is, "butt heads." Thus, if one were to say **paw' tera'nganpu'** ("The Terrans collide"), this would probably be taken to mean that the Terrans butt heads, as unlikely as the image might be. When the subject of **paw'** is anything other than persons, the most likely interpretation is the nonslang one, "collide." If one wanted to say that two persons collide but not imply that they butt heads, the verb **ngeQ** would probably be used along with the suffix **-chuq** ("each other") as in **ngeQchuq tera'nganpu'** ("The Terrans collide with each other"). There is no simple nonslang verb for "butt heads."

pIn "expert, authority"

The word **pIn** is literally "boss." In its slang sense, it is never used alone but always in constructions such as **'Iw HIq pIn** ("expert on bloodwine, somebody who knows all about bloodwine"; literally, "bloodwine boss"). The word **pIn** is also found in nonslang terms referring to crew members on a ship: **QeDpIn** ("science officer"), **QumpIn** ("communications officer"). It is not known whether these words originated as slang and became accepted as the regular terms or whether the use of **pIn** in the sense of "expert, authority" was modeled after the words **QeDpIn** and **QumpIn**. Note that for the crew terms, in one case **pIn** follows a noun (**QeD,** "science"; thus, **QeDpIn** is "science boss"), but in the other, it follows what is found elsewhere only as a verb (**Qum,** "communicate"), suggesting that there may have been a noun **Qum** ("communication") at some point in the past. The nonslang term for an expert is **po'wI'** (literally, "one who is expert, skilled").

> **qang** ("always agree with [someone], always go
> along with [someone], always cooperate with
> [someone]")

The literal meaning of the verb **qang** is "pour into," though the slang usage is influenced by the verb suffix **-qang** ("willing"; compare **QaH,** "He/she helps," and **QaHqang,** "He/she is willing to help"). The slang term may be found in such sentences as **jIHDaq Daqang** ("You always agree with me, you always cooperate with me"; literally, "You pour [something] into me"; **jIHDaq,** "in/at me"; **Daqang,** "You pour [something] into"). To say that someone "pours" ("always agrees") is somewhat derogatory, implying that the agreeing or cooperating may be for ulterior motives. Nonslang equivalents of **qang,** though lacking the negative connotation, are **reH Qochbe'** ("always agree"; **reH,** "always"), **reH yeq** ("always cooperate"), and **reH jIj** ("always be cooperative").

> **qu'** ("be great, wonderful, excellent, superlative,
> splendid")

The verb **qu'** literally means "be fierce." In its slang sense, it may be used adjectivally, as in **taj qu'** ("excellent knife"; literally, "fierce knife"), or as the main verb in a sentence, as in **qu' taj** ("the knife is excellent"; literally, "the knife is fierce"). Though, from the Klingon point of view, equating being "fierce" with being "great, wonderful," and so on seems quite natural, the slang meaning of **qu'** probably receives further support because it sounds just like the verb suffix **-qu',** which is used for emphasis

Even in the midst of ferocious Jem'Hadar, there is no doubt who is the fiercest warrior. *Robbie Robinson*

(compare **Qatlh,** "difficult," and **Qatlhqu',** "very difficult"). When applied to people or animals, it is not always clear whether the slang or nonslang meaning of **qu'** is intended. That is, **SuvwI' qu'** ("fierce warrior") could be interpreted literally, or it could mean "excellent warrior." When applied to anything other than people or animals, the slang meaning is more likely. Thus, **may' qu'** ("fierce battle") is really a way of saying "excellent battle." In Klingon, only a participant in a battle, not the battle itself, can literally be described as "fierce." The word **qu'** may also be used as an exclamation ("Great!" "Wonderful!"). In this sense, it seems to be interchangeable with **chong** (literally, "be vertical"; see page 148). The slang usage of **qu'** is currently extremely common among Klingons, and it has pretty much displaced another slang term with the same set of meanings ("excellent, wonderful, etc."), **Huv** (literally, "be clear, not obstructed"), which was in vogue not all that long ago. The use of **Huv** for "excellent" is now considered old-fashioned. This is also the case with **nong** ("passionate"), an even older slang term for "excellent." (As of this writing, the slang usage of **nong** seems to be making a comeback, but it is still too early to say whether this will really happen.) Nonslang verbs expressing similar ideas are **Dun** ("be wonderful, great"), **pov** ("be excellent"), and, as an exclamation, **maj!** ("Good!").

QaD ("be safe, protected")

Literally meaning "be dry," the word **QaD** may be applied to just about anything: a person, object, place, and so forth. For example, **QaD puq** ("The child is dry") means that the child is safe; **vengHom QaD** ("dry village") means that the village is protected. This slang meaning may have developed in part because of the Klingon association of water with weakness (as opposed to the strength of blood or ale, for that matter) and in part because of the phonetic similarity of **QaD** to **Qan** ("protect"). In the Krotmag dialect, source of many idiomatic expressions, **QaD** would be pronounced almost as if **Qan** (see the chapter on The Fiction of Klingon Conformity, under "Pronunciation," pages 18–23).

Qom ("be hazardous, perilous, treacherous")

The word **Qom** literally means "experience a tremor" or, using an old Terran phrase, "experience an earthquake." The word is used in its slang sense of "perilous, treacherous" when applied to a mission or voyage. For example, **Qom Qu'** (literally, "The mission experiences a tremor") means "The mission is perilous." Likewise, **Qom He** (literally, "The route experiences a tremor") generally means "The route is treacherous," implying that the journey is treacherous. The word can also be applied to the state of a structure or a vessel following a

Trafficking with the Romulans shows that B'Etor's (Gwynyth Walsh) mission will be **Qom**. *Robbie Robinson*

disastrous encounter, though in this case the verb usually takes the perfective suffix **-pu'**, indicating that the action has been completed. Thus, **Qompu' Duj** (literally, "The ship has experienced a tremor") may be used to mean "The ship is hazardous, has been left in a hazardous condition." The fact that in the Krotmag dialect (see the chapter on The Fiction of Klingon Conformity, under "Pronunciation," pages 18–23) the word **Qob** ("be dangerous") would be pronounced **Qom** is probably not unrelated to the origin of the idiomatic usage of **Qom**, though the basic meaning of **Qom** itself certainly carries with it the notion of potential danger. Note that despite its slang meaning of "be hazardous, treacherous," the way the verb is used grammatically is based on its standard, literal sense. That is, while it is acceptable to say **He Qob** ("dangerous route"), using **Qob** ("be dangerous") adjectivally, it is ungrammatical to say **He Qom** for ("perilous route"). The verb **Qom** still means "experience a tremor" and must be used in a grammatical structure appropriate to that meaning.

Qop ("be dead" [referring to food])

The word **Qop** means "be worn out" and is usually applied to old weapons, tools, mechanical devices, and the like. It is also used to mean "be dead," but only in reference to an animal that one was expecting to eat live. If a bowl of dead **qagh** (*"gagh,* serpent worms") is placed before a Klingon, the disappointed diner will probably criticize the cook for preparing **qagh Qop** ("dead *gagh*"). The normal way to say "be dead," referring to a person or animal, is by using the form **Heghpu'** ("has died"): **Heghpu' SuvwI'** ("The warrior has died"). It is not appropriate to say **SuvwI' Qop** ("dead warrior, worn-out warrior.")

SaS ("be shallow, superficial, uncritical"; also "not good, unfortunate")

This word, literally meaning "be horizontal," refers to someone's intellect. To describe someone as **SaS** is certainly insulting, as in **SaS DIvI' HoD** ("The Federation captain is shallow"—that is, literally, "The Federation captain is horizontal"; **DIvI'**, "federation"; **HoD**, "captain"). This slang expression has apparently been in use for quite a while and is fairly common. Indeed, for this usage of the term, there is no known standard equivalent. **SaS** is also used as an exclamation to express disapproval, comparable to the standard **Do'Ha'** ("unfortunate"). For example, upon hearing that a ship has been destroyed, one may say simply **SaS** (literally, "horizontal" but suggesting "That's bad, that's unfortunate"). A slang word with a meaning similar to **SaS** is **natlh** (literally, "consume, use up" [see page 155]). The opposite meaning—that is, "profound, thorough" and "good"—is often expressed by the slang verbs **chong** (literally, "be vertical") and **qo'** (literally, "be fierce").

SIj ("be insightful, clever, have a keen mind")

This verb literally means "slash, slit (with a blade)." When used in its slang sense, it does not take an object: **bISIj** ("You are insightful, you have a keen mind"; literally, "You slash"). Nonslang counterparts are **val** ("be clever, smart") and **'ong** ("be cunning, sly").

Sub ("be brave, bold, heroic, valiant, intrepid")

Literally meaning "be solid," as opposed to gaseous or liquid, **Sub**, in its slang usage, may be applied to a person. Thus, **SuvwI' Sub** is "brave warrior" (literally, "solid warrior"; **SuvwI'**, "warrior") and **Sub SuvwI'** means "The warrior is brave" (literally, "The warrior is solid"). It is inappropriate to use the word to describe anything other than a person; a phrase such as **may' Sub** (**may'**, "battle") would mean only "solid battle" and would probably be considered a meaningless utterance. The slang meaning of **Sub** is probably influenced by the phonetically identical noun **Sub,** meaning "hero." Non-slang equivalents for **Sub** are **yoH** ("be brave") and **jaq** ("be bold"), which can be used pretty much interchangeably.

tlham ("structure, order")

The word **tlham**, literally meaning "gravity," is used to mean "order" or "structure" in the sense of an ordered or well-structured society. In the same way that gravity holds one to a planet (or, in the case of artificial gravity, to the floor of a space vessel), the structure of a society holds its members in, preventing them from going off in all directions. In other words, it ensures that a society function properly by keeping it from coming apart. The word is used in phrases such as **tlham ghaj** ("have gravity"—that is, "have structure, order") or **tlham Hutlh** ("lack gravity" or "lack structure, order"). A very well ordered society may be said to have **tlham'a'** ("big gravity") or **tlham HoS** ("strong gravity"), while a society that is judged to be falling apart may have **tlhamHom** ("little gravity") or **tlham puj** ("weak gravity.")

tlhuH ("be exhilarated, stimulated, invigorated")

Literally meaning "breathe," this word is used in such expressions as **jItlhuH** ("I am exhilarated, it's exhilarating to me"; literally, "I breathe"). Perhaps a near equivalent in standard Klingon is **Sey** ("be excited").

vonlu' ("fail utterly")

This verb literally means "be trapped, entrapped." The verb **von**, usually translated as "trap, entrap," means "put (someone) in a position from which there is no escape." For a Klingon, to be in such a position, to be unable to fight back, is most dishonorable, especially since he or she is likely to be viewed in a helpless state. Thus, it is a sign of utter failure. The slang expression is used in such constructions as **bIvonlu'pu'** ("You have failed completely"; literally, "You have been trapped"). In standard Klingon, the same idea may be expressed by saying **lujbej** ("certainly fail"), **lujchu'** ("fail perfectly"), or **lujqu'** ("really fail"), all based on **luj** ("fail"). Note that **luj** is also used to mean "lose" (as in "lose at a game"). To say "I lose" is **jIluj** (**jI-**, "I"); to say "I lose in a big way" is **jIlujqu'** or **jIlujchu'**. The slang term **vonlu'** is not used in reference to games. It means "perform most inadequately, ineffectually, unsuccessfully" and is applied to one's performance as a warrior, tactician, political usurper, and the like.

> **yeb** ("wrist" [derogatory])
> **ngIb** ("ankle" [derogatory])

The words referring to the joints at the ends of arms and legs have slightly negative connotations. Likening a person or situation to either is to say something unflattering. It is not uncommon, therefore, to hear references to them in insults on the order of **yeb Darur** ("You resemble a wrist") or **ngIb ghaH verengan'e'** ("The Ferengi is an ankle"). To say **SuvwI' yoH law' ngIb yoH puS** ("The warrior is braver than an ankle") is far from complimentary. One theory as to the reason for this negative association is that wrists and ankles, being joints, are flexible and pliant, while being rigid—maintaining one's principles and goals against all odds—is a virtue. A more likely scenario, however, is that the meanings of the words were influenced by the distinctive speech of the Krotmag region, which has been shown to be responsible for some other common idioms and slang as speakers of other dialects incorporate certain Krotmag pronunciations (see the chapter on The Fiction of Klingon Conformity, under "Pronunciation," pages 18–23). In the Krotmag dialect, **yeb** ("wrist") is pronounced **yem**, identical to the verb **yem** ("sin"). In parallel fashion, **ngIb** ("ankle") is pronounced **ngIm**, identical to the verb **ngIm** ("be putrid"). Thus, the wrist gained an association with sinning, or dishonorable behavior; the ankle, with putridity, perhaps moral decay.

yIv ("annoy, bother, irk, irritate")

This verb literally means "chew." In its slang sense, it is found in such constructions as **choyIv** ("You bother me"—literally, "You chew me"; **cho-,** "You [do something to] me") or **muyIv romuluS Ha'DIbaH** ("The Romulan dog irks me"; literally, "The Romulan animal chews me," where "Romulan animal" is a derogatory way to refer to a Romulan; **mu-,** "He/she [does something to] me"; **romuluS,** "Romulus"; **Ha'DIbaH,** "animal"). The subject of **yIv** can be only a person or creature, not an inanimate object or a situation. Thus, it is inappropriate to say something like **muyIv 'Iw HIq bIr** ("cold bloodwine chews me"; **'Iw HIq,** "bloodwine"; **bIr,** "be cold"). Standard ways to express the same idea are **nuQ** ("annoy, bother") and **berghmoH** ("irritate").

'Igh ("be cursed, jinxed")

This is a slang term with no known origin. It can be applied to just about anything—persons, missions, ships, and so on—when everything seems to be going wrong. Since Klingons consider self-control a great virtue, declaring oneself to be cursed is comparable to an admission of weakness and utterly uncharacteristic (though not unknown). To say that someone else is cursed, on the other hand, is to attribute weakness to that person. Accordingly, **bI'Igh** ("You are cursed, you are jinxed"; **bI-,** "you") is quite insulting. In standard Klingon, the same idea may be expressed by saying **Do'Ha'moHlu'** ("be made unlucky" or "someone/something causes [someone/something] to be unlucky"), as in **DaDo'Ha'moHlu'** ("You've been made unlucky," or "someone/something causes you to be unlucky"; **Da-** along with the impersonal subject suffix **-lu'** means "someone/something [does something to] you").

THE CHANGING RULES:
ACCEPTABLE DEVIATION

Though not "proper," judging by its frequency of use, slang would have to be deemed acceptable when used in appropriate contexts. Similarly, certain departures from normal grammatical structure are also commonly heard. These may be categorized into four types. First, some of these formations are correlated with certain social groupings, such as social class or generation. These are discussed in the chapter on The Fiction of Klingon Conformity, under "Societal Variation," pages 36–43, and this chapter, under "Generational Differences: Pronunciation and Grammar," pages 138–142). Second, some instances of grammatical variation, even though generally regarded as errors, seem to be rather mild infractions. Some of these may well become acceptable at some time in the future, much to the chagrin of the more traditional members of Klingon society. Third, some nonstandard varieties of language are used quite frequently and by most Klingons, but only in a restricted set of circumstances. Finally, some deviations are definitely ungrammatical but are not errors; they are uttered with full knowledge and understanding of what the rules prescribe, perhaps a sort of grammatical slang. These constructions are used in restricted contexts or for rhetorical effect or both.

Common Errors: The Case of *lu-*

Among the more tolerated grammatical errors is one involving the pronominal prefix **lu-**, whose use is rather complex. In colloquial Klingon, however, it is sometimes not used in instances in which grammar books would say it is required. It is well known that Klingon pronominal prefixes indicate both the subject and object of the verb. For example, the prefix **mu-** means that the subject (per-

The Jem'Hadar have made the error of underestimating a Klingon warrior. *Robbie Robinson*

former of the action) is "he/she" or "they" and that the object (recipient of the action) is "me," as in **muHIv** ("He/she attacks me," or "they attack me"; **HIv,** "attack"). The subject of a sentence with **muHIv**, then, could be **SuvwI'** ("warrior") or **SuvwI'pu'** ("warriors"): **muHIv SuvwI'** ("The warrior attacks me"), **muHIv SuvwI'pu'** ("The warriors attack me"). If the object in these sentences is "you" (singular) instead of "me," there are two different prefixes, depending on whether the attacker is singular or plural: **Du-** ("He/she [does something to] you") and **nI-** ("They [do something to] you"), as in **DuHIv** ("He/she attacks you"), **nIHIv** ("They attack you"). These verb forms are correctly used in such sentences as **DuHIv SuvwI'** ("The warrior attacks you") and **nIHIv SuvwI'pu'** ("The warriors attack you"). It is ungrammatical to use **Du-** with a plural subject or **nI-** with a singular subject. That is, both **DuHIv SuvwI'pu'** ("The warriors attacks you") and **nIHIv SuvwI'** ("The warrior attack you") are as inappropriate as their Federation Standard translations.

When the subject of the verb is third person ("he, she, it, they") and there is either no object or else the object is also third person, except for imperatives, there is usually no prefix attached to the verb. Thus, **HIv**—the verb alone, with no prefix—could mean "He/she attacks," "They attack," "He/she attacks him/her," "He/she attacks them," or "They attack them." When the third person subject is plural but the object is singular, however, the prefix **lu-** is used: **luHIv** ("they attack him/her"). In short, no prefix should be attached to the verb unless a plural subject acts upon a singular object:

> **HIv tlhIngan.** ("The Klingon attacks"; **tlhIngan,** "Klingon")
> **HIv tlhInganpu'.** ("The Klingons attack"; **tlhInganpu',** "Klingons")
> **romuluSngan HIv tlhIngan.** ("The Klingon attacks the Romulan"; **romuluSngan,** "Romulan")

romuluSnganpu' HIv tlhIngan. ("The Klingon attacks the Romulans"; **romuluSnganpu'**, "Romulans")

romuluSnganpu' HIv tlhInganpu'. ("The Klingons attack the Romulans.")

but:

romuluSngan luHIv tlhInganpu'. ("The Klingons attack the Romulan.")

If the indefinite subject suffix **-lu'** (phonetically similar, but unrelated to the prefix) is used, indicating that someone or something unknown or unstated performs the action, things get a little more complicated. In these instances, the prefix **lu-** indicates that the *object* is plural: **romuluSnganpu' luHIvlu'** ("Someone attacks the Romulans," or "The Romulans are attacked").

Because Klingon nouns may be plural even if they lack a plural suffix (**-pu'** in the examples above), sometimes sentences, if taken out of context, are ambiguous. Thus, **romuluSngan HIv tlhIngan** could, theoretically, mean "The Klingon attacks the Romulan," "The Klingon attacks the Romulans," or "The Klingons attack the Romulans." It could not mean "The Klingons attack the Romulan," however, because that meaning would require the prefix **lu-** on the verb: **romuluSngan luHIv tlhIngan**. Since the subject and object are not otherwise distinguished as singular or plural, **lu-** is what makes the meaning clear. Similarly, if the verb has the indefinite subject suffix **-lu'** and the object of the sentence lacks a plural suffix, only the presence of the prefix **lu-** makes it clear that it is plural: **romuluSngan luHIvlu'** ("Someone attacks the Romulans," or "The Romulans are attacked").

In those instances, however, when clarity is not an issue—that is, if the object is unambiguously singular (when the subject is known) or unambiguously plural (when the subject is indefinite)—the prefix **lu-** is sometimes left off: **wa' romuluSngan HIv tlhInganpu'** ("The Klingons attack one Romulan"; **wa'**, "one"); **romulu-Snganpu' HIvlu'** ("Someone attacks the Romulans," or "The Romulans are attacked"). Though this makes the sentences fall in line with other third-person subject/ third-person object sentences in that there is no verb prefix, these are still regarded as errors; the correct sentences are **wa' romuluSngan luHIv tlhInganpu'** and **romuluSnganpu' luHIvlu'**. Except in formal situations, however, the omission of **lu-** in such cases is often overlooked. Though technically an error, and jarring to many Klingons' ears, it causes no confusion as to the intended meaning of the sentence. It is important to note that this does not mean that the use of **lu-** is optional; it is left off only under specific conditions.

Klingon grammarians refer to the rule that governs the use of pronominal prefixes as the rule of **rom** (literally, "accord"). Grammarians of Federation Standard and many Earth languages call the phenomenon "agreement." Thus, in the case of Klingon, the prefix used must "agree" with the noun to which it refers; if the object noun is plural, for example, the prefix must be one that is used with plural objects. Agreeing is not a trait typically associated with Klingon nature, however, and apparently, at least under certain circumstances, this may extend to grammar as well.

Restricted Contexts: Clipped Klingon

One form of nonstandard speech that is heard rather frequently is what is called **tlhIngan Hol poD** ("Clipped Klingon") or simply **Hol poD** ("clipped language"). In Clipped Klingon, certain grammatical elements are left out, but sentences otherwise match the standard formations. Clipped Klingon differs from those patterns associated with a particular generation or social class or found only in certain regions, however, because it is restricted

The battle to save the *Starship Defiant* demonstrates a Klingon proverb to Worf. *Elliott Marks*

contextually. That is, it is associated not with certain groups of speakers but instead with certain situations. In particular, Clipped Klingon is heard in situations where quick communication is desirable and certain phrases are expected to be heard, such as on the bridge of a ship during a battle.

The element most likely to be missing from a Clipped Klingon utterance is the pronominal prefix. Thus, **yaj'a'** (consisting of the verb **yaj** ["understand"] plus **-'a'**, the interrogative suffix) would mean "Does he or she understand?" in Standard Klingon but could also mean "Do you understand?" in Clipped Klingon, with the pronominal prefix **bI-** ("you" [singular]) or **Su-** ("you" [plural]) left off.

Precisely because certain elements are absent, Clipped Klingon phrases cannot be properly interpreted unless the meaning that would have been expressed by the missing pieces is understood by all involved in the conversation. Accordingly, Clipped Klingon is typically used only in such situations. For example, a captain's command to fire a torpedo is most commonly just **baH!** ("Fire [a torpedo]!") rather than **yIbaH!**, the full form with the imperative prefix **yI-**, or even the lengthier and more explicit **peng yIbaH!** ("Fire the torpedo!") In the throes of battle, by the time the order to fire a torpedo is given, all concerned are expecting to hear that order. The torpedo has already been loaded into the torpedo tube, the weapon has been aimed, and the firing mechanism has been readied. All that is left is for the gunner to actually discharge the weapon. Thus, the only information that must be conveyed at this point is when to fire; the person doing the firing and the object to be fired are already known by all. Clipped Klingon accommodates this need quite nicely.

On the other hand, it would be inappropriate to use Clipped Klingon when first ordering a drink at a bar. To approach the bartender and say simply **qang!** ("Pour!") does not convey enough information. What should be poured? Does the speaker want the bartender to pour the drink, or does the speaker want to do it him- or herself? Once a context has been established, however, the clipped command form works adequately. Thus, if the bartender has already poured two or three glasses of bloodwine for a patron and these have been consumed, the customer's shout of **qang!** would probably be correctly interpreted as "Pour me one more drink of bloodwine!"

The role of context in determining whether to use Clipped Klingon is both crucial and subtle. For example, in the bar scenario mentioned above, to order an additional drink by saying **'Iw HIq yIqang!** ("Pour the bloodwine!") rather than simply **qang!** ("Pour!") carries no particular connotation. On the other hand, if the patron had used the clipped form on one or more occasions and, for some reason, was displeased with the bartender's response, use of the longer form the next time would convey this annoyance, as if to say, "I will be very explicit so there is no misunderstanding this time: pour the bloodwine." Such a switch from Clipped Klingon to the fuller form is often interpreted as a challenge to one's honor, so it should not be done unless one is prepared to deal with the consequences.

Clipped Klingon is also frequently found in song lyrics. There are two possible reasons for this. First, songs are often associated with situations in which spoken (that is, not sung) Clipped Klingon would probably be found, such as battles and drinking. Second, resorting to Clipped Klingon may make it easier to fit the words of a song to the melody. For example, in a song traditionally sung by Klingon warriors at the beginning of a mission (sometimes called "The Warrior's Anthem" or "**SuvwI' van bom**"), the opening lines are in Clipped Klingon:

Qoy qeylIS puqloD
Qoy puqbe'pu'

Compare these with the nonclipped version:

peQoy qeylIS puqloD
peQoy puqbe'pu'

These lines mean "Hear, sons of Kahless!/Hear, daughters!" In the song, the first word in each line is **Qoy** ("hear"), a command in clipped form; the imperative prefix **pe-** is left off.

Actually, these lyrics are an illustration of another way context is important when using clipped Klingon. In theory, the full form of the clipped verb **Qoy** ("hear") could be either **yIQoy** or **peQoy**. The prefix **yI-** indicates a command when addressing one person; **pe-** is used when addressing a group. The phrase **qeylIS puqloD** by itself is ambiguous; it means either "son of Kahless" or

"sons of Kahless" (**qeylIS**, "Kahless"; **puqloD**, "son") because nouns in Klingon, even if intended to refer to more
than one, do not require a plural suffix. Thus, the clipped
phrase **Qoy qeylIS puqloD** may mean either "Hear, son
of Kahless!" or "Hear, sons of Kahless!" In the context of
the song, however, it is clear that the plural meaning is
intended since in the second line, the word **puqbe'pu'**
("daughters") has the plural suffix **-pu'** and is not ambiguous at all. If the lyrics were sung in their nonclipped
form, with the prefix **pe-** used with the verb **Qoy**, there
would be no misunderstanding. Even though **puqloD**
alone is "son" or "sons," **peQoy qeylIS puqloD**, containing the prefix **pe-,** which is used only with plural address-
ees, could mean only "Hear, sons of Kahless!"

Intentional Ungrammaticality

Sometimes words or phrases are coined for a specific
occasion, intentionally violating grammatical rules in
order to have an impact. Usually these are never heard
again, though some gain currency and might as well be
classified as slang. Klingon grammarians call such forms
mu'mey ru' ("temporary words"). Sometimes, **mu'mey
ru'** fill a void—that is, give voice to an idea for which
there is no standard (or even slang) expression; sometimes, like slang, they are just more emphatic ways of
expressing an idea. A common way to create these constructions is to bend the grammatical rules somewhat,
violating the norm in a way that is so obvious that there
is no question that it is being done intentionally. To do
this is expressed in Klingon as **pabHa'** ("misfollow [the
rules], follow [the rules] wrongly").

Several of these made-up words involve constructions normally restricted to numbers. The suffix **-DIch** is
attached to a number to form an ordinal number: **wa'**
("one"), **wa'DIch** ("first"); **cha'** ("two"), **cha'DIch** ("second"); **vagh** ("five"), **vaghDIch** ("fifth"). Ordinal numbers

follow the noun with which they are associated, as in **'avwI' vaghDIch** ("fifth guard"), **nentay wa'DIch** ("First Rite of Ascension"). Sometimes the suffix is heard attached to **pagh** ("zero, none"), producing the technically ungrammatical term **paghDIch** ("zeroth"). It is used to describe something that was expected to occur but has not, or that could conceivably occur but has not. For example, one might say **pawpu' 'avwI' paghDIch** ("the zeroth guard has arrived"; **pawpu',** "has arrived"), implying that no guard has arrived even though one (and probably more than one) is expected. Similarly, one might describe how to wield a painstik during the Rite of Ascension by saying:

> **'oy'naQ DaQeqDI' mIw wa'DIch Data', 'ach**
> **'oy'naQ Dachu'DI' mIw paghDIch Data'.**
> ("When you aim the painstik, you accomplish the first step, but when you turn the painstik on, you accomplish the zeroth step"; **'oy'naQ,** "painstik"; **DaQeqDI',** "when you aim it"; **mIw,** "procedure"; **wa'DIch,** "first"; **Data',** "You accomplish it"; **'ach,** "but"; **Dachu'DI',** "when you activate it")

The implication here is that activating the painstik must be done before beginning the ritualistic part of the ceremony.

On the other extreme, when **-DIch** is attached to **Hoch** ("all"), the resulting word, **HochDIch** ("allth") is used as an alternate for **Qav** ("be final, last") to refer to the final one of a series whose members either were counted or could have been counted, as in **pIpyuS pach HochDIch DaSoppu'** ("You've eaten the last *pipius* claw"; **pIpyuS pach,** *"pipius* claw"; **DaSoppu',** "You've eaten it"). The word also may be used to describe the final step of a process. Speaking of the Rite of Ascension, one might say **'oy'naQ Dachu'Ha'DI' mIw HochDIch Data'** ("When you turn the painstik off, you accomplish the last step"; **Dachu'Ha'DI',** "when you deactivate it").

The suffix **-logh,** when attached to numbers, is used to count the number of instances of something: **wa'logh** ("once"), **cha'logh** ("twice"), **vaghlogh** ("five times"). When **-logh** is attached to **pagh** ("zero"), the resulting form, **paghlogh** ("zero times") is used as an emphatic alternate for **not** ("never"), as in **paghlogh jegh tlhIngan SuvwI'** ("a Klingon warrior surrenders zero times"; **jegh,** "surrender"; **SuvwI',** "warrior"; **tlhIngan,** "Klingon"); compare **not jegh tlhIngan SuvwI'** ("a Klingon warrior never surrenders"). Similarly, when **-logh** is attached to **Hoch** ("all"), the resulting word, **Hochlogh** ("all times"), is used in the same way as **reH** ("always"), as in **Hochlogh no' yIquvmoH** ("All times honor your ancestors"; **no',** "ancestors"; **yIquvmoH,** "Honor them!" [actually, this is "Honor him/her!"; the inherently plural noun **no',** "ancestors," takes a singular pronoun]); compare **reH no' yIquvmoH** ("Always honor your ancestors").

Another kind of bending of the grammar involves the comparative construction—that is, the way to say that something is more or greater than something else. In Klingon, this is expressed by a grammatical formula: A Q **law'** B Q **puS,** where A and B are the two items being compared as to a specific quality (Q), A having the greater amount of this quality (expressed by **law',** "be many"), B the lesser (expressed by **puS,** "be few"): **tlhIngan yoH law' verengan yoH puS** ("The Klingon is braver than the Ferengi"; **tlhIngan,** "Klingon"; **yoH,** "be brave"; **verengan,** "Ferengi"). As a form of word play, antonyms (that is, words with opposite meanings) other than **law'** and **puS** are sometimes plugged into the formula. The resulting phrases literally make no sense at all, but because of the uniqueness of the **law'**/**puS** phrases within Klingon grammar, they are always understood. Constructions such as the following might be heard, all meaning, though not literally, "The Klingon is braver than the Ferengi":

tlhIngan yoH HoS verengan yoH puj. (HoS, "be strong"; **puj,** "be weak")

tlhIngan yoH pIv verengan yoH rop. (pIv, "be healthy"; **rop,** "be sick")

tlhIngan yoH Daj verengan yoH qetlh (Daj, "be interesting"; **qetlh,** "be dull")

Such fanciful use of words is found with the superlative construction (something is the most or the best) as well. In the superlative, the noun **Hoch** ("all") fits into the B slot, as in the normal sentence **tlhIngan yoH law' Hoch yoH puS** ("Klingons are the bravest of all"). It is possible, however, for rhetorical effect, to say such things as **tlhIngan yoH HoS Hoch yoH puj (HoS,** "be strong"; **puj,** "be weak").

If one state of affairs is not inherently better or worse than its opposite, the terms may occur in either order. Once again comparing the brave Klingon and the not-so-brave Ferengi:

tlhIngan yoH jen verengan yoH 'eS or **tlhIngan yoH 'eS verengan yoH jen** (**jen,** "be high"; **'eS,** "be low")

tlhIngan yoH ghegh verengan yoH Hab or **tlhIngan yoH Hab verengan yoH ghegh** (**ghegh,** "be rough"; **Hab,** "be smooth")

Some conditions, on the other hand, are more highly regarded than others. In those instances, it is essential to get the terms in the correct order. For example, among Klingons, a task that is difficult (**Qatlh**) is more highly valued than one that is easy (**ngeD**). Accordingly, in these creative comparative and superlative constructions, **Qatlh** is associated with the quality that is "many" and **ngeD** with the quality that is "few." To say "The Klingon is braver than the Ferengi," one would have to say **tlhIngan yoH Qatlh verengan yoH ngeD**. Reversing the order of **Qatlh** and **ngeD** would produce the phrase

tlhIngan yoH ngeD verengan yoH Qatlh, which, if interpretable at all, would mean "The Klingon is less brave than the Ferengi." Even if one really meant it, uttering such a phrase could lead to unfortunate consequences.

Some speakers of Klingon never use such nonconformist constructions. Some use a few from a stock set. Others seem to be somewhat creative. Among Klingons, there is a fine line between creative use of the language and silliness, however, and Klingons are rather intolerant of the latter. Accordingly, the visitor to a Klingon planet is advised to avoid making such constructions until he or she is very well versed in Klingon culture. Not only will this preclude being viewed as less than serious, it will also prevent inadvertently making comparisons backward.

A final type of intentional ungrammaticality may occur as a result of an attempt to circumvent a grammatical rule. One such rule involves the manner in which verb suffixes may or may not be used together in the same word. Excluding a small set of suffixes that may occur just about anywhere, if a verb has more than one suffix, the order of the suffixes is fixed. For example, if both **-nIS** ("need") and **-bej** ("certainly") occur in the same word, **-nIS** must always precede **-bej**, as in **maSopnISbej** ("We certainly need to eat"; **ma-,** "we"; **Sop,** "eat"). Putting the suffixes in the wrong order, as in **maSopbejnIS**, produces an unacceptable form (just as *talkser* is an ungrammatical way to make the plural of *talker* in Federation Standard; only *talkers* is acceptable). In addition, there are suffixes that can never occur in the same word; they can neither precede nor follow one another. For instance, one cannot use **-nIS** ("need"), as in **maSopnIS** ("We need to eat") and **-rup** ("ready"), as in **maSoprup** ("We are ready to eat"), in the same word, just as in Federation Standard one cannot use both *-s* (third-person present-tense indicator), as in *talks,* and *-ed* (past-tense indicator), as in *talked,* in the same word. Saying

maSoprupnIS or **maSopnISrup** is as impossible to a Klingon speaker as saying *talksed* or *talkeds* would be to a speaker of Federation Standard.

Among those suffixes that can never occur together are **-lu'** (indefinite subject indicator) and **-laH** ("can, able"). The former is used when the subject is unknown or indefinite, often translated into Federation Standard by means of the passive voice: **jagh jonlu'** ("One captures the enemy," or "The enemy is captured"; **jagh,** "enemy"; **jon,** "capture"). The latter is used to express ability: **jagh jonlaH** ("He/she can capture the enemy"). If it is desirable to express the ideas of "indefinite subject" and "ability" at the same time, such as in the sentences "One can capture the enemy" or "The enemy can be captured," it is not uncommon to use the noun **vay'** ("somebody, anybody") as the subject of the sentence: **jagh jonlaH vay'** ("Somebody can capture the enemy," or "Anybody can capture the enemy"). Nevertheless, some speakers seem to want to put the two concepts into a single word, and, on rare occasion, they will do so. Rather than violating the rules by using the two suffixes sequentially (that is, **-lu'laH** or **-laHlu'**), however, these speakers will say either **-luH** or **-la'**, employing totally artificial, made-up suffixes formed by fusing **-lu'** and **-laH**, as in **jagh jonluH** or **jagh jonla'** ("The enemy can be captured"). No one accepts such constructions as grammatical; their inappropriateness, the way they grate on the Klingon ear, is exactly what gives them elocutionary clout. A visitor may hear one of these odd suffixes occasionally, but, as with other intentionally ungrammatical forms, it is best to avoid using them until one is extremely comfortable with the nuances of Klingon style.

Ritualized Speech

As noted earlier (in the chapter on The Fiction of Klingon Conformity, pages 7–43), in some ritualistic settings tradition overrides any tendency for change or variation. The language of such ceremonies, **no' Hol** ("ancestors' language"), has not changed for centuries, though different forms of **no' Hol** are heard, depending on when the ceremony originated. For other rituals, however, the standard version of modern Klingon, **ta' Hol**, is used. Even though the words and grammar are the same as those used in everyday speech, in ritualistic settings, the sentences are set. Each Klingon who undergoes the Rite of Ascension, for example, follows the same script, beginning with **DaHjaj SuvwI''e' jIH** ("Today I am a warrior"). The lines must be said in the same way each time, with little room for variation. Over time, as the language changes, the current versions of these phrases may become fossilized and be considered examples of **no' Hol**, but for the time being, they are just highly formal examples of Standard Klingon.

One type of occasion on which ritualized speech is heard is the induction ceremony or initiation rite (**muvtay**). For example, in the ceremony to induct new members into the Order of the *Bat'leth* (**betleH 'obe'**), the highest honor that the government bestows on a Klingon, the presiding official, usually the leader of the Klingon High Council, first reads a name from the **naD tetlh** ("Commendation List"), always calling out the inductee's name in the most formal way (given name plus father's name, such as **tI'vIS barot puqloD** ["T'vis, son of Barot"]). The inductee approaches, and the official says—with no variation—**pInaDqu' tuqlIj wInaDqu' je** ("Glory to you and your house"; literally, "We praise you highly; we also praise your house highly").

A ritual of a less majestic sort occurs on a Klingon vessel when a new set of officers takes over and a mission is about to begin. With the bridge crew assembled but the captain not yet present, the first officer states his or her name and then says **DaH yaS wa'DIch vIgheS** ("I now take my place as first officer" or, literally, "Now I

Chancellor Gowron presides over the awarding of the Order of the *Bat'leth*. *Brian D. McLaughlin*

assume the responsibilities of first officer"; **DaH,** "now"; **yaS wa'DIch,** "first officer"; **vIgheS,** "I assume the duties of, I take on the responsibilities of"). The first officer then requests the ship's **may' ta** ("record of battle"), which is presented by a crew member. The first officer reviews it. Soon the captain enters. The first officer says, **beq may' ta vIlajpu'** ("I have accepted the crew's record of battle"; **beq,** "crew"; **vIlajpu',** "I have accepted it"), pledges the crew's lives to the captain, and concludes by saying, **juDev 'ej Dujvam ra'wI' DagheS 'e' vItlhob** ("I ask you to lead us as commander of this ship" or, literally, "I request that you lead us and that you assume the duties of commander of this ship"; **juDev,** "You lead us"; **'ej,** "and"; **Dujvam,** "this ship"; **ra'wI',** "commander"; **DagheS,** "You assume the duties of"; **'e',** "that"; **vItlhob,** "I request it"). The captain replies, **ghopDu'wIjDaq yInmeyraj vIlaj** ("I accept your lives into my hands"; **ghopDu'wIjDaq,** "in my hands"; **yInmeyraj,** "your lives"; **vIlaj,** "I accept them") and then reverts to the ancient language form **no' Hol** and says, **Delaq Do',** meaning something like "Take your stations," a phrase never heard in any other context.

Finally, another sort of ritualized speech consists of ways of starting or concluding conversations. Though, as is well known, there are really no Klingon greetings along the lines of "hello," "how're things?" or the like, Klingons sometimes begin a conversation by saying **nuqneH,** an idiomatic expression meaning "What do you want?" (If fully grammatical, "What do you want?" would be rendered as **nuq DaneH.**) The usual response to **nuqneH** is neither a repetition of the expression nor is it an answer to the question. There is often no particular response at all; the "greeted" party simply begins speaking about the topic at hand. Sometimes the response is **yIjatlh!** ("Speak!"), after which the person who began the conversation continues. If the addressee has reason to be angry with the "greeter," the most likely response is silence. The lack of a response is not necessarily an indication of ill will, however; it may just be that the person to whom **nuqneH** is said can think of nothing to say and is waiting for the greeter to go on.

Similarly, at the end of a conversation, there is no Klingon equivalent for "good-bye" or "catch you later" or "have a nice day." If anything of a concluding nature is said at all, however, it will certainly be **Qapla'** ("success"), a customary send-off that has its origins in ship captains' dispatching their crews on dangerous and, most assuredly, glorious missions.

Robbie Robinson

AVOIDING GAFFES

Despite the diversity exhibited by speakers of Klingon who belong to different groups or who come from different parts of the Empire, despite the acceptability of different pronunciations, terminology, and even grammar, there are still some aspects of language use for which the speaker must be sure to adhere to all the rules rather meticulously. For example, care must be taken when pronouncing some words and phrases to ensure that they cannot be mistaken for other words or phrases with completely different meanings. When choosing words, one must be aware that there are expressions that may be used when speaking to certain people but must be avoided when speaking to others. In addition, when translating to or from Klingon, there are some concepts that tend to cause a certain amount of difficulty simply because there are no words for the concept in one or the other of the languages. This may result in ungrammatical constructions whose use clearly marks one as an outsider and therefore probably as one not to be trusted. It is important for anyone visiting a Klingon settlement to be aware that saying the wrong thing or saying it in the wrong way may not only lead to communication difficulties but also may be detrimental to one's health.

PHONETIC PERILS

When learning to speak a new language, one has a tendency to pronounce sounds in a familiar, comfortable way, as if they were sounds in a language already spoken. For example, someone who speaks Federation Standard may mispronounce Klingon **q** as *k* because the two sounds are similar and the Federation Standard speaker is accustomed to making the *k* sound toward the back of the mouth but is not accustomed to making a **q** sound even farther back. In the same fashion, a Federation Standard speaker may mispronounce Klingon **D**, made with the tip of the tongue touching the roof of the mouth, as if it were the similar but not identical Federation Standard *d*, made with the tip of the tongue somewhat behind the upper teeth. Unless the Federation Standard speaker learns to overcome old habits, then, he or she is likely to pronounce the word **qoD** ("interior"), which has unfamiliar consonants, as if it were Federation Standard *code*. To pronounce Klingon words with Federation Standard sounds is to speak Klingon with a Federation Standard accent. For the most part, speaking Klingon with an alien accent will not lead to any misunderstanding. If one were to say *pa code* for Klingon **pa' qoD** ("room's interior, inside of a room"), one's pronunciation would betray his or her non-Klingon status, and one would risk being judged too lazy to learn Klingon properly, but the idea of "inside of a room" would still be conveyed.

Mispronunciation may turn dangerous, on the other hand, if one Klingon sound is substituted for another. This is most likely to happen if both of the sounds are initially unfamiliar to the language learner—that is, if they are lacking from the learner's native tongue. For example, the Klingon sounds **H** and **Q** are not found in Federation Standard, and some students of Klingon at first have a hard time distinguishing the two, even though they are, to a Klingon's ear, quite distinct. (The **Q** has a sudden onset, is produced farther back in the mouth, and is louder than is **H**.) If **Q** is misused for **H** or vice versa, one might accidentally say **bIjeH** ("You are absent-minded") when one intends to say **bIjeQ** ("You are self-confident"), or perhaps one will issue the command **yI-Qotlh!** ("Disable it!") when one intends **yIHotlh!** ("Scan it!") Depending on the circumstances, such utterances could be fatal errors for the speaker.

Sometimes even sounds familiar to a language learner cause problems. Federation Standard speakers generally have no problem distinguishing the Klingon vowel sounds **e** and **I** simply because these sounds are distinct in Federation Standard as well (for example, *pet* versus *pit*). Nevertheless, when one is learning Klingon words, it is not uncommon to confuse words with **e** with words with **I**, just as in some dialects of Federation Standard *pen* and *pin* sound pretty much alike. All too frequently, one hears rumors about the fate of a student of Klingon who intended to say **yo' qIj** ("Black Fleet") but accidentally said **yo' qej** ("grouchy fleet") instead. (In Klingon mythology, the Black Fleet is a band consisting of warriors who have died bravely and honorably and, in a sort of afterlife, carry on glorious battles forever.)

As a practical matter, most mispronunciations will not cause problems, simply because context will make one word rather than the other the only possible choice. Thus, if the occupant of a room heard a door chime, there would probably be no misunderstanding as a result of his or her saying **yI'Il!** ("Be sincere!") rather than the correct **yI'el!** ("Enter!"). In the situation at hand, only "Enter!" makes any sense. Sometimes grammar makes the context clear. For example, saying **joQpu'** rather than **joHpu'** for "Lords, Ladies" (**joH,** "Lord, Lady"; **-pu',** plural suffix) probably would not be misinterpreted as saying "ribs" (**joQ,** "rib") because the plural suffix **-pu'** is used only with nouns indicating beings capable of using language. The reverse is likewise true. That is, if one said **joHDu'** rather than **joQDu'** for "ribs," the meaning of "ribs" would probably be understood because the plural suffix **-Du'** is used only for body parts. In identical fashion, mispronouncing **joHwI'** ("my Lord" or "my Lady") as **joQwI'** would probably not cause the listener to think that "my rib" was the intended meaning, because the suffix **-wI'** ("my") is used only with nouns capable of using language. The suffix meaning "my" used with other nouns is **-wIj**, as in **joQwIj** ("my rib"). To stay out of trouble, however, it is important to get the grammar right. If, for instance, one did not understand the appropriate usages of the plural suffixes **-pu'** versus **-Du'** or of the possessive suffixes **-wI'** versus **-wIj**, there could be unfortunate repercussions even if one's pronunciation were perfect. Addressing "my Lord" or "my Lady" as **joHwIj** rather than **joHwI'** is insulting indeed, since it implies that "my Lord" or "my Lady" is a lower order of being. Similarly, a group of heads of households would probably not appreciate being referred to as **joHDu'**, since that would be the appropriate way to say "Lords" or "Ladies" only if they were body parts. The only thing worse would be combining mispronunciation with grammatical blundering, such as by saying **joQDu'wIj** ("my ribs")—with **Q** rather than **H**, **-Du'** rather than **-pu'**, and **-wIj** rather than **-wI'**—when **joHpu'wI'** ("my Lords, my Ladies") is intended. Mistakes of this kind are simply not tolerated and there are no recorded instances of anyone living long enough to repeat the offense.

Of course, not all pronunciation errors are egregious. Some produce semantically peculiar utterances and, therefore, are usually recognizable as errors. Thus, if a would-be captain were to shout **yIbaQ!** rather than **yIbaH!** ("Fire [the torpedo]!"; **baH,** "fire [a torpedo]"), he or she would be saying "Be just picked!" The consequences of such an error would be trivial, however, since the verb **baQ** ("be fresh, just picked") applies only to fruit or vegetables and is utterly incongruous in the context of torpedo launching. Indeed, since **yIbaH** is what one would expect to hear in such a situation, the mispronunciation would probably go unnoticed or else be considered a mere slip of the tongue.

On the other hand, one should not rely on context or semantic weirdness as always being available to bail one out of a sticky situation that results from articulating a word incorrectly. When dealing with Klingons, it is safest to avoid putting oneself in such a situation in the first place by being aware of which mispronunciations one is most likely to make. To that end, the following sections contain pairs of words and phrases of which to be particularly wary. The lists are by no means complete and are weighted in favor of the mistakes most common among those whose first language is Federation Standard. The best course of action for a visitor to a Klingon planet is to assume that all mispronunciations lead to trouble and to be careful with enunciation under all circumstances.

e/I

bej ("watch")/**bIj** ("punish")
    qabej. ("I watch you.")
    qabIj. ("I punish you.")

Del ("describe")/**DIl** ("pay for")
    Soj yIDel! ("Describe the food!")
    Soj yIDIl! ("Pay for the food!")

Hej ("rob")/**HIj** ("deliver, transport goods")
    HejwI' ("robber")
    HIjwI' ("delivery person")

meQ ("burn")/**mIQ** ("deep-fry")
    to'waQ meQ vutwI'. ("The cook burns the tendon.")
    to'waQ mIQ vutwI'. ("The cook deep-fries the tendon.")

While tendon or ligament (**to'waQ**) that has been deep-fried is one of the few hot dishes enjoyed by most Klingons, burnt tendon is definitely a culinary gaffe.

ngev ("sell")/**ngIv** ("patrol")
    tlhIlHal yIngev! ("Sell the mine!")
    tlhIlHal yIngIv! ("Patrol the mine!")

regh ("bleed")/**rIgh** ("be lame")
  regh SuvwI'. ("The warrior bleeds.")
  rIgh SuvwI'. ("The warrior is lame.")

Note that for a Klingon warrior, bleeding is an indication of a particularly exhilarating battle, not a symbol of defeat. A lame warrior, on the other hand, is often considered an object of pity.

Care in pronunciation may extend to grammatical elements as well. Thus, **qaleghneS** ("I see you honorably" or, perhaps more naturally, "I am honored to see you"; **qalegh,** "I see you"), which ends in the honorific suffix **-neS,** is different in meaning from **qaleghnIS** ("I need to see you"), which ends in the suffix **-nIS** ("need, must"). Furthermore, since **-neS** is used only in addressing a superior, saying **-neS** rather than **-nIS** may be bestowing honor inappropriately.

gh/H

chegh ("return")/**cheH** ("defect")
  wa'leS jIchegh. ("Tomorrow I will return.")
  wa'leS jIcheH. ("Tomorrow I will defect.")

ghew ("bug")/**Hew** ("statue")
  ghew vIHo' ("I admire the bug.")
  Hew vIHo' ("I admire the statue.")

ghIch ("nose")/**HIch** ("pistol, handgun")
  ghIchDaj yIQotlh! ("Disable his/her nose!")
  HIchDaj yIQotlh! ("Disable his/her handgun!")

ghob ("wage war")/**Hob** ("yawn")
  ghob tlhIngan SuvwI'pu'. ("Klingon warriors wage war.")
  Hob tlhIngan SuvwI'pu'. ("Klingon warriors yawn.")

gho' ("step on")/**Ho'** ("admire")
  ghew vIgho'. ("I step on the bug.")
  ghew vIHo'. ("I admire the bug.")

qagh ("*gagh,* serpent worm" [food])/**qaH** ("sir")
  lu', qagh! ("Yes, serpent worm!")
  lu', qaH! ("Yes, sir!")

Mispronouncing **qaH** as **qagh** has often led to particularly unfortunate results.

Qagh ("err, make a mistake")/**QaH** ("help")
  Qagh yaS wa'DIch. ("The first officer errs.")
  QaH yaS wa'DIch. ("The first officer helps.")

regh ("bleed")/**reH** ("play")
  regh puqpu'. ("The children bleed.")
  reH puqpu'. ("The children play.")

'ugh ("be heavy")/**'uH** ("have a hangover")
  'ugh SuvwI' qan. ("The old warrior is heavy.")
  'uH SuvwI' qan. ("The old warrior has a hangover.")

H/Q

HIv ("attack")/**QIv** ("be inferior")
  HIv SuvwI'pu'. ("The warriors attack.")
  QIv SuvwI'pu'. ("The warriors are inferior.")

Hoj ("be cautious")/**Qoj** ("make war")
  yIHoj! ("Be cautious!")
  yIQoj! ("Make war!")

Huch ("money")/**Quch** ("forehead")
  Huch DaHutlh. ("You lack money.")
  Quch DaHutlh. ("You lack a forehead.")

The remark "You lack a forehead" would be considered extremely offensive to a Klingon, calling into question his or her very identity. Since there are any number of phrases involving money that could be taken the wrong way if **Huch** is pronounced **Quch**, many tourists follow the Klingon practice of using the term **DarSeqmey** (*"darseks"*), the plural form of **DarSeq** (*"darsek"*, a Klingon unit of currency) to refer to money in general. Thus, "You lack money" would be **DarSeqmey DaHutlh** (literally, "You lack *darseks*").

> **taH** ("continue, endure, survive")/**taQ** ("be weird")
>> **taH tlhIngan wo'.** ("The Klingon empire survives.")
>> **taQ tlhIngan wo'.** ("The Klingon empire is weird.")

There is a story, perhaps apocryphal, of a non-Klingon actor who attempted to play the lead in the original Klingon version of Shakespeare's *Hamlet* but was shouted off the stage when he began the famous soliloquy by saying, **taQ pagh taQbe'** ("To be weird or not to be weird"), rather than the correct **taH pagh taHbe'** ("To be or not to be"; literally, "[one] continues or [one] does not continue").

> **veH** ("boundary, border")/**veQ** ("garbage")
>> **jogh veH lungIv.** ("They patrol the quadrant border.")
>> **jogh veQ lungIv.** ("They patrol the quadrant garbage.")

> **'IH** ("be beautiful")/**'IQ** ("be sad")
>> **'IH be'nallI'.** ("Your wife is beautiful.")
>> **'IQ be'nallI'.** ("Your wife is sad.")

Glottal Stop: '

Many nonnative speakers of Klingon, especially those for whom Federation Standard is a first language,

Unbowed, Worf stoically witnesses the Borgification of the Earth.
Elliott Marks

seem to have trouble with **'**, the glottal stop, at the end of a word. Articulated correctly, **'** is simply a very abrupt cessation of vocalization. The most common mispronunciation of **'** is as **q**, though some newer speakers leave **'** off altogether. Errors of this type could lead to confusion or confrontation.

> **ro** ("torso")/**ro'** ("fist")
>> **rolIj HI'ang!** ("Show me your torso!")
>> **ro'lIj HI'ang!** ("Show me your fist!")

"Show me your fist" is an idiomatic expression used to challenge someone to take action in a manner consistent with something he or she has just said. Substituting "torso" for "fist" by mispronouncing **ro'** as **ro** would produce a phrase that would be interpreted only literally. Ordering a Klingon to reveal his or her torso is probably not a good idea.

paw ("arrive")/**paw'** ("collide")
   paw Dujmey. ("The ships arrive.")
   paw' Dujmey. ("The ships collide.")

Suy ("merchant")/**Suy'** (*"shooy,"* a type of animal)
   Suy SoH. ("You are a merchant.")
   Suy' SoH. ("You are a *shooy.*")

Calling someone a **Suy'** is quite derogatory, comparable to using the word "pig" in Federation Standard. Mistakenly calling someone a **Suy** ("merchant") when the intent is to be insulting and call him or her a **Suy'** will have the effect of making the speaker appear to be foolish and, therefore, weak and hardly in a position to be ridiculing someone else. Furthermore, the speaker may inadvertently offend a nearby merchant.

HI' ("dictator")/**HIq** ("liquor")
   romuluS HI' vImuS. ("I detest the Romulan dictator.")
   romuluS HIq vImuS. ("I detest Romulan ale.")

pu' ("phaser")/**puq** ("child, offspring")
   reH pu' vIqem. ("I always bring a phaser.")
   reH puq vIqem. ("I always bring a child.")

lu' ("Yes, I will")/**luq** ("Yes, I will")/**lu** ("fall [from power]")
   lu' joHwI'. ("Yes, my Lord.")
   luq joHwI'. ("Yes, my Lord.")
   lu joHwI'. ("My Lord falls from power.")

Because there are two forms of the word meaning "Yes, I will"—**lu'** and **luq**—no confusion can result from mispronouncing **'** as **q**. On the other hand, if **'** is left off entirely and the word is pronounced **lu**, it may be taken to be the verb **lu,** meaning "fall (from power)," a status one probably does not want to attribute to someone in a position to give orders or grant requests.

DIRECT ADDRESS

When addressing someone directly—that is—when speaking to that person—it is sometimes appropriate to refer to him or her by name, title, or other term of respect. For example, if the president of the United Federation of Planets happens to be a human named Joseph Smith, he may be addressed as *Mr. Smith*, *Mr. President*, *President Smith*, or *sir*. His friends are more likely to call him *Joseph* or *Joe*. Members of his family may refer to him by any number of terms: *Uncle Joe*, *Dad* (or *Father* or *Daddy*), *Grandfather* (or *Grandpa* or *Granddad*), and so on. Finally, his closest associates, including anyone with whom he may be romantically involved, may use special nicknames, perhaps *Joey*, or even pet names (*sweetheart* and the like).

A similar range of terms of address exists among Klingons. It is crucial that the right terms be used in the right contexts, however. To call a Klingon by an inappropriate name or title is to dishonor him or her and is never tolerated. The correct choice is based on a number of factors such as the gender of the speaker and addressee, the official position of either participant, and the degree of intimacy the two share.

It is always proper to call somebody by his or her name alone: **Qugh, ghawran, lurSa', be'etor, qeng, vIq-SIS**, and so on. (In Federation Standard, these names are usually rendered as Kruge, Gowron, Lursa, B'Etor, Kang, and Vixis, respectively.) During formal occasions, it is also not uncommon to refer to someone by his or her father's name, such as **mogh puqloD** ("son of Mogh") or a combination of given name plus father's name, such as **HuS 'atrom puqbe'** ("Huss, daughter of A'trom").

If someone has an official title, such as a military

rank or a position in the government, this title follows the name; for example, **martaq Sa'** ("General Martok"), **ghawran Qang** ("Chancellor Gowron"). When addressing such a person, the title is left off only when the occasion is decidedly nonofficial. As was discussed earlier (see the chapter on The Fiction of Klingon Conformity, under "Societal Variation," pages 36–43), the head of a house is afforded the title **joH** ("Lord, Lady"), which, when one is addressing such a personage, may be used either after the name (as in **qamor joH** ["Lord Kahmor"]) or without the name if followed by the possessive suffix **-wI'** ("my"), as in **joHwI'** ("my Lord, my Lady"). In those situations in which a lower-ranked speaker addresses a higher-ranked person (regardless of the basis of the ranking system), a term or phrase of direct address is, if not required, certainly expected. For example, a lower-ranking member of a military unit addresses a superior by name plus rank (such as **tlha'a HoD** ["Captain Klaa"]), by rank alone (e.g., **HoD** ["captain"]), or, as an alternative, by saying **qaH** ("sir"). The word **qaH** is interesting because it is never heard except in direct address. Thus, while one might say **yoH qor HoD** ("Captain Kor is brave") or **yoH HoD** ("The captain is brave"), one would never say **yoH qaH** ("Sir is brave.")

In addition to names (which, as noted above, are always appropriate to use), there are a few common words friends or family members employ when speaking to one another. Within the family, a child usually addresses his or her mother as **SoS** ("Mother" and father as **vav** ("Father"), though it is not uncommon for younger children to use the words **SoSoy** ("Mommy") and **vavoy** ("Daddy"). These are the regular words for "mother" and "father" followed by the suffix **-oy,** which indicates endearment. Most older children drop the **-oy** around the time of their Age of Ascension, though some continue to use it even after that, especially when addressing the parent of the opposite sex. By the same token, a parent may address a son as **puqloDoy** (**puqloD,** "son," plus **-oy**) and a daughter as **puqbe'oy** (**puqbe',** "daughter," plus **-oy**). As with the terms for parents, the **-oy** form is seldom used past the child's Age of Ascension. Though almost always heard as terms of direct address (as in **SoSoy jIghung** ["Mommy, I'm hungry"]), kinship terms with the suffix **-oy** are occasionally used as subjects or objects of sentences, particularly in the speech of younger children. For example, a proud child may say, **SuvwI' ghaH vavoy'e'** ("My daddy is a warrior").

The word for "husband" is **loDnal** and that for "wife" is **be'nal**. Though there are occasional exceptions, for the most part, neither of these words is used in direct address (in a sentence such as **loDnal HIghoS** ["Husband, come here"]) and neither of them typically takes the suffix of endearment **-oy** (as in **be'naloy** ["wifey"]). A similar pattern is observed for **parmaqqay**, which means "someone involved in a romantic relationship with a specific other person" ("romantic partner," perhaps). The word **parmaqqay** is formed from **parmaq**, conventionally translated "love" or "romance" (though the Klingon concept is far more aggressive than the Federation Standard translations imply), plus **qay**, an otherwise unknown element. One may refer to one's "romantic partner" as **parmaqqaywI'** ("my **parmaqqay**"), but one rarely uses the word in direct address (as in, say, **parmaqqay HIghoS** ["**parmaqqay**, come here"]). Instead, couples (officially married and otherwise) tend to call each other by pet names (sometimes called endearments or hypocorisms or, in Klingon, **bang pongmey** ["beloveds' names"]). A **bang pong** (the singular form, "beloved's name") is usually couple-specific—that is, the set of expressions used by one couple is different from that used by another couple. Pet names are almost never uttered unless the two members of the couple are alone and, therefore, are seldom known by anyone else. Indeed, one of the defining characteristics of a **bang pong** is that it

Jadzia is not the **parmaqqay** that Worf expects. *Danny Feld*

be secret, known only by the two members of the couple. The phenomenon of the **bang pong**, however, is not secret. Usually, parents teach their children how the system works and have to give examples in doing so, though it is not known whether the example pet names are actual pet names used by the parents doing the teaching. Sometimes, however, children learn about the custom from other children. In particular, younger children often tell each other pet names they have heard. A child who has a reputation for revealing pet names is usually quite popular among other children, though older Klingons, upon finding out about his or her lack of propriety, will certainly take disciplinary action. As children grow older and start to experience **parmaq** ("love, romance") themselves, they tend to become quite protective of their own **bang pongmey**.

Primarily because of the conversations of children,

but also because, despite all precautions, one member of a couple is on rare occasion overheard saying a **bang pong**, it is possible to give a small number of examples. A **bang pong** is formed by attaching **-oy**, the suffix indicating endearment, to an everyday noun. Most of the resulting terms make very little sense to anyone not in the particular relationship, and none translates well. Some pet terms are based on words for kinds of food, such as **chatlhoy** (from **chatlh** ["soup"]) and **'awje'oy** (from **'awje'** ["root beer"]). Perhaps these words could be rendered in Federation Standard as "soupy" and "poppy" (from "soda pop"), though neither translation conveys the intimacy and intensity of the Klingon. Other terms consist of words for weapons plus **-oy**; for example: **yanoy** (**yan,** "sword"), **HIchoy** (**HIch,** "pistol"), **tajoy** (**taj,** "knife"), **jorwI'oy** (**jorwI',** "explosive"). A third type involves body parts, Klingon or otherwise, as in **'uSoy** (**'uS,** "leg"), **'aDoy** (**'aD,** "vein"), **pIpoy** (**pIp,** "spine"), **pachoy** (**pach,** "claw"). Another term based on a body part, **Ho'oy** (from **Ho'** ["tooth"]), is one of the few that makes sense to a non-Klingon if it is remembered that **Ho'** is a slang term for "hero, idol." (It is also enormously important that this word be pronounced correctly so that it is not misconstrued as **Ho''oy'** ["toothache"]).

Because of the nature of the **parmaq** relationship, misusing a **bang pong** is a serious cultural offense. This could mean, among other things, revealing a **bang pong** to someone other than one's **parmaqqay**, revealing a third party's **bang pong** (regardless of how this information was acquired), addressing one's **parmaqqay** by the wrong pet name, or using a **bang pong** in a public setting. Unless a visitor gets involved in a serious relationship with a Klingon, it is strongly advised that one avoid saying anything that can be misinterpreted as a misused **bang pong**.

For terms of address among friends outside of a family or romantic relationship, there are a number of options, and a number of rules governing their use. The normal word for "friend" is **jup** and it may be used in direct address in sentences such as **jup 'Iw HIq yItlhutlh** ("Friend, drink the bloodwine"). It commonly occurs with the possessive suffix **-wI'** ("my"): **jupwI' 'Iw HIq yItlhutlh** ("My friend, drink the bloodwine"). The word **jup**, however, does not necessarily connote a close friend. For this, one may add the noun suffix **-na'** ("definite") to the word and say **jupna'** ("real friend, good friend"): **jupna' 'Iw HIq yItlhutlh** ("Good friend, drink the bloodwine") or **jupna'wI' 'Iw HIq yItlhutlh** ("My good friend, drink the bloodwine"). In addition, however, there are some other terms used for very close friends, and the correct usage depends, among other things, on the gender of the speaker and the addressee.

The word **maqoch**, sometimes translated as "buddy" or "pal," is used most often by a male addressing another male who is a good friend, as in **maqoch 'Iw HIq yItlhutlh** ("Pal, drink the bloodwine"). When used in such a context, it signifies genuine companionship. If, however, it is used by someone who is definitely not a good friend, such as a member of a house with which one has been feuding, it is considered offensive. Furthermore, if used by a casual acquaintance, it may be taken as a sign of aggression; Klingons are generally apprehensive about those showing too much friendship. A Klingon female would address someone as **maqoch** only if she intended to insult him or her. A Klingon male with any honor at all would never address a female as **maqoch**. The word **maqoch** itself may derive from **may' qoch** (literally, "battle partner"), so perhaps it originally meant something like "war buddy."

There is a word that Klingon females use in a pattern paralleling the males' use of **maqoch**. This word is **chaj**, a close female friend of a female. As with **maqoch**, it is used only in addressing a true friend. If uttered by a fe-

Chief O'Brien (Colm Meaney) and Worf have served together and have shared many battles. *Robbie Robinson*

male adversary, it is insulting; if uttered by a casual acquaintance it is presumptuous. A male Klingon would address a female Klingon as **chaj** only to offend her. If a male were to be addressed as **chaj**, by either a male or a female, he would consider his honor to be attacked and would react accordingly.

It is not uncommon for a Klingon father to address his son as **maqoch** or for a Klingon mother to address her daughter as **chaj**. The reverse, however, is not true. That is, a son would never call his father **maqoch,** nor would a daughter address her mother as **chaj**.

Because of the dangers inherent in using **maqoch** and **chaj** inappropriately, it is suggested that visitors be quite sure of the status of their relationships with individual Klingons before uttering or reacting to either of these words.

The expression of Worf says it all: there is no Klingon word for *jolly*. *Robbie Robinson*

MISMATCHED CONCEPTS

When translating from one language to another, some concepts are easily conveyed. For example, the Klingon word **mIn** means the same thing as its usual Federation Standard translation—*eye*, **Hov** refers to the same celestial object as *star*, and either **cha'pujqutmey** or *dilithium crystals* will work in a warp drive system. On the other hand, some concepts do not translate easily at all. Thus, Federation Standard has no word meaning the same as Klingon **tova'Daq**, a sort of mind sharing or insight into one another's thoughts; Klingon has no word corresponding exactly to the Federation Standard *hypochondria*. In order to avoid unfortunate misunderstandings, it is essential that a traveler to a Klingon planet be aware of instances in which Klingon and his or her native language do not quite match up.

The differences between cultures plays a critical role here. Some words lack direct equivalents simply because they refer to concepts embedded in one culture but not the other. Thus, though conventional translations exist, there are not really one-for-one matches for various weapons, food-preparation implements, and so on. Klingon has at least two words, **maHpIn** and **Duq**, corresponding to Federation Standard *bowl*, but no single word to refer to both; Federation Standard lacks distinctive vocabulary for the two vessels, so it must add on adjectives or descriptive phrases: *large bowl for serving, small bowl for eating from*.

There are various other ways of dealing with concepts that do not have direct equivalents. For example, one language may borrow (and, in the process, phonetically modify) a word for a concept is lacks, such as Federation Standard *bat'leth* for the Klingon weapon **betleH**, or Klingon **qa'vIn** ("coffee"), which seems to be taken from Federation Standard *caffeine*. A similar technique is to not incorporate the word of one language into the other, but to simply use the foreign word itself, pronouncing it with greater or lesser accuracy, depending on the linguistic skill of the speaker. For instance, the **jInaq**, an amulet given to a Klingon girl to symbolize her coming of age, may be pronounced correctly or else "Federationized" to sound something like "gin knack," but there is no word *jinak* or the like in Federation Standard. A third approach is for one language to translate the item in question, such as Federation Standard *painstik*, which is a pretty exact translation of Klingon **'oy'naQ** (**'oy'**, "pain"; **naQ**, "cane, staff").

Often, when no exact equivalent is available, a near equivalent is used. For example, as noted earlier (see the chapter on Argot: Specialized Vocabulary, under the section on "Food," pages 83–103), the Klingon verb **vut** is conventionally translated "cook," but heat is seldom involved in the activity. Similarly, the Klingon words **jaj**,

jar, and **DIS** are normally translated as "day," "month," and "year," respectively, but the length of a Klingon day, month, or year is not the same as the Terran counterpart. Calculating the length of a Klingon day, month, or year is not at all a straightforward exercise, but suffice it to say that a period of five months is not the same amount of time as a period of **vagh jarmey** (**vagh,** "five"; **-mey,** plural indicator).

Even if cultural differences are not involved, or at least not involved in any obvious way, terms may be lacking in one language or the other. For example, in both Klingon and Federation Standard, there is a verb for "consume solid food" (*eat,* **Sop**) and another for "consume liquid" (*drink,* **tlhutlh**). In Klingon, but not in Federation Standard, there is a third verb in this set, **'ep**, which refers to consuming soup or, more accurately, to consuming Klingon **chatlh**, which contains less liquid than the typical Terran *soup*. (It should be noted that although the Federation Standard verb *slurp* may well apply to how a Klingon consumes **chatlh**, it is not an accurate translation of **'ep,** since it refers to eating and drinking noisily, not to the consumption of soup in particular.)

It is also quite common for a language to not make a terminological distinction in the same way the another does. Thus, Federation Standard uses the single word *day* to refer to both a period of 24 Earth hours (generally reckoned from midnight to midnight) and to that part of the 24-hour period which is light (*day* as opposed to *night*). In Klingon, there are two distinct terms: **jaj** is the period from dawn to dawn; **pem** is that part of a **jaj** which is light (as opposed to **ram** ["night"]). Although Federation Standard also makes use of the locutions *daytime* and *nighttime*, when a speaker of Federation Standard is counting periods of daytime, only *day* is used. Thus, *three days*, with no further context, is ambiguous, for it can refer to three 24-hour periods (as in "They wandered for three days") or three periods of daylight (as in "They wandered for three days and three nights"). In Klingon, **wej jajmey** (**wej,** "three"; **-mey,** plural indicator) means only three stretches from dawn to dawn; **wej pemmey** means "three periods of daylight" (as opposed to **wej rammey** ["three nights"]).

Finally, there are some words that simply do not translate. One must resort to descriptions rather than simple one- or two-word translations, and one must be a quite facile in the language and knowledgeable of the culture to understand the concepts. The Klingon notion of sharing of minds noted above, **tova'Daq,** is an example of such a word. So is **parmaq,** the Klingon term for an aggressive sort of romantic feeling. Sometimes seemingly ordinary concepts cannot be expressed easily. For example, the Klingon verb **mI'** may be translated "dance," but it also means "exercise, do calisthenics, do martial arts movements." The central idea of **mI'** is that a physical activity is performed that results in no change, other than, perhaps, in the well-being of the person performing the action. Thus, it is wrong to use **mI'** for "run to a place," though it is quite appropriate to use it for "run in place." No term in Federation Standard means quite the same thing as Klingon **mI'**. By the same token, no word in Klingon means quite the same thing as Federation Standard *dance*. At many Klingon festivals, a popular group of performers is called the **qul mI'wI'pu'**, usually translated as "fire dancers" (**qul,** "fire"; **mI'wI'**, "dancer, exerciser"; **-pu'**, plural indicator). Since what the performer is doing is properly designated by the verb **mI'** but not really accurately described by the translation *dance*, the visitor—particularly one who learned the Klingon word only by its usual Federation Standard translation—is in for quite a surprise when the show begins.

Robbie Robinson

ADDENDUM TO THE DICTIONARY

The following vocabulary lists are intended to supplement the original *Klingon Dictionary* published some years ago. They contain a number of words verified after the compilation of that book as well as words discussed and exemplified in earlier chapters of this volume. Though the Federation's knowledge of Klingon vocabulary is certainly increasing, it must be emphasized that there is still a great deal of information about Klingon that is not yet documented or well understood. Thus, the lists, even when joined with those in the *Dictionary*, must still be considered incomplete.

There are two parts to this dictionary addendum: one with words arranged alphabetically by Klingon, the other with words arranged alphabetically by Federation Standard. The abbreviations, notational conventions, and Klingon alphabetical ordering system used in the original *Dictionary* are retained here. Words regarded as slang are so marked, as are words found in certain regions but not used throughout the Empire. In some cases, words listed here are also in the original *Dictionary* to provide clarification or to illustrate a broader range of meanings than was originally known.

KLINGON–FEDERATION STANDARD

bachHa'	err, make a mistake (n) (slang)
baj	earn, (actively) work for (v)
bal	jug, jar, bottle (n)
bang bom	love song (n)
bang pong	pet name, endearment (n)
baq	terminate, discontinue (v)
baqghol	type of liquor, *bahgol* (n)
baQ	toss *bat'leth* from one hand to the other (v)
baQ	be fresh, be just picked (fruit, vegetable) (v)
bargh	flat-bottomed pot for food preparation (n)
batlhHa'	dishonorably (adv)
bej	be sure, be definite, be positive, be certain (v) (slang)
bem	sole of foot (n)
ben	years old (n)
beqpuj	type of mineral, *bekpuj* (orange in color) (n)
bey	howl, wail (n)
bey'	ceremonial display (n)
bIm	second tone of nonatonic musical scale (n)
bIQ bal	water jug (n)
bIQDep	fish (n)

bIraqlul	*brak'lul* (redundancy in body parts) (n)
bIreqtal	*Brek'tal* ritual (n)
bI'	sweep (away) (v)
bochmoHwI'	sycophant, flatterer (n) (slang)
boD	forehead (n) (regional)
bol	drool (v)
bolwI'	traitor (n) (slang)
bom	song, chant (n)
bom	sing, chant (v)
bom mu'	lyric, lyrics (n)
boq	bloc, coalition (n)
boq ru'	coalition (n)
boqrat	type of animal, *bokrat* (n)
bortaS DIb	Right of Vengeance (n)
botjan	shields (force field on ship) (n)
bo'Dagh	scoop, scooping implement (to serve food) (n)
burgh quD	naturally produced *kud* (n)
buSHa'	ignore (v)
buy'	be full, be filled up (v)
buy' ngop	good news, it's good to hear that (excl) (slang)
chab	invention, innovation (n) (slang)
chaDvay'	radio frequency (n)
chaj	close female friend of a female (n)
cham	technology (n)
chanDoq	marinade (n)
chaQ	thrust upward with end of *bat'leth* (v)
char	be slimy (v)
charghwI'	victor, conqueror (n)
chatlh	nonsense, balderdash (n) (slang)

chatlh	soup (thick) (n)
cha'nob	ritual gifts (n)
chechtlhutlh	type of liquor, *baceh'tluth* (n)
chej	liver (n)
chelwI'	accountant, financier (n) (slang)
chemvaH	type of animal, *chemvah* (n)
chenmoH	form, make, create (v)
chenmoHwI'	creator, maker (n)
cheSvel	coat, jacket (n) (regional)
cheSvel	type of coat (n)
chetvI'	spear-throwing device (n)
che'	preside (v)
che'ron	battlefield (n)
choghvat	stairway leading to door of a ship, gangplank (n)
chon	hunt (n)
chon bom	hunting song (n)
chonnaQ	hunting spear (n)
chontay	ritual hunt (n)
chong	be good, be excellent (v) (slang)
chong	be profound, be thorough, be careful (v) (slang)
choptaH	gnaw (v)
chor	ceramic flat-bottomed pot (n) (regional)
chor bargh	ceramic flat-bottomed pot (n) (regional)
chorgh	eighth tone of nonatonic musical scale (n)
chuH	explain clearly to, clarify for, specify for (v) (slang)
chuH	throw (a spear) at, hurl (a spear) at (v)
chu'	play (a musical instrument) (v)
chu'wI'	player (of an instrument) (n)

Dab	dwell in/at, reside in/at (v)
Dach	be not attentive, be distracted, lack focus (v) (slang)
Daghtuj	mixture of animal parts (n)
DaHjaj gheD	dish in a restaurant, "catch of the day" (n)
Dap bom	nonsense song (n)
Daqtagh	warrior's knife, *d'k tahg* (n)
Dargh HIvje'	teacup (n)
DarSeq	*darsek,* unit of currency (n)
DayquS	type of plant, dikus plant (n)
Degh	act without a plan, improvise (v) (slang)
DeH	be ripe, be overripe (fruit, vegetable) (v)
DeS	ax handle (n)
DeSqIv	elbow (n)
DevwI'	leader (n)
DIb	right, privilege (n)
DIghna'	type of plant (n)
DIj	slide sword blade along opponent's blade (v)
DIj	use a pigment stick, paint with pigment stick (v)
DIron	bagpipes (n)
Dov'agh	flute, fife (n)
Do'Ha'	unfortunately (adv)
DuDwI'	stirring stick (n)
Duj ngaDHa'	irresponsible person, undisciplined person (n) (slang)
Duq	bowl (small) (n)
DuQ	touch (emotionally) (v)
DuQwI'	spike (n)
Du' naH	produce (n)
ghab	meat from midsection of animal (n)

ghab tun	meat from midsection of animal, no bones (n) (regional)
gham	limb (of an animal) (n)
ghanjaq	mace (stick, club) (n)
ghaw'	insecure one, one full of self-doubt (n) (regional) (slang)
ghaw'	*igvah* liver soup (n)
gha'tlhIq	ode of respect (n)
gheD	prey (n)
ghel	ask (a question) (v)
gheS	assume duties of, take on responsibilities of (v)
ghevI'	sauce for *gagh* (n)
ghe'naQ	opera (n)
ghe'tor	Gre'thor (where spirits of dishonored go) (n)
ghIgh	assignment, task, duty (n) (slang)
ghIlab ghew	glob fly (n)
ghIntaq	battle spear, *Gin'tak* (n)
ghIqtal	to the death (excl) (archaic)
ghISDen	scales (animal covering) (n)
ghIt	ax blade (n)
ghIt	open, flat hand (n)
ghItlh	engrave, incise, mark (v)
gho	hoop (n)
ghob	fight, battle, do battle, wage war (v)
ghob	virtue (n)
ghom	band, group, party (n)
ghonDoq	type of knife (slender blade) (n)
ghoq	spy on (v)
ghoQ	be fresh, be just killed (meat) (v)
ghuS	lower (spear) to horizontal to attack (v)

HaH	soak, drench (v)
HaH	marinate (v)
HajDob	leg (served as food) (n)
Haq	intervene in (a situation) (v) (slang)
Haq	perform surgery (on) (v)
Hargh	fight, battle (major confrontation) (v)
Ha'DIbaH	dog, cur, inferior person (n) (slang)
Ha'quj	baldric, sash (n)
Heghbat	ritual suicide (n)
Heghtay	death ritual (n)
Heng	finger (holes, strings of instrument) to vary sound (v)
Hew	statue (n)
Hew chenmoHwI'	sculptor (n)
HIq	ale, beer, wine (n)
HIvDuj	attack fighter (vessel) (n)
HIvje' bom	drinking song (n)
HochHom	most, greater part (n)
HolQeD	linguistics (n)
Hom	weakling, runt, scrawny one, skinny one (n) (slang)
HovpoH	stardate (n)
Ho'	idol (n) (slang)
HuH	slime (n)
HurDagh	stringed instrument (general term) (n)
Hur'Iqngan	Hur'q (person) (n)
Hur'Iq	outsider, foreigner (n) (slang)
Hutlh	lack, be without, to not have (v)
Huy'Dung	forehead (n) (regional)

jabwI'	food server, waiter, waitress (n)
jaD	throw around, hurl about (v)
jan	musical instrument (n)
jargh	forehead (n) (regional)
jat	speak incoherently, mumble (v) (slang)
jatyIn	spiritual possession (n)
jav	sixth tone of nonatonic musical scale (n)
jav	prisoner (n) (slang)
jeD	be thick, be dense, be viscous (v)
jejHa'	be dull, be blunt (of blades) (v)
jengva'	plate (for eating) (n)
jeq	protrude from (v)
jeqqIj	club, bludgeon (n)
jey'naS	double-headed ax (n)
jIj	be cooperative (v)
jInaq	amulet symbolizing a girl's coming of age (n)
jIr	rotate, twirl (v)
jIrmoH	twirl *bat'leth*, cause *bat'leth* to rotate (v)
joH	Lady, female head of house (n); Lord, male head of house (n)
jom	install (a device) (v)
jonpIn	engineering officer (n)
jop	lunge, thrust (v)
joQ	strip of material in a *susdek* instrument (n)
joQ	rib (n)
jornub	warhead (of a torpedo) (n)
lajQo'	reject (v)
lat	shrine (n)
lav	shrub (n)

lay'Ha'	break one's word (v)
lem	hoof (n)
leSpal	type of stringed instrument (n)
letlh	stairs, stairway (n)
letlh	stairway leading to door of a ship (n) (regional)
lev	move *bat'leth* from vertical to horizontal orientation (v)
ley'	nose (n) (regional)
le'be'	be unexceptional, be nonspecific (v)
lIch	pour (into/onto anything) (v)
lIghon	Ligon (n)
lIghon DuQwI' pogh	glavin, Ligonian spike glove (n)
lIngta'	type of animal, *lingta* (n)
lIt	get on(to) (v)
lItHa'	get off (of) (v)
lIw	substitute, stand-in, temporary surrogate (n)
lop	celebration (n)
lop	observe, celebrate (a ritual) (v)
lopno'	party, celebration (n)
loS	fourth tone of nonatonic musical scale (n)
lu	fall (suffer loss of status) (v)
luH	intestine (n)
luH	cause (someone) to confess or reveal a secret (v) (slang)
luj	lose (not win) (v)
lul	fight, battle (relatively major fight) (v)
lung	type of animal, *loong* (lizardlike) (n)
lupwI'	jitney, bus (n)
luSpet	black hole (astronomical phenomenon) (n)

maHpIn	bowl (large) (n)
maqoch	buddy, pal, close male friend of a male (n)
matlhHa'	be disloyal (v)
mavje'	liver (n) (regional)
may' bom	battle song (n)
may'luch	battle gear, panoply, complete set of armor and weapons (n)
may'ron	accordion, concertina (n)
mebpa'mey	hotel (n)
melchoQ	marrow, bone marrow (n)
meq	motive (n)
meqleH	type of weapon, *mek'leth* (n)
meSchuS	large wind instrument (n)
mIl'oD	type of animal, sabre bear (n)
mIp	wealth, richness (n)
mIQ	deep-fry (v)
mIQ	forehead (n) (regional)
mIv	metal flat-bottomed pot (n) (regional)
mIv bargh	metal flat-bottomed pot (n) (regional)
mIv'a'	crown (n)
mIw	step, stage (in a process) (n)
mI'	dance, run in place, do calisthenics (v)
moH	exert undue influence on (v) (slang)
mon	smile, grin, sneer (v)
moq	beat (something with an implement) (v)
moQbara'	*Mok'bara* (martial arts form) (n)
motlh	usually, typically, as expected (adv)
mov	top of foot (n)
mo'	motive, motivation, grounds, reason, rationale (n) (slang)

much	perform (music) (v)
muchwI'	musician (n)
muD	weather (in general) (n)
muD Dotlh	weather (at any given moment) (n)
mum	taste, sense flavors (v)
mupwI'	hammer (n)
mupwI'Hom	mallet (for striking a musical instrument) (n)
muq	have a volume of (v)
mu'mey qhoQ	slang
mu'qaD	curse (n)
naD tetlh	Commendation List
nagh beQ	stone panel (artwork, similar to a painting) (n)
nagh DIr	shell (of an animal) (n)
nagh	ceramic material (n)
naghboch	gemstone (n)
naH taj	vegetable knife, fruit knife (small knife) (n)
naHlet	nut, nuts (n)
najmoHwI'	lullaby (n)
nalqaD	mate challenge (n)
namwech	paw (n)
nan	gouge (v)
nanwI'	chisel (n)
naQ	ponytail (n) (slang)
naQHom	stick (used to strike percussion instrument) (n)
naQjej	spear (n)
natlh	use up, consume, expend (v)
natlh	be reprehensible, be disgusting, be contemptible (v) (slang)
na'	be salty, be brackish (v)

na'	be sure, be definite, be positive, be certain (v) (slang)
na'ran	type of fruit (n)
neHjej	thistle (n)
nen	be mature, be grown-up, be adult (v)
nen	growth, maturation (n)
nenchoH	mature, grow up (v)
nevDagh	type of pot with handles (used for food preparation) (n)
nIbpoH	déjà vu (n)
nIm	milk (n)
nISwI'	disruptor (n)
nISwI' beH	disruptor rifle (n)
nISwI' HIch	disruptor pistol, hand-held disruptor (n)
nIt	be plain, be pure, be uncorrupted, be unsullied (v)
nItlh naQ	pigment stick (n) (slang)
nItlhpach	flat end of a pigment stick (n)
nobHa'	give back, return (v)
noH	war (an individual war) (n)
norgh	type of animal, *norg* (sharklike sea creature) (n)
noS	eat in small mouthfuls, nibble (v)
nov	alien, outsider, foreigner (n)
no' DIr	ancestor hanging (wall ornament) (n)
no' Hol	ancient language (n)
no"och	forehead (n) (regional)
nugh	society; group of people with shared culture (n)
nughI'	twist knuckle into someone's head (v)
nuH	possibility (n)
nuHpIn	weapons officer (n)
ngaD	be stable, be balanced (v)

ngaDmoH	stabilize (v)
ngaDmoHwI'	stabilizer (component of a ship) (n)
ngagh	mate with (v)
ngaj	be short (in duration) (v)
ngal	be chewy (v)
ngaQ	be locked, be sealed, be secured, be fastened (v)
ngat	herbed granulated cartilage (for food preparation) (n)
ngawDeq	mixing stick with flattened, paddlelike end (n)
ngep'oS	stairs, stairway (except at ship door) (n) (regional)
ngeQ	bump into, run into, collide with (v)
ngIb	ankle (also a slang term of deprecation) (n)
ngI'	have a weight of, weigh (v)
ngoH	paint using fingers (v)
ngol	move *bat'leth* from horizontal to vertical orientation (v)
ngop	plates (for eating) (v)
ngoQ	purpose (n)
ngujlep	mouthpiece (of a wind instrument) (n)
ngup	authority, power, one in authority or in charge (n) (slang)
nguv	be dyed, be stained, be tinted (v)
nguvmoH	dye, stain, tint (v)
pagh	no one (n)
pang	pluck (a stringed instrument) (v)
parmaq	love, romance (n)
parmaqqay	romantic companion, romantic partner (n)
paS	be late (v)

patlh	level, layer, standing (n)
paw'	butt heads (v) (slang)
pa'	enclosed area (n)
peb'ot	type of fruit (n)
pel'aQ	shell (of an egg) (n)
per yuD	code name (n)
pe'meH taj	cutting knife (n)
pe"egh	keep score (v)
pID	coat (food) with herbed mixture (v)
pIj	frequently (adv)
pIjHa'	seldom, infrequently (adv)
pIl	be stimulated, be inspired, be motivated (v)
pIlmoH	stimulate, inspire, motivate (v)
pIn	expert, authority (n) (slang)
polHa'	discard (v)
por	leaf (of a plant) (n)
puq poH	generation (n)
qaD	resist, oppose, confront, face (v)
qaD	test of one's abilities (n)
qajunpaQ	courage, audacity (n)
qang	always agree with, always cooperate with (v) (slang)
qang	pour (from one container into another) (v)
qarDaS	Cardassia (n)
qarDaSngan	Cardassian (person) (n)
qat	accompany (singing) with instrumental music (v)
qat	encase (v)
qa'	spirit (n)
qa'meH	replacement (permanent) (n)

qa'vaQ	*qa'vak* (traditional game) (n)
qa'vIn	coffee (n)
qeb	squeeze (windbag instrument) (v)
qegh	vat, barrel (for storage of liquor) (n)
qettlhup	type of sauce (n)
qevpob	jowl, cheek (n)
qeylIS betleH	Sword of Kahless (n)
qID	joke (n)
qID	joke, make a joke, tell a joke (v)
qItI'nga'	*K'Tinga* class (vessel) (n)
qIvon	body part (not further identified) (n)
qIvo'rIt	*K'Vort* class (vessel) (n)
qoD	inside, interior (n)
qogh	ear (external, cartilaginous flap) (n)
qompogh	type of food (n)
qon	compose (v)
qotlh	deserve, warrant (v)
quD	type of sauce (n)
quH	heritage (n)
qul mI'wI'	fire dancer (n)
qurgh	bean, beans (n)
qutlh	be cheap (v)
quvHa'	be dishonored (v)
quvHa'ghach	dishonor (n)
qu'	be great, be wonderful, be excellent, be splendid (v) (slang)
Qach	wield or swing (a weapon) (v)
QaD	be safe, be protected (v) (slang)
QaD	be dried out (v)

Qaj	type of animal, *kradge* (n)
Qaj tlhuQ	type of food, *kradge* tail (n)
Qap	win (v)
Qap	operate, be in operation (v)
Qatlh	be complex (v)
Qa'Hom	type of animal (similar to a *Qa'*, but smaller) (n)
Qa'raj	type of animal (n)
Qeb	ponytail holder (n) (slang)
Qenvob	ground-up, dried-up mixture for brewing tea (n)
Qeq	aim (v)
Qev	stew (v)
QIH	wrong, treat unjustly (v)
QIm	egg (n)
QIn	message (n)
QIn	spearhead (n)
QIS	wavy-bladed knife (n)
QoghIj	brain (organ) (n)
Qoj	make war (v)
Qom	be hazardous, be perilous, be treacherous (v) (slang)
QongDaq	bed (n)
Qop	be worn out (v)
Qop	be dead (referring to food) (v) (slang)
QoQ	music (n)
Qor	fight, battle (very minor fight) (v)
Qorwagh	window (n)
ragh	rust, corrode (v)
raHta'	type of food, *racht* (n)
ram	be insignificant (v)

raQ	manipulate by hand, handle (v)
raS	table (n)
ra'taj	coffee with liquor (n)
regh	bleed (v)
ret'aq	handle, hilt (of knife, *bat'leth*) (n)
rey	squeeze and stretch out (windbag instrument) (v)
rItlh	pigment, paint, dye (n)
rItlh naQ	pigment stick (n)
roD	customarily, habitually, regularly (adv)
rogh	ferment (v)
roghmoH	cause to ferment (v)
roS	lick (v)
roSHa'moH	paralyze (v)
run	be short (in stature) (v)
runpI'	teapot (n)
rut	occasionally (adv)
ru'Ha'	be permanent (v)
Sargh	*sark* (n)
SaS	be shallow, be superficial, be uncritical (v) (slang)
SaS	be unfortunate, be not good (v) (slang)
Saw'	have a depth of (v)
Sech	torch (n)
SeDveq	barbed spearhead (n)
Separ	type of gemstone (n)
SeQ	be formal, be ritualistic, be ceremonial (v)
SIj	be insightful, be clever (v) (slang)
SIjwI'	type of knife (used for food preparation) (n)
SIQwI'	celebrant, recipient (n)

SIrgh	string, thread, filament (n)
Soch	seventh tone of nonatonic musical scale (n)
Soj qub	haute cuisine (n)
SopwI'pa'	mess hall (n)
Sor Hap	wood (n)
Sorya'	Sauria (n)
Sub	be brave, be heroic, be bold, be valiant, be intrepid (v) (slang)
Sub	hero (n)
Sum	be near, be nearby (v)
Supghew	type of stringed instrument (n)
Suqqa'	prepare *kud* in a specific way (v)
SuS	blow (into wind instrument) to produce sound (v)
SuSDeq	windbag, bellows (n)
Suy'	type of animal, *shooy* (n)
Su'lop	type of food (n)
taH	survive (v)
tajtIq	type of knife (n)
talarngan	Talarian (person) (n)
tap	mash, squash (v)
ta'	deed, accomplishment (n)
ta' Hol	standard dialect (n)
tebwI'	food server in a *Dok'e* (fast-food restaurant) (n)
teghbat	type of animal, *teg'bat* (n)
teS	ear (internal, organ of hearing) (n)
tetlh	roll, scroll, list (n)
tey	scrape (v)
teywI'	file (n)
tIH	shaft (of spear) (n)

tIngDagh	type of stringed instrument (n)
tIqnagh	type of animal, *tknag* (n)
tI'qa' vIghro'	type of animal, *tika* cat (n)
toj	bluff (v)
tonSaw'	fighting technique (n)
toppa'	type of animal, *topah* (n)
toqvIr lung	type of animal, Tokvarian skink (n)
tova'Daq	mind sharing (n)
to'baj	type of animal, *tobbaj* (n)
to'waQ	ligament, tendon (n)
tuq	tribe, house, ancestral unit (n)
tuq Degh	family crest (n)
tuqvol	forehead (n) (regional)
tu'HomI'raH	something useless (n)
tu'lum	teacup (n) (older or upper-class word)
tlhach	sect, faction (n)
tlhagh	fat, animal fat (n)
tlham	order, structure (societal) (n) (slang)
tlhaS	fight, battle (relatively minor fight) (v)
tlhatlh	type of food, *gladst* (n)
tlhaw'	hit (percussion instrument) with fist (v)
tlhay	sleeve (n)
tlher	be lumpy (v)
tlhevjaQ	type of spear (thrown with aid of a special tool) (n)
tlhImqaH	type of food, *zilm'kach* (n)
tlhIq	stew (n)
tlhIS	spit out (v)
tlhombuS	type of food (n)

tlhop	front, area in front of (n)
tlhorgh	be pungent (referring to food) (v)
tlhorghHa'	be bland (referring to food) (v)
tlhoS	almost, nearly, virtually, not quite (adv)
tlhuD	emit (energy, radiation, etc.) (v)
tlhuH	be exhilarated, be stimulated, be invigorated (v) (slang)
tlhuQ	tail (n)
vagh	fifth tone of nonatonic musical scale (n)
vaH	sheath, knife case (n)
vaHbo'	lava (n)
van bom	anthem, hymn (n)
vaQ	be effective, be vigorous (v)
vatlh DIS poH	century (n)
vay	fight, battle (midlevel ferocity) (v)
veb	be next (in a series, sequence) (v)
veD	fur (n)
veDDIr	pelt (skin with fur still attached) (n)
veragh	rivet (n)
veS	war, warfare (n)
vIghro'	type of animal, *v'gro* (like a cat) (n)
vIttlhegh	proverb (n)
vIychorgh	juice, sap of a plant (n)
vI'	decimal point (n)
von	trap, entrap (v)
vonlu'	fail utterly (v) (slang)
voQSIp	nitrogen (n)
vutmeH 'un	flat-bottomed pot for food preparation (n) (regional)
vut'un	flat-bottomed pot for food preparation (n) (regional)

wagh	be expensive (v)
waH	taste, try out (food) (v)
waH	try out, test, use experimentally (v)
wamwI'	hunter (n)
warjun	type of knife (used for food preparation) (n)
way'	parry, deflect a lunge (v)
wech	serve fermented food at its peak (v)
wep	shirt with sleeves (n) (regional)
weq	hit (percussion instrument) with palm (v)
wey	company (military unit) (n)
wIb	be bitter, be tart (v)
wItlh	break (something) off (v)
wob	hurl a spear by means of a *chetvi* (v)
woj	sterilize (v)
wornagh	*warnog,* Klingon ale (n)
wup	burst into song (v)
yach	strum (a stringed instrument) (v)
yaD	sword (n) (slang)
yan	sword (n)
yan	use or manipulate a sword (v)
yatlh	be pregnant (v)
yeb	wrist (also a slang term of deprecation) (n)
yejHaD	institute, institution (n)
yej'an	society (e.g., scholarly society) (n)
yInSIp	oxygen (n)
yIrIDngan	Yiridian (person) (n)
yIv	annoy, bother, irk, irritate (v) (slang)
yIvbeH	sleeveless shirt (n) (regional)
yoHwI'	brave one (n)

yu	first (and last) tone of nonatonic musical scale (n)
yub	husk, rind, peel, shell (of fruit, nut) (n)
'aD	have a length of, measure (v)
'agh	show, demonstrate, display (v)
'alngegh	ax with spike at end (n)
'ampaS	academy (n)
'aqleH	type of weapon (half ax, half *bat'leth*) (n)
'aqnaw	type of knife (general purpose) (n)
'aQlo'	forehead (n) (regional)
'atlhqam	type of fungus (n)
'awje'	type of beverage (root beer) (n)
'ay'	part, component, piece (n)
'eb	chance, opening (n)
'egh	third tone of nonatonic musical scale (n)
'elpI'	serving platter (n)
'em	behind, area behind (n)
'ep	consume soup (v)
'eq	be early (v)
'eS	be low (v)
'etlh	blade (n)
'ey	be good, be delicious, be tasty, be harmonious (v)
'Ib	tub (n)
'Igh	be cursed, be jinxed (v) (slang)
'IghvaH	type of animal, *igvah* (n)
'Im	render, boil fat (v)
'In	percussion instrument (drum, bell) (n)
'Iwghargh	bloodworm (n)
'I'	armpit (n)

'obe'	order, group officially recognized by government (n)
'obmaQ	ax (n)
'oDwI'	arbitrator (n)
'om	resist, fend off (v)
'op	some, an unknown or unspecified quantity (n)
'oQqar	root, tuber (n)
'o'lav	type of drum (n)
'uch	hold, grasp (v)
'uD	laser (n)
'uj	*uj* (unit of linear measure, about 35 centimeters) (n)
'ul	electricity (n)
'un	pot (for food preparation) (general term) (n)
'un naQ	stirring stick, mixing stick (n)
'un quD	artificially produced *qud* (n)
'up	be unsavory, be disgusting, be repugnant, be loathsome, be icky (v)
'uQ'a'	banquet, feast (n)
'uSu'	sauce for *gladst* (n)

FEDERATION
STANDARD–KLINGON

academy (n)	'ampaS
accompany (singing) with instrumental music (v)	qat
accomplishment, deed (n)	ta'
accordion, concertina (n)	may'ron
accountant, financier (n) (slang)	chelwI'
act without a plan, improvise (v) (slang)	Degh
[be] adult, be mature, be grown-up (v)	nen
agree with routinely, always cooperate with (v) (slang)	qang
aim (v)	Qeq
ale, beer, wine (n)	HIq
ale: Klingon ale, *warnog*	wornagh
alien, foreigner, outsider (n)	nov
almost, nearly, virtually, not quite (adv)	tlhoS
amulet symbolizing a girl's coming of age (n)	jInaq
ancestor hanging (wall ornament) (n)	no' DIr
ancestral unit, tribe, house (n)	tuq
ancient language (n)	no' Hol
animal parts mixed together (n)	Daghtuj

animal: types of animals	boqrat, chemvaH, lIngta', lung, mIl'oD, norgh, Qaj, Qa'Hom, Qa'raj, Sargh, Suy', teghbat, tIqnagh, tI'qa' vIghro', toppa', toqvIr lung, to'baj, vIghro', 'IghvaH, 'Iwghargh
ankle (also used as slang term of deprecation) (n)	ngIb
annoy, bother, irk, irritate (v) (slang)	yIv
anthem, hymn (n)	van bom
arbitrator (n)	'oDwI'
armor and weapons, complete set (n)	may'luch
armpit (n)	'I'
artificially produced *qud* (n)	'un quD
ask (a question) (v)	ghel
assignment, task, duty (n) (slang)	ghIgh
assume duties of, take on responsibilities of (v)	gheS
attack fighter (vessel) (n)	HIvDuj
audacity, courage (n)	qajunpaQ
authority, power, one in authority or in charge (n) (slang)	ngup
authority, expert (n) (slang)	pIn
ax (n)	'obmaQ
ax blade (n)	ghIt
ax handle (n)	DeS
ax with double head (n)	jey'naS
ax with spike at end (n)	'alngegh

bagpipes (n)	**DIron**
bahgol (type of liquor) (n)	**baqghol**
[be] balanced, be stable (v)	**ngaD**
balderdash, nonsense (n) (slang)	**chatlh**
baldric, sash (n)	**Ha'quj**
band, group, party (n)	**ghom**
banquet, feast (n)	**'uQ'a'**
barrel, vat (for storage of liquor) (n)	**qegh**
battle, do battle, fight, wage war (v)	**ghob**
battle gear, complete set of armor and weapons (n)	**may'luch**
battle, fight (minor fight) (v)	**Qor**
battle, fight (major confrontation) (v)	**Hargh**
battle, fight (relatively major fight) (v)	**lul**
battle, fight (midlevel ferocity) (v)	**vay**
battle, fight (relatively minor fight) (v)	**tlhaS**
battle song (n)	**may' bom**
battle spear, *gin'tak* (n)	**ghIntaq**
battlefield (n)	**che'ron**
bean, beans (n)	**qurgh**
beat (something with an implement) (v)	**moq**
bed (n)	**QongDaq**
beer, ale, wine (n)	**HIq**
behind, area behind (n)	**'em**
bekpuj (type of mineral, orange in color) (n)	**beqpuj**
bellows, windbag (n)	**SuSDeq**
beverage: type of beverage (root beer) (n)	**'awje'**
beverage: type of beverage (coffee) (n)	**qa'vIn**
beverage: type of beverage (coffee with liquor) (n)	**ra'taj**

[be] bitter, be tart (v)	wIb
black hole (astronomical phenomenon) (n)	luSpet
blade (n)	'etlh
blade of ax (n)	ghIt
[be] bland (referring to food) (v)	tlhorghHa'
bleed (v)	regh
bloc, coalition (n)	boq
bloodworm (n)	'Iwghargh
blow (into wind instrument) to produce sound (v)	SuS
bludgeon, club (n)	jeqqIj
bluff (v)	toj
[be] blunt, be dull (of blades) (v)	jejHa'
body part (not further identified) (n)	qIvon
boil fat, render (v)	'Im
bokrat (type of animal) (n)	boqrat
[be] bold, be brave, be heroic, be intrepid (v) (slang)	Sub
bone marrow (n)	melchoQ
bother, irk, irritate, annoy (v) (slang)	yIv
bottle, jug, jar (n)	bal
bowl (large) (n)	maHpIn
bowl (small) (n)	Duq
[be] brackish, be salty (v)	na'
brain (organ) (n)	QoghIj
brak'lul (redundancy in body parts) (n)	bIraqlul
[be] brave, be heroic, be bold, be intrepid (v) (slang)	Sub
brave one (n)	yoHwI'
break (something) off (v)	wItlh
break one's word (v)	lay'Ha'

Brek'tal ritual (n)	bIreqtal
buddy, pal, close male friend of a male (n)	maqoch
bump into, run into, collide with (v)	ngeQ
burst into song (v)	wup
bus, jitney (n)	lupwI'
butt heads (v) (slang)	paw'
[do] calisthenics, run in place, dance (v)	mI'
Cardassia (n)	qarDaS
Cardassian (person) (n)	qarDaSngan
cartilage, herbed granulated cartilage (for food preparation) (n)	ngat
cause to ferment (v)	roghmoH
cause (someone) to confess or reveal a secret (v) (slang)	luH
celebrant, recipient (n)	SIQwI'
celebrate, observe (a ritual) (v)	lop
celebration (n)	lop, lopno'
century (n)	vatlh DIS poH
ceramic material (n)	nagh
ceremonial display (n)	bey'
[be] ceremonial, be formal, be ritualistic (v)	SeQ
[be] certain, be sure, be positive, be definite (v) (slang)	bej, na'
chance, opening (n)	'eb
chant, sing (v)	bom
chant, song (n)	bom
[be] cheap (v)	qutlh
chech'tluth (type of liquor) (n)	chechtlhutlh
cheek, jowl (n)	qevpob
[be] chewy (v)	ngal

chisel (n)	nanwI'
clarify for, specify for, explain clearly to (v) (slang)	chuH
[be] clever, be insightful (v) (slang)	SIj
close female friend of a female (n)	chaj
close male friend of a male (n)	maqoch
club, bludgeon (n)	jeqqIj
coalition (n)	boq ru'
coalition, bloc (n)	boq
coat, type of coat (n)	cheSvel
coat (food) with herbed mixture (v)	pID
coat, jacket (general term) (n) (regional)	cheSvel
code name (n)	per yuD
coffee (n)	qa'vIn
coffee with liquor (n)	ra'taj
collide with, bump into, run into (v)	ngeQ
Commendation List	naD tetlh
company (military unit) (n)	wey
[be] complex (v)	Qatlh
component, piece, part (n)	'ay'
compose (v)	qon
concertina, accordion (n)	may'ron
confront, resist, oppose, face (v)	qaD
conqueror, victor (n)	charghwI'
consume soup (v)	'ep
consume, use up, expend (v)	natlh
[be] contemptible, be disgusting, be reprehensible (v) (slang)	natlh
cooperate with routinely, always agree with (v) (slang)	qang
[be] cooperative (v)	jIj

corrode, rust (v)	ragh
courage, audacity (n)	qajunpaQ
create, make, form (v)	chenmoH
creator, maker (n)	chenmoHwI'
crest, family crest (n)	tuq Degh
crown (n)	mIv'a'
cur, dog, inferior person (n) (slang)	Ha'DIbaH
currency: unit of currency, *darsek* (n)	DarSeq
curse (n)	mu'qaD
be cursed, be jinxed (v) (slang)	'Igh
customarily, habitually, regularly (adv)	roD
d'k tahg, warrior's knife (n)	Daqtagh
dance, run in place, do calisthenics, exercise (v)	mI'
darsek, unit of currency (n)	DarSeq
[be] dead (referring to food) (v) (slang)	Qop
death ritual (n)	Heghtay
decimal point (n)	vI'
deed, accomplishment (n)	ta'
deep-fry (v)	mIQ
[be] definite, be sure, be positive, be certain (v) (slang)	bej, na'
deflect a lunge, parry (v)	way'
déjà vu (n)	nIbpoH
[be] delicious, be good, be tasty, be harmonious (v)	'ey
demonstrate, show, display (v)	'agh
[be] dense, be thick, be viscous (v)	jeD
[have a] depth of (v)	Saw'
deserve, warrant (v)	qotlh
dikus plant (n)	DayquS

discard (v)	polHa'
discontinue, terminate (v)	baq
[be] disgusting, be contemptible, be reprehensible (v) (slang)	natlh
[be] disgusting, be unsavory, be repugnant, be loathsome, be icky (v)	'up
dish in a restaurant, "catch of the day" (n)	DaHjaj gheD
dishonor (n)	quvHa'ghach
dishonorably (adv)	batlhHa'
[be] dishonored (v)	quvHa'
[be] disloyal (v)	matlhHa'
display, show, demonstrate (v)	'agh
disruptor (n)	nISwI'
disruptor pistol, hand-held disruptor (n)	nISwI' HIch
disruptor rifle (n)	nISwI' beH
[be] distracted, lack focus (v) (slang)	Dach
dog, cur, inferior person (n) (slang)	Ha'DIbaH
drench, soak (v)	HaH
[be] dried out (v)	QaD
drinking song (n)	HIvje' bom
drool (v)	bol
drum, type of drum (n)	'o'lav
[be] dull, be blunt (of blades) (v)	jejHa'
duty, assignment, task (n) (slang)	ghIgh
dwell in/at, reside in/at (v)	Dab
dye, stain, tint (v)	nguvmoH
dye, pigment, paint (n)	rItlh
[be] dyed, be stained, be tinted (v)	nguv
ear (external, cartilaginous flap) (n)	qogh
ear (internal, organ of hearing) (n)	teS

[be] early (v)	'eq
earn, (actively) work for (v)	baj
eat in small mouthfuls, nibble (v)	noS
[be] effective, be vigorous (v)	vaQ
egg (n)	QIm
elbow (n)	DeSqIv
electricity (n)	'ul
emit (energy, radiation, etc.) (v)	tlhuD
encase (v)	qat
enclosed area (n)	pa'
end of a pigment stick (flattened) (n)	nItlhpach
endearment, pet name (n)	bang pong
engineering officer (n)	jonpIn
engrave, incise (v)	ghItlh
entrap, trap (v)	von
err, make a mistake (v) (slang)	bachHa'
exact a confession, cause (someone) to confess (v) (slang)	luH
[be] excellent, be good (v) (slang)	chong, qu'
exercise, dance, do calisthenics, run in place (v)	mI'
exert undue influence on (v) (slang)	moH
[be] exhilarated, be stimulated, be invigorated (v) (slang)	tlhuH
expectedly, typically, usually	motlh
expend, consume, use up (v)	natlh
[be] expensive (v)	wagh
expert, authority (n) (slang)	pIn
explain clearly to, clarify for, specify for (v) (slang)	chuH
face, confront, oppose, resist (v)	qaD
faction, sect (n)	tlhach

fail utterly (v) (slang)	vonlu'
fall (suffer loss of status) (v)	lu
family crest (n)	tuq Degh
[be] fastened, be locked, be secured, be sealed (v)	ngaQ
fat, animal fat (n)	tlhagh
feast, banquet (n)	'uQ'a'
fend off, resist (v)	'om
ferment (v)	rogh
fife, flute (n)	Dov'agh
fight, battle, do batle, wage war (v)	ghob
fight, battle (v) (midlevel ferocity)	vay
fight, battle (v) (minor fight)	Qor
fight, battle (v) (relatively minor fight)	tlhaS
fight, battle (v) (major confrontation)	Hargh
fight, battle (v) (relatively major fight)	lul
fighting technique (n)	tonSaw'
filament, string, thread (n)	SIrgh
file (n)	teywI'
[be] filled up, be full (v)	buy'
financier, accountant (n) (slang)	chelwI'
finger (holes, strings of instrument) to vary sound (v)	Heng
fire dancer (n)	qul mI'wI'
fish (n)	bIQDep
flatterer, sycophant (n) (slang)	bochmoHwI'
flute, fife (n)	Dov'agh
food server in a *Dok'e* restaurant (n)	tebwI'
food server, waiter, waitress (n)	jabwI'
food: type of food, *gladst* (n)	tlhatlh

food: type of food, *kradge* tail (n)	Qaj tlhuQ
food: type of food, *racht* (n)	raHta'
food: type of food, *zilm'kach* (n)	tlhImqaH
food: types of food (n)	qompogh, Su'lop, tlhombuS
forehead (n) (regional terms)	boD, Huy'Dung, jargh, mIQ, no"och, tuqvol, 'aQlo'
foreigner, alien, outsider (n)	nov
foreigner, outsider (n) (slang)	Hur'Iq
form, make, create (v)	chenmoH
[be] formal, be ritualistic, be ceremonial (v)	SeQ
frequency, radio frequency (n)	chaDvay'
frequently (adv)	pIj
[be] fresh, be just killed (meat) (v)	ghoQ
[be] fresh, be just picked (fruit, vegetable) (v)	baQ
friend, close female friend of a female (n)	chaj
friend, close male friend of a male (n)	maqoch
front, area in front of (n)	tlhop
fruit knife, vegetable knife (small knife) (n)	naH taj
fruit: types of fruit (n)	na'ran, peb'ot
fry, deep-fry (v)	mIQ
[be] full, be filled up (v)	buy'
fungus: type of fungus (n)	'atlhqam
fur (n)	veD
game: *qa'vak* (n)	qa'vaQ
gemstone (n)	naghboch
gemstone: type of gemstone (n)	Separ

generation (n)	puq poH
get on(to) (v)	lIt
get off (of) (v)	lItHa'
gifts, ritual gifts (n)	cha'nob
Gin'tak, battle spear (n)	ghIntaq
give back, return (v)	nobHa'
gladst (type of food) (n)	tlhatlh
glavin, Ligonian spike glove (n)	lIghon DuQwI' pogh
glob fly (n)	ghIlab ghew
gnaw (v)	choptaH
[be] good, be delicious, be tasty, be harmonious (v)	'ey
[be] good, be excellent (v) (slang)	chong, qu'
good news, good to hear that (excl) (slang)	buy' ngop
gouge (v)	nan
grasp, hold (v)	'uch
Gre'thor (where spirits of dishonored go) (n)	ghe'tor
[be] great, be wonderful, be excellent (v) (slang)	chong, qu'
grin, sneer, smile (v)	mon
grounds, motive, motivation, reason, rationale (n) (slang)	mo'
grow up (v)	nenchoH
[be] grown-up, be mature, be adult (v)	nen
growth, maturation (n)	nen
habitually, customarily, regularly (adv)	roD
hammer (n)	mupwI'
handle, hilt (of knife, *bat'leth*) (n)	ret'aq
handle, ax handle (n)	DeS

handle, manipulate by hand (v)	raQ
[be] harmonious, be good, be delicious (v)	'ey
haute cuisine (n)	Soj qub
have a depth of (v)	Saw'
have a length of, measure (v)	'aD
have a volume of (v)	muq
have a weight of, weigh (v)	ngI'
[be] hazardous, be perilous, be treacherous (v) (slang)	Qom
heritage (n)	quH
hero (n)	Sub
[be] heroic, be brave, be bold, be intrepid (v) (slang)	Sub
hilt, handle (of knife, *bat'leth*) (n)	ret'aq
hit (percussion instrument) with fist (v)	tlhaw'
hit (percussion instrument) with palm (v)	weq
hold, grasp (v)	'uch
hoof (n)	lem
hoop (n)	gho
hotel (n)	mebpa'mey
house, tribe, ancestral unit (n)	tuq
howl, wail (n)	bey
hunt (n)	chon
hunt, ritual hunt (n)	chontay
hunter (n)	wamwI'
hunting song (n)	chon bom
hunting spear (n)	chonnaQ
Hur'q (person) (n)	Hur'Iqngan
hurl a spear by means of a *chetvi* (v)	wob
hurl about, throw around (v)	jaD

hurl (a spear) at, throw (a spear) at (v)	chuH
husk, rind, peel, shell (of fruit, nut) (n)	yub
hymn, anthem (n)	van bom
idol (n) (slang)	Ho'
ignore (v)	buSHa'
igvah (type of animal) (n)	'IghvaH
igvah liver soup (n)	ghaw'
improvise, act without a plan (v) (slang)	Degh
incise, engrave (v)	ghItlh
inferior person, dog, cur (n) (slang)	Ha'DIbaH
influence, exert undue influence on (v) (slang)	moH
infrequently, seldom (adv)	pIjHa'
innovation, invention (n) (slang)	chab
insecure one, one full of self-doubt (n) (regional) (slang)	ghaw'
inside, interior (n)	qoD
[be] insightful, be clever (v) (slang)	SIj
[be] insignificant (v)	ram
inspire, stimulate, motivate (v)	pIlmoH
[be] inspired, be stimulated, be motivated (v)	pIl
install (a device) (v)	jom
institute, institution (n)	yejHaD
instrument, musical instrument (n)	jan
instrument: large wind instrument (n)	meSchuS
instrument: percussion instrument (drum, bell) (n)	'In
instrument: stringed instrument (general term) (n)	HurDagh
instrument: types of stringed instruments (n)	leSpal, Supghew, tIngDagh

interior, inside (n)	qoD
intervene in (a situation) (v) (slang)	Haq
intestine (n)	luH
[be] intrepid, be brave, be heroic, be bold (v) (slang)	Sub
invention, innovation (n) (slang)	chab
[be] invigorated, be exhilarated, be stimulated (v) (slang)	tlhuH
irk, annoy, bother, irritate (v) (slang)	yIv
irresponsible person, undisciplined person (n) (slang)	Duj ngaDHa'
irritate, irk, annoy, bother (v) (slang)	yIv
jar, jug, bottle (n)	bal
[be] jinxed, be cursed (v) (slang)	'Igh
jitney, bus (n)	lupwI'
joke (n)	qID
joke, make a joke, tell a joke (v)	qID
jowl, cheek (n)	qevpob
jug, jar, bottle (n)	bal
juice, sap of a plant (n)	vIychorgh
K'Tinga class (vessel) (n)	qItI'nga'
K'Vort class (vessel) (n)	qIvo'rIt
ka'raj (type of animal) (n)	Qa'raj
knife case, sheath (n)	vaH
knife: cutting knife (n)	pe'meH taj
knife: type of knife (n)	tajtIq
knife: type of knife (general purpose) (n)	'aqnaw
knife: type of knife (slender blade) (n)	ghonDoq
knife: types of knives (used for food preparation) (n)	SIjwI', warjun

knife: vegetable knife, fruit knife (n)	**naH taj**
knife: warrior's knife, *d'k tahg* (n)	**Daqtagh**
knife: wavy-bladed knife (n)	**QIS**
kradge (type of animal) (n)	**Qaj**
lack focus, to not pay attention, be distracted (v) (slang)	**Dach**
lack, be without, to not have (v)	**Hutlh**
Lady, female head of house (n)	**joH**
laser (n)	**'uD**
late, be late (v)	**paS**
lava (n)	**vaHbo'**
layer, level, standing (n)	**patlh**
leader (n)	**DevwI'**
leaf (of a plant) (n)	**por**
leg (served as food) (n)	**HajDob**
[have a] length of (v)	**'aD**
level, layer, standing (n)	**patlh**
lick (v)	**roS**
ligament, tendon (n)	**to'waQ**
Ligon (n)	**lIghon**
Ligonian spike glove, glavin	**lIghon DuQwI' pogh**
limb (of an animal) (n)	**gham**
lingta (type of animal) (n)	**lIngta'**
linguistics (n)	**HolQeD**
liquor: type of liquor, *bahgol* (n)	**baqghol**
liquor: type of liquor, *chech'tluth* (n)	**chechtlhutlh**
list, roll, scroll (n)	**tetlh**
liver (n)	**chej**
liver (n) (regional)	**mavje'**

loathsome, be loathsome, unsavory, disgusting (v)   **'up**

[be] locked, be sealed, be secured, be fastened (v)   **ngaQ**

Lord, male head of house (n)   **joH**

lose (not win) (v)   **luj**

love, romance (n)   **parmaq**

love song (n)   **bang bom**

[be] low (v)   **'eS**

lower (spear) to horizontal to attack (v)   **ghuS**

lullaby (n)   **najmoHwI'**

[be] lumpy (v)   **tlher**

lunge, thrust (v)   **jop**

lyric, lyrics (n)   **bom mu'**

mace (stick, club) (n)   **ghanjaq**

make, create, form (v)   **chenmoH**

maker, creator (n)   **chenmoHwI'**

mallet (for striking a musical instrument) (n)   **mupwI'Hom**

manipulate by hand, handle (v)   **raQ**

manipulate or use a sword (v)   **yan**

marinade (n)   **chanDoq**

marinate (v)   **HaH**

mark (v)   **ghItlh**

marrow, bone marrow (n)   **melchoQ**

martial arts form, *Mok'bara* (n)   **moQbara'**

mash, squash (v)   **tap**

mate with (v)   **ngagh**

mate challenge (n)   **nalqaD**

maturation, growth (n)   **nen**

mature, grow up (v)   **nenchoH**

[be] mature, be grown-up, be adult (v)	nen
measure, have a length of (v)	'aD
meat from midsection of animal (n)	ghab
meat from midsection of animal, no bones (n) (regional)	ghab tun
mek'leth (type of weapon) (n)	meqleH
mess hall (n)	SopwI'pa'
message (n)	QIn
milk (n)	nIm
mind sharing (n)	tova'Daq
mineral: type of mineral, *bekpuj* (n)	beqpuj
mistake, make a mistake, err (v) (slang)	bachHa'
mixing stick, stirring stick (n)	'un naQ, DuDwI'
mixing stick with flattened, paddlelike end (n)	ngawDeq
mixture of animal parts (n)	Daghtuj
mixture (ground up and dried up) for brewing tea (n)	Qenvob
Mok'bara (martial arts form) (n)	moQbara'
most, greater part (n)	HochHom
motivate, inspire, stimulate (v)	pIlmoH
motive, motivation, grounds, reason, rationale (n) (slang)	mo'
motive (n)	meq
mouthpiece (of a wind instrument) (n)	ngujlep
move *bat'leth* from horizontal to vertical orientation (v)	ngol
move *bat'leth* from vertical to horizontal orientation (v)	lev
mumble, speak incoherently (v) (slang)	jat
music (n)	QoQ

musical instrument (n)	jan
musician (n)	muchwI'
naturally produced *qud* (n)	burgh quD
[be] near, be nearby (v)	Sum
nearly, virtually, almost, not quite (adv)	tlhoS
[be] next (in a series, sequence) (v)	veb
nibble, eat in small mouthfuls (v)	noS
nitrogen (n)	voQSIp
no one (n)	pagh
nonsense, balderdash (n) (slang)	chatlh
nonsense song (n)	Dap bom
[be] nonspecific, be unexceptional (v)	le'be'
norg (type of animal, sharklike sea creature) (n)	norgh
nose (n) (regional)	ley'
[be] not attentive, be distracted (v) (slang)	Dach
[be] not good, be unfortunate (v)	SaS
[to] not have, to lack, be without (v)	Hutlh
not quite, almost, nearly, virtually (v)	tlhoS
nut, nuts (n)	naHlet
observe, celebrate (a ritual) (v)	lop
occasionally (adv)	rut
ode of respect (n)	gha'tlhIq
open, flat hand (n)	ghIt
opening, chance (n)	'eb
opera (n)	ghe'naQ
operate, be in operation (v)	Qap
oppose, resist, confront, face (v)	qaD
order, structure (societal) (n) (slang)	tlham

order, group officially recognized by government (n)	'obe'
outsider, foreigner (n) (slang)	Hur'Iq
outsider, alien, foreigner (n)	nov
oxygen (n)	yInSIp
paint using fingers (v)	ngoH
paint, dye, pigment (n)	rItlh
paint with a pigment stick (v)	DIj
pal, buddy, close male friend of a male (n)	maqoch
panel, stone panel (artwork, similar to a painting) (n)	nagh beQ
panoply, battle gear, complete set of armor and weapons (n)	may'luch
paralyze (v)	roSHa'moH
parry, deflect a lunge (v)	way'
part, component, piece (n)	'ay'
party, celebration (n)	lopno'
paw (n)	namwech
peel, shell, husk, rind (of fruit, nut) (n)	yub
pelt (skin with fur still attached) (n)	veDDIr
percussion instrument (drum, bell) (n)	'In
perform (music) (v)	much
perform surgery (on) (v)	Haq
[be] perilous, be treacherous, be hazardous (v) (slang)	Qom
[be] permanent (v)	ru'Ha'
piece, component, part (n)	'ay'
pigment, paint, dye (n)	rItlh
pigment stick (n) (slang)	nItlh naQ
pigment stick (n)	rItlh naQ

[be] plain, be pure, uncorrupted, unsullied (v)	**nIt**
plant: type of plant (n)	**DIghna'**
plant: dikus plant (n)	**DayquS**
plate (for eating) (n)	**jengva'**
plates (for eating) (n)	**ngop**
platter, serving platter (n)	**'elpI'**
play (a musical instrument) (v)	**chu'**
player (of an instrument) (n)	**chu'wI'**
pluck (a stringed instrument) (v)	**pang**
ponytail (n) (slang)	**naQ**
ponytail holder (n) (slang)	**Qeb**
[be] positive, be sure, be definite, be certain (v) (slang)	**na', bej**
possibility (n)	**nuH**
pot (for food preparation, general term) (n)	**'un**
pot with handles (used for food preparation) (n)	**nevDagh**
pot: ceramic flat-bottomed pot (n) (regional)	**chor, chor bargh**
pot: flat-bottomed pot for food preparation (n)	**bargh**
pot: flat-bottomed pot for food preparation (n) (regional)	**vutmeH 'un, vut'un**
pot: metal flat-bottomed pot (n) (regional)	**mIv, mIv bargh**
pour (into/onto anything) (v)	**lIch**
pour (from one container into another) (v)	**qang**
power, authority, one in authority (n) (slang)	**ngup**
[be] pregnant (v)	**yatlh**
prepare *qud* in a specific way (v)	**Suqqa'**
preside (v)	**che'**
prey (n)	**gheD**
prisoner (n) (slang)	**jav**
produce (n)	**Du' naH**

[be] profound, be thorough, be careful (v) (slang)	chong
[be] protected, be safe (v) (slang)	QaD
protrude from (v)	jeq
proverb (n)	vIttlhegh
[be] pungent (referring to food) (v)	tlhorgh
[be] pure, be plain, uncorrupted, be unsullied (v)	nIt
purpose (n)	ngoQ
qa'vak (traditional game) (n)	qa'vaQ
reason, grounds, motive, motivation, rationale (n) (slang)	mo'
recipient, celebrant (n)	SIQwI'
regularly, customarily, habitually (adv)	roD
reject (v)	lajQo'
render, boil fat (v)	'Im
replacement (permanent) (n)	qa'meH
[be] reprehensible, be disgusting, be contemptible (v) (slang)	natlh
[be] repugnant, be unsavory, be disgusting, be icky, be loathsome (v)	'up
reside in/at, dwell in/at (v)	Dab
resist, oppose, confront, face (v)	qaD
resist, fend off (v)	'om
return, give back (v)	nobHa'
rib (n)	joQ
richness, wealth (n)	mIp
right, privilege (n)	DIb
Right of Vengeance (n)	bortaS DIb
rind, peel, shell, husk (of fruit, nut) (n)	yub

[be] ripe, be overripe (fruit, vegetable) (v)	**DeH**
ritual gifts (n)	**cha'nob**
ritual hunt (n)	**chontay**
ritual suicide (n)	**Heghbat**
[be] ritualistic, be formal, be ceremonial (v)	**SeQ**
rivet (n)	**veragh**
roll, scroll, list (n)	**tetlh**
romance, love (n)	**parmaq**
romantic companion, romantic partner (n)	**paramaqqay**
root, tuber (n)	**'oQqar**
rotate, twirl (v)	**jIr**
run into, bump into, collide with (v)	**ngeQ**
run in place, dance, do calisthenics, exercise (v)	**mI'**
runt, wealking, scrawny one, skinny one (n) (slang)	**Hom**
rust, corrode (v)	**ragh**
sabre bear (n)	**mIl'oD**
[be] safe, be protected (v) (slang)	**QaD**
[be] salty, be brackish (v)	**na'**
sap of a plant, juice (n)	**vIychorgh**
sark (type of animal) (n)	**Sargh**
sash (n)	**Ha'quj**
sauce for *gagh* (n)	**ghevI'**
sauce for *gladst* (n)	**uSu'**
sauce: types of sauce (n)	**qettlhup, quD, 'uSu'**
Sauria (n)	**Sorya'**
scales (animal covering) (n)	**ghISDen**
scoop, scooping implement (to serve food) (n)	**bo'Dagh**
score, keep score (v)	**pe"egh**

scrape (v)	tey
scrawny one, weakling, runt, skinny one (n) (slang)	Hom
scroll, roll, list (n)	tetlh
sculptor (n)	Hew chenmoHwI'
[be] sealed, be locked, be secured, be fastened (v)	ngaQ
sect, faction (n)	tlhach
[be] secured, be locked, be sealed, be fastened (v)	ngaQ
seldom, infrequently (adv)	pIjHa'
self-doubter, insecure one (n) (regional) (slang)	ghaw'
sense flavors, taste (v)	mum
serve fermented food at its peak (v)	wech
server of food, waiter, waitress (n)	jabwI'
server of food in a *Doke'* restaurant (n)	tebwI'
serving platter (n)	'elpI'
shaft (of spear) (n)	tIH
[be] shallow, be superficial, be uncritical (v) (slang)	SaS
sheath, knife case (n)	vaH
shell (of an animal) (n)	nagh DIr
shell (of an egg) (n)	pel'aQ
shell, husk, rind, peel (of fruit, nut) (n)	yub
shields (force field on ship) (n)	botjan
shirt, sleeveless shirt (n) (regional)	yIvbeH
shirt with sleeves (n) (regional)	wep
shooy (type of animal) (n)	Suy'
[be] short (in duration) (v)	ngaj
[be] short (in stature) (v)	run

show, demonstrate, display (v)	'agh
shrine (n)	lat
shrub (n)	lav
sing, chant (v)	bom
skinny one, weakling, runt, scrawny one (n) (slang)	Hom
slang (n)	mu'mey ghoQ
sleeve (n)	tlhay
sleeveless shirt (n) (regional)	yIvbeH
slide sword blade along opponent's blade (v)	DIj
slime (n)	HuH
[be] slimy (v)	char
smile, grin, sneer (v)	mon
soak, drench (v)	HaH
society (e.g., scholarly society) (n)	yej'an
society; group of people with shared culture (n)	nugh
sole of foot (n)	bem
some, an unknown or unspecified quantity (n)	'op
something useless (n)	tu'HomI'raH
song, chant (n)	bom
soup (thick) (n)	chatlh
speak incoherently, mumble (v) (slang)	jat
spear (n)	naQjej
spear: battle spear, *gin'tak* (n)	ghIntaq
spear: hunting spear (n)	chonnaQ
spear thrown with aid of a special tool (n)	tlhevjaQ
spear-throwing device (n)	chetvI'
spearhead, barbed spearhead (n)	SeDveq
spearhead (n)	QIn

specify for, explain clearly to, clarify for (v) (slang)	chuH
spike (n)	DuQwI'
spike glove, Ligonian spike glove, glavin (n)	lIghon DuQwI' pogh
spirit (n)	qa'
spiritual possession (n)	jatyIn
spit out (v)	tlhIS
[be] splendid, be wonderful, be excellent (v) (slang)	qu', chong
spy on (v)	ghoq
squash, mash (v)	tap
squeeze and stretch out (windbag instrument) (v)	rey
squeeze (windbag instrument) (v)	qeb
stabilize (v)	ngaDmoH
stabilizer (component of a ship) (n)	ngaDmoHwI'
[be] stable, be balanced (v)	ngaD
stage, step (in a process) (n)	mIw
stain, tint, dye (v)	nguvmoH
[be] stained, be dyed, be tinted (v)	nguv
stairs, stairway (n)	letlh
stairs, stairway (except at ship door) (n) (regional)	ngep'oS
stairway leading to door of a ship, gangplank (n)	choghvat
stairway leading to door of a ship (n) (regional)	letlh
stand-in, substitute, temporary surrogate (n)	lIw
standard dialect (n)	ta' Hol
standing, layer, level (n)	patlh
stardate (n)	HovpoH
statue (n)	Hew

step, stage (in a process) (n)	mIw
sterilize (v)	woj
stew (n)	tlhIq
stew (v)	Qev
stick, stirring stick (n)	DuDwI'
stick (used to strike percussion instrument) (n)	naQHom
stimulate, inspire, motivate (v)	pIlmoH
[be] stimulated, be inspired, be motivated (v)	pIl
[be] stimulated, be exhilarated, be invigorated (v) (slang)	tlhuH
stirring stick, mixing stick (n)	'un naQ, DuDwI'
stone panel (artwork, similar to a painting) (n)	nagh beQ
string, thread, filament (n)	SIrgh
stringed instrument (general term) (n)	HurDagh
strip of material in a *susdek* instrument (n)	joQ
structure, order (societal) (n) (slang)	tlham
strum (a stringed instrument) (v)	yach
substitute, stand-in, temporary surrogate (n)	lIw
suicide ritual (n)	Heghbat
[be] superficial, be uncritical (v) (slang)	SaS
[be] sure, be definite, be positive, be certain (v) (slang)	bej, na'
[perform] surgery (on) (v)	Haq
surrogate (temporary), stand-in, substitute (n)	lIw
survive (v)	taH
sweep (away) (v)	bI'
swing, wield (a weapon) (v)	Qach
sword (n)	yan
sword (n) (slang)	yaD
[use or manipulate a] sword (v)	yan

Sword of Kahless (n)	qeylIS betleH
sycophant, flatterer (n) (slang)	bochmoHwI'
table (n)	raS
tail (n)	tlhuQ
take on responsibilities of, assume duties of (v)	gheS
Talarian (person) (n)	talarngan
[be] tart, be bitter (v)	wIb
task, assignment, duty (n) (slang)	ghIgh
taste, sense flavors (v)	mum
taste, try out (food) (v)	waH
[be] tasty, be good, be delicious, be harmonious (v)	'ey
tea-brewing mixture (n)	Qenvob
teacup (n) (older or upper-class word)	tu'lum
teacup (n)	Dargh HIvje'
teapot (n)	runpI'
technology (n)	cham
tendon, ligament (n)	to'waQ
terminate, discontinue (v)	baq
test, use experimentally, try out (v)	waH
test of one's abilities (n)	qaD
[be] thick, be dense, be viscous (v)	jeD
thistle (n)	neHjej
[be] thorough, be profound, be careful (v) (slang)	chong
thread, filament, string (n)	SIrgh
throw around, hurl about (v)	jaD
throw (a spear) at, hurl (a spear) at (v)	chuH
thrust upward with end of *bat'leth* (v)	chaQ
thrust, lunge (v)	jop

tika cat (n)	tI'qa' vIghro'
tint, stain, dye (v)	nguvmoH
[be] tinted, be stained, be dyed (v)	nguv
to the death (excl) (archaic)	ghIqtal
Tokvarian skink (type of animal) (n)	toqvIr lung
tone: tones of nonatonic musical scale (n) (in order)	yu, bIm, 'egh, loS, vagh, jav, Soch, chorgh, yu
top of foot (n)	mov
torch (n)	Sech
toss *bat'leth* from one hand to the other (v)	baQ
touch (emotionally) (v)	DuQ
traitor (n) (slang)	bolwI'
trap, entrap (v)	von
[be] treacherous, be hazardous, be perilous (v) (slang)	Qom
treat unjustly, wrong (v)	QIH
tribe, house, ancestral unit (n)	tuq
try out, taste (food) (v)	waH
try out, test, use experimentally (v)	waH
tub (n)	'Ib
tuber, root (n)	'oQqar
twirl, rotate (v)	jIr
twirl *bat'leth*, cause *bat'leth* to rotate (v)	jIrmoH
twist knuckle into someone's head (v)	nughI'
typically, usually, as expected (adv)	motlh
uj (unit of linear measure, about 35 centimeters) (n)	'uj
[be] uncorrupted, be unsullied, be pure, be plain (v)	nIt

[be] uncritical, be superficial, be shallow (v) (slang)	SaS
undisciplined person, irresponsible person (n) (slang)	Duj ngaDHa'
[be] unexceptional, be nonspecific (v)	le'be'
[be] unfortunate, be not good (v) (slang)	SaS
unfortunately (adv)	Do'Ha'
unit of currency, *darsek* (n)	DarSeq
[be] unsavory, be disgusting, be loathsome (v)	'up
[be] unsullied, be uncorrupted, be pure, be plain (v)	nIt
use or manipulate a sword (v)	yan
use up, consume, expend (v)	natlh
useless thing, something useless (n)	tu'HomI'raH
usually, typically, as expected (adv)	motlh
[be] valiant, be brave, be bold, be heroic (v) (slang)	Sub
vat, barrel (for storage of liquor) (n)	qegh
vegetable knife, fruit knife (small knife) (n)	naH taj
victor, conqueror (n)	charghwI'
[be] vigorous, be effective (v)	vaQ
virtually, not quite, almost, nearly (adv)	tlhoS
virtue (n)	ghob
[be] viscous, be dense, be thick (v)	jeD
[have a] volume of (v)	muq
wage war, fight, battle (v)	ghob
wail, howl (n)	bey
waiter, waitress, food server (n)	jabwI'

war, warfare (n)	veS
[make] war (v)	Qoj
war (an individual war) (n)	noH
warhead (of a torpedo) (n)	jorneb
warnog, Klingon ale (n)	wornagh
warrant, deserve (v)	qotlh
warrior's knife, *d'k tahg* (n)	Daqtagh
water jug (n)	bIQ bal
weakling, runt, scrawny one, skinny one (n) (slang)	Hom
wealth, richness (n)	mIp
weapon: type of weapon (n)	'aqleH
weapon: type of weapon, *mek'leth* (n)	meqleH
weapons officer (n)	nuHpIn
weather (in general) (n)	muD
weather (at any given moment) (n)	muD Dotlh
weigh, have a weight of (v)	ngI'
wield or manipulate a sword (v)	yan
wield, swing (a weapon) (v)	Qach
win (v)	Qap
windbag, bellows (n)	SuSDeq
window (n)	Qorwagh
wine, beer, ale (n)	HIq
[be] without, lack (v)	Hutlh
[be] wonderful, be great, be excellent, be splendid (v) (slang)	qu', chong
wood (n)	Sor Hap
work for (actively), earn (v)	baj
[be] worn out (v)	Qop

wrist (also used as slang term of deprecation) (n)   **yeb**

wrong, treat unjustly (v)   **QIH**

years old (n)   **ben**

Yiridian (person) (n)   **yIrIDngan**

zilm'kach (type of food) (n)   **tlhImqaH**